Over Yonder

WANDA JENNINGS

BOOK EIGHT OF THE MAGNOLIA MANOR SERIES

Printed in the United States of America
First Printed June, 2023

Published by:
Between Friends Publishing,
1080 GA Hwy 96, Suite #100,
Warner Robins, Georgia 31088

ISBN: 978-1-956544-54-1

This book is dedicated to my two precious children. To my sweet son who has always been the inspiration behind Wilbur, the most gentle, tender soul in my life. To my precious daughter, may you always have the confidence of Mavis and the wanderlust that drives her.

You both are the best people I have ever known.

Chapter One

"So, Wilbur, have you called Emily yet?" Mavis asked with a sly smile. She stabbed the lone piece of meat left on her plate with her fork and dipped it in ketchup.

It had only been two days since Nadine Waters' funeral where Wilbur had met the most stunning woman, Emily Groves. Her grandmother was Beulah Johnson, Nadine's best friend. Wilbur had been too timid to ask for her phone number after they made small talk in the rain after the service, but Opal had swooped in and saved the day.

Wilbur had every intention of calling Emily, but every time he sat down to do it, he suddenly lost the nerve. Emily was beautiful and smart. Plus, she didn't live in Rhinestone. She was only visiting her grandmother for the time being and Wilbur wasn't sure how long she'd even be around. He wasn't sure where she lived either. Each time he told himself that Emily was way out of his league and he had better save himself the heartburn.

"Of course he's called her," Opal said. "Right Wilbur?"

Wilbur's face lost all color. He dropped his fork onto his plate and the piece of pork chop fell to the floor. He mumbled something under his breath that no one else at the table could quite make out.

"What was that?" Mavis asked. She sopped up the last of the gravy with her biscuit and polished her plate clean as Wilbur shook his head.

"Mavis," he glared at her. He had been avoiding that topic ever since Opal had chased Emily and her grandmother down at a restaurant in Junction last week after the burial.

"Yeah, Wilbur, how are things with Emily?" Maude asked.

"I gave you that piece of paper with her number on it, right?" Opal wondered.

"You did," Maude nodded. "I watched you hand it to him and he put it in his billfold. You remember, Wilbur?"

Wilbur nodded and cleared his throat. "Yes ma'am, and thank you again for that, but," Wilbur began.

"That's right," Opal nodded. "How are things going?"

"There aren't any things with Emily," Wilbur said quietly. He could feel his cheeks flush red with embarrassment as all three women stared at him.

"Are you seeing Emily again soon? I talked to Beulah yesterday and she didn't mention a thing," Maude said. "She usually keeps everyone better informed." She choked slightly on the wad of chewed up pork in her mouth. Opal whacked her on the back and bits of food particles sprayed onto the table.

"Y'all aren't dating yet?" Opal asked. She turned to Maude and shrugged, "Kids these days."

"It's best not to move too fast," Maude countered. "That's how I got married the first time. And the second. Don't rush into marriage."

"Who's getting married?" Opal asked. "No, Wilbur, it's too fast to get married. You just started dating her a few days ago. They'll be time for that later."

"Yes, way too soon," Maude agreed. "You haven't even introduced us yet."

"Well, I," he turned to Maude who dabbed at the table with her napkin. "I mean we aren't actually dating. There's really nothing to tell."

"Did she tell you no?" Maude gasped. "Just you wait until I see her or Beulah again! I'll tell that little hussy how bad she screwed up!"

"Oh, no, that's not it at all," Wilbur stammered.

"He hasn't called her yet to ask her on a date," Mavis explained loudly.

"What on earth are you waiting for?" Opal asked. "She's a great girl. And Beulah's real nice once you get through that tough exterior. You've got a lifetime of experience with tough old birds with Maude here."

Maude shot Opal a dirty look, but Opal was unbothered. "Why haven't you even called her yet?" Maude asked.

"I've been asking him that for days," Mavis

confided to Opal and Maude. Wilbur shot her a look and opened his mouth to try and explain his reasoning to Maude and Opal.

"You didn't lose her number, did you?" Maude demanded.

"Wilbur doesn't usually lose things," Mavis said, defending him unexpectedly. She loved getting under Wilbur's skin, but once Maude and Opal got ahold of a bone, they were like two bulldogs. Mavis had simply intended to encourage Wilbur to make the leap and reach out to Emily, but she hadn't meant to encourage Maude or Opal in the process.

"That would explain it," Opal nodded. "I knew something was amiss."

"Were you embarrassed to tell us you lost her number?" Maude added. She nodded knowingly at Opal who seemed to agree.

"I don't think he lost her number," Mavis said.

Wilbur took a deep breath. "No, I didn't lose her number. That's not it."

"You shouldn't be embarrassed to ask for help, Wilbur," Opal patted his arm.

"Yeah, you know we're always here to help," Maude said. "We're very helpful."

"We sure are," Opal agreed.

"But I don't need any help," Wilbur said.

"It's okay to misplace things. Maude does it all the time," Opal said. "She'd lose her underwear if they weren't so wedged up her, well, you know."

"I don't think he lost her number," Mavis said. She gagged slightly at the idea of Maude's undergarments being lodged anywhere they shouldn't be, but she knew better than to ask any questions.

"No, I didn't lose her number," Wilbur said, but Maude and Opal were ignoring everything Mavis and Wilbur were saying.

"Don't worry, Wilbur. I'll call Beulah and get everything taken care of," Maude reached in her bag and pulled out her cell phone. It was the newest and most up to date phone on the market, and they all knew that she had no idea how to use it.

"Tell her I said hi," Opal said loudly.

"You don't have to call Mrs. Beulah," Wilbur said.

"We'll take care of it. Don't you worry, Wilbur," Maude assured him. "She won't dogfish you on our watch."

"What's dogfish?" Mavis asked, right at the same time that Wilbur repeated, "But I don't need you to call Mrs. Beulah."

While Maude tapped the screen of her smart phone repeatedly and cursed under her breath, Opal launched into a discussion on how Maude had seen a television show about a woman who had been misled on an online meetup.

"I think she means catfished," Mavis whispered to Wilbur.

"Wilbur knows how to catfish," Opal corrected. "This is different. Dogfish is when the boy said he was lean, tan, and rich, but he lied. Lied like a dog!"

"Yea, I saw that show at your house. That man was an old geezer who looked like a tree stump,"

Maude agreed, still mumbling under her breath about the woes of technology.

"Exactly," Opal nodded. "He was a dogfish. It's a serious epidemic in your generation."

"It's a crime," Maude nodded. "We didn't have to deal with that when we were younger. I hope you two aren't out there on the internets doing that to people."

"Wilbur and Mavis wouldn't do that," Opal interjected.

"This Emily better not either. I'll ask Beulah if she's on the internets. Damnt, I can't get this piece of space brick to work," Maude grumbled.

Opal snatched the phone and pressed a few buttons on the screen to connect Maude to Beulah. "I didn't hit the button where you could see her. What if she was on the commode or something?" she frowned.

"I don't need to see any more of that," Maude agreed.

"Whose commode are you looking at?" Mavis gasped.

"On the facelook feature thingy," Opal explained. "Patsy got a new phone and showed us all her cracks and crevices on the phone screen yesterday morning while we were at breakfast. It wasn't pretty."

"Oh God," Mavis shrieked. "Why was Mrs. Patsy on FaceTime in the bathroom?"

"Let it go," Wilbur whispered to Mavis. It wouldn't be the first time that one of the women got a millennial term incorrect. They both knew that it wouldn't do any good to try and correct

Opal's new phrase, and Wilbur didn't want to hear about his best friend's mother on the toilet. It also didn't matter how many times Wilbur told Maude that he didn't need her assistance contacting his crush.

"There it goes!" Maude exclaimed. "Beulah! It's Maude!"

"Oh God," Wilbur sighed. Every head in the restaurant turned to watch them.

"But, Ms. Maude," Mavis began.

"You gotta be louder than that," Opal said. She took a deep breath and bellowed loudly, "Hey Beulah!"

Mavis and Wilbur both cowered at the loud bellow. "Beulah is a little hard of hearing," Opal explained.

Wilbur glared at Mavis and shook his head. "I'm sorry," Mavis whispered.

"I know I just saw you!" Maude hollered into the phone. She rolled her eyes at Beulah's lack of couth. She picked the food out of her teeth with her knife as Beulah drawled on about the sales price she got on her new muumuu.

Opal snatched the phone and said, "Is Emily still there? She is? That's great!" She looked at Wilbur and gave him a big thumbs up as Beulah carried on. "She's there with her, Wilbur. Want to talk to her?"

Wilbur shook his head so fast that he looked like a ping pong ball going back and forth during a heated match.

"He can't come to the phone right now!" Opal yelled into the phone.

"Give me my phone back," Maude snapped. "I'm calling to arrange a playdate!"

"A play what?" Mavis squeaked.

"A playdate!" Maude repeated. "No, not with you, Beulah! It's for Wilbur and Emily!"

"This is it," Wilbur sighed. "I'm in hell."

Mavis couldn't help but laugh at the spectacle in front of her. She hated that it was at Wilbur's expense, but hopefully this would help get Wilbur out of his sudden shyness where Emily was concerned. Mavis hadn't ever seen Wilbur this smitten over anyone. Not that he'd come right out and said it, but it was obvious to anyone with eyes. Wilbur was so lucky to have Mavis in his life to help coach and guide him, but even she hadn't thought of the playdate angle.

"Great! See you both tomorrow!" Maude yelled. She pressed the big red button on the screen and put the phone back in her purse. "It's scheduled for tomorrow! Me and Beulah will chaperone!" Maude howled.

"Where at?" Opal asked. "And what time? Because I already have plans for tomorrow morning."

"The more the merrier," Mavis giggled.

"I didn't invite you," Maude huffed at Opal.

"Oh hush, if Wilbur's going on a playdate, I'm coming, too!" Opal replied. "After I finish with my chickens."

"Fine, you can come, too. But your chickens can wait!" Maude huffed. She turned to Wilbur who had gone paler than Mavis had ever seen. "Opal's gotta dip her chickens in this flea bath tomorrow. Vet's orders. They got eat up with fleas. I didn't even know chickens could get fleas!"

"They can," Opal nodded. "But Wilbur comes first."

"We'll pick you up at noon," Maude explained.

"I don't, I mean, y'all," Wilbur stuttered. He looked at Mavis for help, but she was giggling too hard. "I've never been so mortified," he whispered.

"Just wait til tomorrow," she replied. "Where's this, um, date at?" Mavis asked Maude.

"Beulah suggested the pizza place over off Highway Nine," Maude said. "It's got the best homemade sauce. I eat there twice a week."

"She does," Opal nodded. "I can go for pizza tomorrow. That'll be a good place. Mavis, you want to come, too?"

"Uh, well," Mavis swallowed hard. "I don't know if this is the best idea." Wilbur widened his eyes and silently begged her to intervene in this setup. "Why don't I take you both and Mrs. Beulah for pizza and Wilbur can take Emily somewhere else?"

"Then who's going to chaperone?" Maude asked quickly. "No, that doesn't sound like a good idea. Wilbur already said he needed our help."

"I don't remember saying," Wilbur started, but he was cut off again by Maude ordering dessert from a passing waiter.

"Banana pudding for us all," she directed. The waiter nodded and hurried off to the kitchen to retrieve her order.

"Get me out of this, Mavis," Wilbur wheezed.

Mavis didn't know what else to do other than change the subject. "Did I tell yall that I bought one of those ancestral DNA test things a few days ago?"

"I've heard about those," Maude said. "I won't be doing one of those. Don't even ask me to."

"Maude's afraid she'll find out that she's related to livestock or something," Opal shrugged.

Maude swatted at Opal right as the waiter set down the tray of bowls containing their banana pudding. "Party foul!" Opal yelled as one of the bowls flew across the table and landed in Wilbur's lap.

The waiter apologized profusely and brought Wilbur a new bowl of pudding and napkins to try and clean himself off. "Fix this, Mavis," he huffed as he stood up to walk to the bathroom.

"She can't be fixed," Opal said affirmatively ⬚ and gestured towards Maude.

Wilbur ignored them and rushed off to the bathroom. While he was gone, Mavis calmly explained that it would be best for Wilbur and Emily to meet up and talk on their own. Wilbur was in his mid-forties after all. By the time Wilbur came out of the bathroom ten minutes later, Maude had agreed to allow Wilbur and Emily to have lunch together, but not before she got to meet her in person and make sure she wasn't one of those treacherous internet sneaks. Wilbur sat back down and tried to steer the conversation back to Mavis and her quest to find out more about her heritage.

"I did the test the same day I bought it. Sent it

out in the mail that afternoon. I should be getting the results back in four to six weeks," Mavis squealed in delight. "It's the neatest thing. It can show me all of my distant relatives out there and show where my ancestors came from!"

"Ruby's family was Irish," Maude volunteered. "Jameson's family had some German in there, but if I remember correctly, his grandmother's family was Creek."

"I'm still working through the family trees," Mavis nodded. "There's so much to go through. I called Judy and we talked for a few hours yesterday about it all."

Judy was Ruby's niece who lived in Colorado. She was the oldest daughter of Ruby's deceased older brother. Mavis had been raised by her grandparents, Ruby and Jameson Montgomery, but she had never been into ancestry or history until recently. Judy shared her own research and helped Mavis fill out a few branches of the Lawrence family tree on Ruby's side.

"I bought Wilbur a test, but he hasn't taken it yet," Mavis said. "You need to do it and send it in. You could have all kinds of relatives out there."

Wilbur shrugged and ate his banana pudding. "I'm honestly content with the family I have," he explained. "As long as y'all don't try to arrange any more dates for me."

"That's so sweet," Opal smiled. She patted Wilbur's hand and nodded. "Sometimes you can choose your family."

Chapter Two

Wilbur took forever figuring out what to wear when he woke up the next morning. He wasn't even sure if Emily would show up to the restaurant. Part of him hoped she didn't show up because there was no telling what Maude and Opal were liable to do or say. Then again, if she didn't show up, Maude would probably show up at Beulah's house and demand an audience with her. If he didn't show up, Maude would definitely show up at his house and continue the embarrassment. None of those outcomes sounded pleasant.

He finally settled on his favorite pair of jeans and a nice plaid button up shirt. He grabbed a jacket on his way out and stopped again to spray some extra cologne on just to be sure. He left his house at half past eleven just in case he encountered any traffic. When he passed by the ☐ Manor, he saw that Mavis' car was still parked beneath the signature magnolia tree. She had assured him that she would corral the older ladies so that he could try and convince Emily that he wasn't as crazy as the rest of them once she arrived. Instead of stopping, he drove straight to the restaurant and wasn't at all surprised to see Maude and Opal waiting at the door. Maude had her arms crossed over her chest. She looked aggravated, or at least more aggravated than usual. He stepped out of his truck and asked her what the matter was.

"They don't open til noon," she huffed. Wilbur looked at his watch and saw that it was only fifteen minutes until noon, but Maude didn't care. She did not like to be kept waiting when it came to food. "Tried to get here early for a good table, but they won't even come to the door," Maude continued. "We need a big table for all of us."

Wilbur looked over his shoulder to see if Mavis was pulling in. If she didn't hurry up and get here, he might sweat out of his jacket. "Well, remember now that we aren't all going to be eating together today," he reminded her.

"I told her, but you know how she is," Opal offered.

"I've been thinking about that," Maude said. "And I just don't think we ought to leave you alone with a stranger. Beulah said Emily's from up north and I'm sure she's nice and all, but you just never know."

"Ms. Maude, I think I can handle it," Wilbur said, but Maude kept going on and on about how Ruby would never forgive her if something happened to Wilbur. She had clearly watched too many crime dramas for her own good. He didn't think Emily would set out to harvest his organs on the first date, but Maude wasn't altogether convinced. She patted Wilbur on the arm and said she knew how to fend off any attackers. She leaned in and smelled Wilbur's shirt closely. "Did you leave any cologne in the bottle? More is less," she coughed. "You'll probably ward her off yourself with all that."

Wilbur sighed inwardly and looked around for any sign of Mavis, but she didn't arrive for another ten minutes. She practically flew into the parking lot next to Wilbur's truck. Wilbur met her at the door and told her about Maude's comment. She stepped out of the car and smiled at Wilbur. "It's going to be fine. I'll handle it. Anyway, you look nice, Wilbur. Now don't be nervous. Just be yourself and it will be fine," Mavis said sweetly.

A teenage girl came to open the restaurant's front door. She looked far too timid to deal with a hangry Maude. "About time!" Maude shouted.

"I'm not just worried about me. I'm more worried about Thelma and Louise over there," he jerked his thumb in the direction of Maude and Opal. His watch showed that it was exactly noon. Emily was late. That would not be a good sign for Maude's checklist. She considered it the height of rudeness to be late to a meal. "Where are they?" he asked Mavis.

"They'll be here," Mavis assured him. She followed Maude and Opal into the restaurant where Maude promptly sat down at the largest table in the front.

"And you're going to take them to a different restaurant, right?" Wilbur asked again. He needed to be sure of the plan, but Mavis' expression did nothing to assure him.

"Well, I don't think Maude's going to leave. She seems to have her heart set on this place. You might have to go elsewhere," Mavis shrugged.

Wilbur didn't have the time to argue because seconds later he saw a white SUV pull into the parking lot. Emily stepped out of the driver's side and walked around to open the door for Beulah. Emily was wearing dark-colored jeans and a vibrant purple sweater. Her new cowboy boots matched the deep shade of purple of her sweater. Her dark brown hair was pulled back into a low ponytail revealing feathered earrings that hung down to her shoulders. She helped Beulah walk up the steps to the door and then held the door open for the older lady.

"There they are!" Maude grumbled. "It's about durn time."

"Be nice, Maude," Opal said gently. "Not everyone relies on their stomach to tell time."

"I am being nice. They're late," Maude said firmly.

"Sorry I'm late! I had to find my teeth!" Beulah explained, loud enough for the people across the street to hear.

This was not how Wilbur had envisioned his first date with Emily. He did not expect to be chaperoned by three endearing, but slightly crazy old women. He wanted to crawl underneath the table.

"Beulah, don't be uncouth. This is a playdate for the kids!" Maude told her.

"Maude, remember Mavis told us not to call it a playdate," Opal reminded her.

"I found them, didn't I!" Beulah hollered. "You know how it goes."

"I have all my teeth!" Maude huffed back.

"Let's all calm down," Mavis said politely. "This is for Wilbur, remember."

"Oh yeah, well as long as Emily doesn't try any of that dogfishing mess," Maude began. "Reminds me, I need to ask her about her time on the internets."

"Oh dear God," Wilbur put his face in his hands.

"Dogfishing?" Emily said with a slight smile.

"Ms. Maude, I told you it's catfishing and nobody is doing that," Mavis explained.

"This isn't a fish place. Right? What kind of pizza place serves fish? Beulah asked.

"I'm so sorry," Wilbur told Emily.

"What in the world are they talking about?" Emily asked.

"Mavis has a fish," Opal said.

"We're not talking about Mavis' fish," Maude said.

"But he's a catfish," Opal explained. "I've swam with him before."

Maude couldn't argue that point. She had been at the Manor the day that Opal had stripped down and jumped into the massive aquarium with the giant catfish. It had only been a few weeks from one of Opal's strokes and she hadn't been exactly right when she had done that, but the more Maude thought about it, Opal in her best mind would have done the same thing.

"Catfish sounds good. What do you want

Emily?" Beulah bellowed. She sat down at the table next to Maude and looked back at Emily who was still standing. "You eat fish, right?"

"Grandma, this is a pizza place. They don't serve fish," Emily explained. "At least, I don't think they do."

"Opal just said they did," Beulah said. She flipped the plastic menu upside down looking for any sign of fish.

"I did not. I said Clive is a catfish," Opal corrected.

"Who in tarnation is Clive?" Beulah asked.

"Clive is my pet catfish, Mrs. Beulah," Mavis explained.

"I don't think we should eat any of your pets," Beulah said, shaking her head.

"I wasn't suggesting that," Mavis said meekly. She loved Clive with all of her heart and wouldn't let anyone eat him. "Wilbur, why don't y'all slip out while I distract them. Oh heavens, they're already distracted enough. Just go!"

"I'm so sorry, Emily," Wilbur apologized again. "I can understand if you want to go back home."

"Why in the world would I want to do that? You can't get this kind of entertainment anywhere else," Emily smiled.

Mavis shot Wilbur another look urging him to leave while Maude and Beulah were distracted by the menus that the young waitress was trying to explain. Opal sat down next to Mavis and waved discreetly at Wilbur. It was now or never. Wilbur took a deep breath and asked, "Can we maybe go somewhere else for lunch?" Wilbur glanced over at Maude and Beulah. "Maybe somewhere a lot quieter?"

There was a small Chinese restaurant across the street that Wilbur had been to a few times. It was quiet and had a great selection of food. They also wouldn't be too far from the women in case they accidentally burned the pizza place down or got thrown out.

"Y'all go ahead," Mavis told Emily. "I'll stay here and make sure they don't get in too much trouble. But you owe me, Wilbur," she hissed.

"Are you sure?" Emily asked.

"Absolutely!" Mavis said. "Go and have fun."

Wilbur stood up and waited for Emily to get her bag.

"Where're y'all going?" Beulah asked.

Mavis and Opal looked at each other. Somehow they both knew if they told Beulah that Wilbur and Emily were going across the street, the entire group would move there as well. Best to steer her off at the pass, but Maude was quicker than they were. "They're going on their playdate! They reckon they're old enough to not need chaperoning," she yelled to Beulah. Before Emily and Wilbur could make it to the front door, Maude added, "But I've got my eyes on you! I know all about the internets."

"I'm so sorry," Wilbur muttered again. He held the door open and followed Emily outside.

"I can't wait to hear this story," Emily said as she walked across the parking lot. "By the way, it's nice to see you again."

They found a corner booth and sat down away

from the rest of the patrons. After they had ordered their drinks, Emily turned to Wilbur and smiled. "So, what exactly is this about a playdate?"

"Oh dear God," Wilbur hung his head. "I'm so sorry about that."

"What is going on?" Emily laughed.

"So, yeah, um," Wilbur began. "Your grandmother and my, well, Maude and Opal." Wilbur couldn't even finish his thought.

"It can't be that bad," Emily offered.

"Yeah, but you might not want to talk to me again after this," Wilbur admitted. He was still so embarrassed.

"That all depends on what dogfishing is," Emily laughed again. "And whatever is going on with the interwebs or internets, or whatever Ms. Maude said."

"It's a figment of Maude's imagination. She saw some news report about online catfishing and for the life of her she can't remember that term. Somehow that became dogfishing, and well, here we are," Wilbur explained.

"Why do y'all think I'm catfishing anyone?" Emily looked at him a bit more seriously.

"I don't. Honestly, that's the furthest thing from my mind," Wilbur told her. "Neither does Mavis or Opal, but when Maude hears about any new thing on the news, suddenly she thinks everyone is in danger."

"She thinks you're in danger from me?" Emily took a sip of her tea.

"No. She thinks she's helping me," Wilbur admitted. He shook his head and hoped that

Emily's tea would stay in the glass and not end up in his face.

"Helping you how?" Emily asked.

Wilbur took a deep breath and began to explain the whole thing. He explained how Opal had gone and gotten her number when he was too shy to at the restaurant after him telling them all about this mysterious granddaughter of Beulah Johnson from the funeral.

"I remember that, but when I didn't hear from you, I thought Ms. Opal might have imagined the whole thing," Emily said. "My grandmother says she has quite the imagination." She saw the look of on Wilbur's face and smiled, "Don't worry, she's very fond of Opal Tyler."

"She is definitely a character," Wilbur agreed. He continued catching her up on the conversation yesterday and how Maude had decided that the two kids needed a playdate since he hadn't worked up the courage to ask her out on his own.

"A playdate?" Emily laughed. "What are we? Six?"

"They must think so," Wilbur nodded.

"So this is a date?" Emily smiled. "Or are you dogfishing me?"

"I'm so sorry. I should have just asked you out properly instead of waiting until Maude decided to help, but to be honest, I didn't think you were going to stay in the area for long. I thought you were going back up north once the funeral was over," Wilbur explained.

"I'm actually moving down here. I'm staying with my grandmother until my place is ready,"

Emily explained. "The company I work for merged with a larger outfit in Montgomery. It worked out perfectly because my grandparents are so close by. I enjoy spending time with them. Rhinestone's the cutest little town. My brother and I used to come here during the summers and stay."

They talked like old friends until the waitress brought their entrees and came to refill their drinks. Emily told him about her marketing business. She worked with small businesses and entrepreneurs all over the country to create an active online presence.

"Oh, so you know all about the internets?" Wilbur laughed.

"Something like that," she smiled. "I really love my job. It gives me a lot of freedom."

"I bet," Wilbur agreed.

"So Wilbur, tell me all about you. I've heard quite a bit from my grandmother, but as you can probably tell, she too has a vivid imagination," Emily giggled.

Wilbur was dying to ask what Beulah had shared with her, but he knew it couldn't be too awful if she had agreed to go out with him. "Well, I'm not sure what all you'd like to know. I will say that I don't usually let anyone schedule my dates for me," he chuckled.

"That's refreshing to hear," Emily teased. She leaned in closer and her eyes sparkled. "What makes you happy, Wilbur?"

"What makes me happy?" Wilbur repeated. He thought about when he was happiest and the answer came to him. "I love to be out in nature.

And I love my family, as unconventional as they may be. What about you?"

"I love to travel," she breathed. "And I love to fly."

"You fly?" Wilbur asked.

"Yep," she nodded. "I just spread my wings and jump!" She laughed at her own joke which made Wilbur smile. She had such a great laugh that reminded him of bells ringing.

"There's something about being behind the controls of a plane," she explained. "Have you ever flown before, Wilbur?"

"Mavis has drug me on a few trips," Wilbur mentioned.

"I'll have to get you up in the air sometime," Emily smirked.

Wilbur was surprisingly excited at the offer.

Chapter Three

While Wilbur had a wonderful time on his first date with Emily, Mavis was up to her ears in the gossip of Rhinestone from the perspective of three women in their eighties. It was not a conversation for the faint of heart.

"Can you believe she dyed her hair purple?" Beulah yelled.

"Well, it matches the veins in her legs," Maude said.

"You're one to talk. Your legs look like a road map of Atlanta," Opal added quickly.

"Hey, these legs used to be the talk of the county," Maude countered.

"It wasn't your legs they were talking about," Beulah said. The women burst into a fit of laughter, ignoring everyone else in the restaurant who had been staring at them.

"But you know, back in the 80s, every old woman we knew had purple hair whether they wanted it or not," Maude said.

"At least until your Color Me Crazy line came out and fixed those problems once and for all," Beulah said to Opal proudly.

"You sure were successful with that," Maude said.

"You did Rhinestone proud alright," Beulah said. "But did you hear about Myrtle's grandson? Apparently, he got caught snackchapping some woman who was not his wife. Can you believe that!"

"What's snackchapping?" Maude wanted to know.

"It's one of those picture things for your phone," Opal said. She knew all the lingo thanks to her late-night television shows.

"These kids sure do come up with some weird names for these things," Maude said. "Snackchapping and dogfishing. What in the world are they going to come up with next?"

Mavis didn't have the energy to try to explain SnapChat to them. By the time the waitress brought the drinks and appetizers to the table, she knew all about every senior citizen in the tri-county area and their personal business, which was more than she had ever wanted to know.

After the waitress explained three different times that they didn't serve fish, Mavis took it upon herself to order for the table. She placed the order for two large pizzas, one with extra cheese and the other with half pepperoni for Maude and half pineapple for Opal. Beulah said there was no way that they would be able to eat all of that, but the other three knew that it wouldn't be a problem.

After the brief interruption of ordering, the women were off again on their conversation with Beulah yelling loud enough for everyone in the county to hear. Mavis' head was splitting and she was thankful when the waitress finally brought out the pizzas and the women quieted enough to eat. She wasn't sure how much longer she could take this kind of excitement. All was well until Beulah started making strange faces.

"Good Lord, what's the matter with you Beulah?" Maude yelled. "You choking?"

"The international symbol for choking is like this," Opal said as she grabbed at her throat with both hands.

"No, I got something caught in my teeth," Beulah said, still making a very peculiar face. Before Mavis could process the scene before her, Beulah pulled out her dentures and dropped them in her glass of ice water. She swirled the glass around several times then plopped them back in her mouth. She smacked her gums a few times. "There! That's better!" She wedged them in tightly and hoped they didn't fall out after such a good picking.

"Those came out way too easily," Mavis gagged. "Oh my heavens!" Mavis brought her napkin up to her mouth quickly. She gagged again slightly and had to look away. There wasn't much that could cause Mavis to lose her appetite, but that did it.

"I've got something that will make sure they don't pop out," Opal said sagely. "I'll bring it to your house next week."

"Y'all want anything for dessert?" the waitress asked.

"No, thank you," Mavis answered quickly, still looking a little green around the gills.

"I told y'all we'd never finish that," Beulah said.

Mavis needed some fresh air. She was thankful when Maude asked for the bill and promptly paid it. She rushed outside leaving the three ladies inside slowly following her.

"Hold your horses, Mavis! You worried about Wilbur?" Maude asked once she was outside. "We better go find them."

"No ma'am," Mavis replied. "I just needed some air. Let's give them a little more time to get to know each other."

"I need to walk over to that market over yonder," Beulah pointed across the street. "Y'all come on with me."

Mavis mumbled under her breath about how much Wilbur was going to owe her for this afternoon. She escorted Maude, Opal, and Beulah across the street to the sprawling flea market full of peddlers and salesmen. The flea market always had a terrible smell emanating from it that made Mavis' head hurt. She had been to the market many times when she worked for the antique store in town. There were definitely some good deals to be found, but there were also a lot of scams.

"That sign says they buy gold!" Beulah announced as they passed the first booth. "Doesn't look like gold to me." She turned her nose up at the man behind the counter.

"What exactly are you looking for?" Mavis asked her.

"I've been looking for one of those giant rugs," Beulah said. "I'll know it when I see it."

"Oh, like a flying carpet?" Opal asked. "Those are really nice. Everybody needs a flying carpet."

"She doesn't want a flying carpet," Maude replied.

"They are really hard to clean," Opal nodded, ignoring Maude.

"And besides, there ain't no such thing!" Maude said.

"Of course there are. I have one," Opal said.

"You don't have a flying carpet," Maude yelled.

"Just because it hasn't revealed its powers to you, doesn't mean I'm not in possession of one of the ancient wonders," Opal nodded.

"You ought to be in possession of a straitjacket," Maude mumbled.

"Well, I'm looking for one to go under my dining room table so it better not go anywhere," Beulah said. She wanted it fully known that no carpet of hers needed to galivant all over the place.

"Wonderful," Mavis muttered. She wished that she had a flying carpet so that she could be anywhere else. She hurried to keep up with the three women who had left her in the dust.

They passed racks of fur coats, rows of shoes and purses, and a counter that had boxes full of DVDs and old VHS tapes. They stopped briefly at one booth that boasted the world's largest coin collection, but Opal shook her head immediately when the man tried to sell her currency from Nepal. Little did this stranger know that Opal was a world traveler and had an expansive coin and currency collection of her own.

They walked the length of the main aisle, and to Beulah's dismay, the booth that sold rugs had been boarded up. She almost considered the trip a lost cause until she glimpsed a faded sign that had been tacked haphazardly onto a low counter. "Oh! You know I can't pass this up!" she howled.

Mavis' eyes widened as the older woman practically dove into the rack of skimpy bathing suits that looked like they hadn't been worn since 1980. The three older ladies ogled the different pieces and asked the wizened old man sitting in the chair what else he had to offer.

"I got some great deals for ladies of your caliber," he nodded. He disappeared behind the curtain and reappeared a few minutes later with a dusty box that had duct tape falling off it. "Check out what's in here!"

Mavis held her breath as Opal slowly peeled the rest of the tape off. There was no telling what was in that ancient box. She hoped that a rat didn't pop out. She backed away just to be safe.

"What in the world!" Maude coughed. A shower of dust and what looked to be spider eggs rained down on her as Beulah took over opening the box. "Are those? Are those slingshots?"

"No ma'am," the man said slowly. "Those are the finest and most genuine pairs of lady underpants on the market."

Mavis dared to peek in the box and nearly gagged again. The box was half full of underwear of all shapes and sizes, with three thongs on the top. "I'm good," she said. "No thanks."

"How much?" Beulah asked.

"Beulah!" Opal gasped. "It's a bunch of dirty laundry!"

"They're probably eat up with malaria or whatever other disease things like that carry," Maude huffed. "Come on, Opal, let's go look at those 8-track tapes over there." She and Opal scurried across the aisle leaving Mavis to choose who to follow.

The smells coming from the clothing booth were becoming too much. It was a mixture of moth balls, stale tobacco, and insect repellent. "Mrs. Beulah, I'm going to go see what they're getting into over here. Just walk over when you're done."

Beulah nodded and shooed Mavis away. She was about to haggle with this man. Mavis didn't know who to feel worse for. She held her nose and hurried after Maude and Opal who were having an intense conversation with the woman at the counter.

"It's a collector's item!" the woman explained.

"Negative," Maude said. "I won't pay more than five for that one."

"I can't sell it to you for that low," the woman snapped.

"Then I guess you won't sell it!" Maude huffed. She grabbed Opal's arm and tugged her towards a booth a few stalls down.

"Wait for me!" Mavis cried. Maude moved faster than someone a third of her age.

Thankfully the next booth had prices that were more akin to Maude's liking. She began to amass a small stack of records on the counter in front of her. After another ten minutes of searching through the box in front of her, she turned to Opal and showed her a record that looked to be in pristine condition.

"Y'all find any good deals?" Beulah asked suddenly. Maude had a stack of vinyl records in front of her that she was studying. "Oh, that's a good one!" Beulah pointed out.

"Did you find what you were looking for?" Mavis asked Beulah.

"No," Beulah said sadly. But her sadness was soon forgotten as she dove into the boxes to help Maude search for a Patsy Cline album.

After another ten minutes of looking through box after box and hearing Maude and Beulah haggle over pennies, Mavis couldn't take it any longer. "I think it's time to go check on the lovebirds," Mavis announced. She was at her wit's end.

"Lovebirds?" Opal asked warily, but she too was ready to leave the stale smell behind.

Thankfully the other two women agreed and carried their loot outside. Once they crossed the street towards the Chinese restaurant, Maude rubbed her stomach and said she could go for a snack, but Mavis shook her head and hurried them along.

She saw Wilbur and Emily casually talking at one of the first tables. The dishes had already been cleared and they looked like they were having a great time.

"There you are!" Beulah called out. She walked over to Emily's side of the table and sat down next to her.

"How was the food?" Maude asked.

"The food was great," Emily smiled.

"And the company was even better," Wilbur smiled.

Mavis slapped him on the back and grinned, "good one!" She gave him a thumbs up and nodded appreciatively at his compliment to Emily.

Wilbur ignored her and asked them if they had a nice lunch. "We had an interesting one," Mavis responded. "Then we went shopping at the flea market."

"Hate that I missed that," Emily giggled. She could see that Mavis had had one interesting afternoon. She couldn't imagine what all those three women had dragged her into.

"Oh, Emily! I got you something," Beulah said to Emily. "Hold on, let me get it out of my purse." She rummaged around her oversized bag and tossed out a handkerchief, her glasses case, dirty tissues, her house keys, and a half stick of chewing gum. Mavis scrambled to pick up the discarded items off the floor as Beulah continued to dig. "Oh! Here it is." She handed Emily a small plastic bag and beamed at her. "Go ahead and open it!"

Emily peered into the bag and gasped. Her cheeks flushed red and she shook her head fiercely. "Thank you, but um," her voice trailed off.

"Go ahead and show everyone! I got a great deal on them," Beulah said proudly. Emily shook her head again and tried to tuck the bag into her purse, but in a burst of energy, Beulah snatched the bag back and reached inside. "They didn't have my size, but I think these'll fit you right!"

She held up a neon yellow thong that looked like it was made out of rubber. Emily covered her face with her hand as Wilbur roared in laughter. Suddenly he was feeling much better about being embarrassed earlier.

"Now I'm mortified!" Emily whispered to Wilbur. She snatched the thong and the plastic bag and shoved them both into her purse. She flagged down the waitress and Wilbur snatched the bill from her before she could offer to pay.

"You think it'll fit you?" Beulah asked.

"It looks a little small," Maude said. "Go try it on and let us know. We don't have to see it."

Opal and Mavis were howling in laughter. "I think it's time for us to walk outside," Mavis hiccuped. She grabbed Maude's arm and led her and Opal outside so that Wilbur could pay the ticket and Emily could talk to her grandmother in private.

A few minutes later, a very red-faced Emily walked outside with Beulah. Wilbur followed behind, still chuckling. As they crossed the street back to the pizza place where their cars were parked, Opal promised Beulah that she'd get her the denture cream as soon as she could whip up the mixture. Once Beulah was in the car, Emily sighed and turned back to Wilbur and thanked him for lunch.

"I hope we can do this again soon," Emily said. "Well, maybe not all of this." She blushed again and shook her head with a smile. "It's always an adventure with her."

Wilbur nodded his head over at the three women who were watching him with eagle eyes. "Trust me, I know," he laughed. He hugged her goodbye and promised to call her.

"I'd like that," Emily said. She hopped in the driver's seat and slowly backed out of the parking lot. Beulah waved from the passenger seat happily.

Once the SUV was out of sight, Wilbur turned back to Maude, Opal, and Mavis.

"Well?" Mavis asked.

"Well what?" Wilbur smiled.

Mavis hit him playfully in the arm and asked," You didn't run her off, did you?"

"I think she likes you," Opal offered.

"I hope so," Wilbur grinned. "This afternoon was surely something." He chuckled again to himself and smiled brightly.

"What's so funny?" Maude asked.

Opal looked up at Wilbur as he helped her into the passenger seat of Maude's car. "First date and you already saw her underwear," she said gleefully.

"Wilbur, you know you were raised better than that!" Maude said, opening her car door.

"Mrs. Maude, Opal was talking about the underwear that Mrs. Beulah bought," Mavis explained.

"Oh, okay then. As long as that's it then," Maude said. "Especially at a nice restaurant like that."

"Yes ma'am. I promise that's all it was,"

Wilbur said. Not for the first time that afternoon did he vow never to bring Maude and Opal on a date again for as long as he lived.

Chapter Four

Wilbur didn't waste any time calling Emily later that night once he was home alone and settled in his recliner. He didn't want to make the same mistake twice and have Maude ring up Beulah again and make arrangements. When she answered, he told her that he had such a great time at lunch and hoped that he could take her out to dinner when she was free.

"Think we need chaperones this time?" Emily laughed.

"I think we might want to leave the chaperones out for a bit," he laughed.

"Are you sure? Don't you want to hear about false teeth and underwear that doubles as a weapon?" Emily teased. She couldn't see Wilbur's cheeks blush through the telephone, but she knew she'd caught him off guard.

"Would you believe that that's not the most awkward subject I've ever been a part of?" Wilbur laughed.

"After meeting Maude and Opal, I definitely believe it!" Emily giggled. "I already love them! They made my grandmother laugh so hard. She needed that for sure."

"I know it's been hard on her since Ms. Nadine

passed. I know it's been hard for all of them," Wilbur acknowledged.

"They went way back," Emily said. "I hear she and Maude had quite the friendship."

Wilbur laughed and nodded along. "That's for sure," he chuckled. Everyone who had been anywhere near Maude Cooper and Nadine Waters knew that they were in a lifelong prank war and enjoyed being the thorn in each other's side.

"And I really like Mavis," Emily said suddenly. "I hope we can get to know each other more."

"Mavis is great," Wilbur agreed. "She'd do anything for anyone. I think you two would get along swimmingly."

"I do have a question," Emily mused. "Who is Clive?"

"Oh Lordy! Clive is Mavis' catfish. I hooked him a few years ago on my line and she went berserk. She took him and tossed him in her aquarium and the rest is history," Wilbur explained. It was a wild story, as were most stories that involved Mavis.

"He lives in her home aquarium?" Emily gasped.

"Oh no," Wilbur corrected. "He outgrew that quickly. She finally agreed to let me and my buddy Harry relocate him."

"Relocate him? Did he go to a sanctuary somewhere?" Emily asked.

"Mavis would have never agreed to that," Wilbur laughed. "No, he's in the pond between my cabin and the Manor. Mavis is crazy about that fish. I can't believe I'm going to say this, but I think that fish knows his name. It's like she tamed him or something. Or maybe he just responds to all the food she feeds him."

"When you say he outgrew the aquarium?" Emily began.

"He's huge," Wilbur said. "He's easily the size of a baby whale."

"You're kidding!" Emily laughed.

"I'm serious!" Wilbur laughed loudly. "You'll have to see him one of these days. He's massive."

"I'll be sure to see him with my own eyes," Emily said. "I know many men lie about the size of fish," she giggled.

Wilbur blushed again and shook his head. "He's probably the biggest fish I've ever seen in these parts. You'll have to see her aquarium, too." He told her all about the floor to ceiling aquarium that he and Jameson had helped install for Ruby Montgomery decades ago. He told her all about the colorful fish from around the world that Ruby collected until she passed away and Mavis inherited the Manor. When Mavis rescued Clive from Wilbur's cooler, she released him into the aquarium with Ruby's tropical fish. He promptly ate them all over the next few days, much to Mavis' dismay.

"Now that Clive is in his new home, I ordered Mavis new fish to replace the ones Clive devoured all those years ago," Wilbur explained.

"Wow! You weren't kidding about what you said the other day. Mavis really does keep things exciting," Emily said.

"That's an understatement," Wilbur chuckled. "I need to check with Mauricio and see when the fish will be delivered. I think it's sometime this week."

"I'd love to come see them," Emily said.

"Absolutely," Wilbur said. He knew Mavis wouldn't mind at all. She loved showing off her pets and entertaining guests at the Manor.

"And you can meet the llamas, too," Wilbur added.

"Llamas!" Emily exclaimed. "This is getting even more exciting!"

Wilbur detailed how Mavis had bid for the llamas after the petting zoo owner decided to auction them off after the county fair. Mavis had her own little eclectic slice of heaven at Magnolia Manor.

"So, back to the original question at hand," Wilbur smiled. "Can I take you to dinner one night? No chaperones," he reminded her.

"How about tomorrow night?" Emily offered quickly.

"Tomorrow sounds perfect. I was thinking about driving over to Junction to this German place they have. It's right next to the movie theater," Wilbur mentioned.

"You pick dinner and I'll pick the movie. It's a date!" Emily agreed. Wilbur liked the sound of that.

They spent the two hours talking all about their childhoods, their favorite foods and colors, and everything else two people who didn't feel like strangers could talk about. Wilbur couldn't believe how well this budding relationship was going. When they hung up a few minutes before eleven, Wilbur was elated.

Before he went to sleep that night, he sent Mavis a text message and told her that he was going on an official date the following evening, □ but asked that she keep it on the down low from Maude and Opal just in case they decided to check up on him.

"My lips are sealed," Mavis promised. "Just make sure to keep your elbows off the table and your teeth inside your mouth."

"I'll do my best," Wilbur replied. He could tell that Mavis really liked Emily, even though she hadn't spent much time with her. He knew that she and Emily would have lots to talk about when they got together.

Wilbur slept soundly that night and awoke before his alarm. He had a cup of coffee as he read the newspaper and went through his list of things to do for the day.

The next day passed quickly as Wilbur finished up some last-minute touches on his new barn. It was everything he had ever dreamed of. He had recently acquired an antique Ford tractor and needed a better place to store it. The tractor was a bit of a fixer upper, but Wilbur didn't mind. He enjoyed working on a project that was all his. Now that the new barn was built, he moved Jameson's old Massey Ferguson tractor beside his Ford underneath it. They looked so regal underneath their coverings next to the custom countertops and cabinets he had organized his tools in.

He had always been very handy. He was always looking for new projects to keep his tinkering mind busy. Not that Mavis, Maude, or Opal ever let him get too bored. He checked his watch and figured that he had just enough time to ride over to the Manor and fix the latch on the gate that led to the llama pen. Mavis' new babies, as she referred to them, had already chewed through the original mechanism on the gate. The three llamas were already more of a nuisance than he could have imagined, but Mavis adored them.

When he arrived at the Manor, he didn't see Mavis' car anywhere in sight. She had mentioned that she and Mona were going out to look for antiques at some point this week, so he assumed she was out and about buying more things she didn't have room for. The poor trailer out back was jammed pack with items from her adventures. She was Ruby Montgomery's granddaughter through and through.

Instead he was greeted by Clementine, Winnie, and Morgan who were lazily lounging in the barn in their indoor stall. Mavis had already decorated the large pen with bright colors and photographs of the llamas in different hats and monogrammed bridles. These llamas had hit the jackpot when Mavis Montgomery bid on them at the fair's auction.

Once he had the new latch ready to go, Wilbur jumped back in his truck to head home. He took a quick shower and styled his hair. Then he got dressed and made sure he looked his very best. The nerves were finally starting to set in, but he shook them off and headed to Beulah's house across town to pick up Emily.

Beulah and her husband, Bart, were sitting on the porch when he pulled into the driveway. Bartholomew Johnson was a retired automobile salesman who now owned a few car lots scattered around the southeast. He was Beulah's second husband after her first husband, Emily's grandfather, had passed away twenty or so years ago. Bart was a nice man, a very quiet man, which was the direct opposite of Beulah who perked up the instant she saw Wilbur.

"Hey!" she waved from the front porch. "You here to see Emily?"

"Yes ma'am," Wilbur said. He shook Bart's hand and made small talk with him while Beulah ran inside to check on things with Emily. When she came outside a few minutes later, Wilbur couldn't help but grin. Emily wore a nice pair of jeans and a Halloween sweater that looked comfortable rather than stylish. She didn't seem keen on the high fashion standards of the day that most women fawned over, which suited Wilbur just fine.

Emily hugged Bart and Beulah goodbye and skipped down the steps towards Wilbur's truck. "I'll pick you up next time," she declared to Wilbur.

"So there's already going to be a next time?" Wilbur smiled.

"I don't see why not," Emily shrugged playfully. "Unless you're going to dogfish me or whatever the new trend is. Plus, I want to see those animals you told me about."

Emily was naturally funny. She was extremely witty and kept Wilbur on his toes. They laughed the entire drive to the restaurant in Junction. When they walked in, they felt like they had entered a new Bavarian world. They were seated at a long family style table with other people who looked just as excited as they were. This particular restaurant had a stage in the front center where live musicians played and danced. They ordered their drinks and served themselves from the big bowls on the table in front of them. Bowls full of schnitzel and mushroom gravy, thick sausages, and chewy spaetzle were replenished frequently. They each tried the potato soup and had seconds of sauerkraut. When it came time for dessert, they each had a thick slice of cake topped with whipped cream and raspberries. It was such a filling dinner. It topped Wilbur's list of some of the best food he had ever eaten. Maybe he would take Mavis up on the idea of traveling to Germany one summer.

As the food bowls were cleared away, the stage lights came up and the show began. Three men dressed in lederhosen came onstage carrying three different musical instruments. The first man opened the show with his accordion that instantly made everyone want to dance. The second man played the lute and the third a small flute. When a fourth man stepped on stage and blew into the long alphorn, the crowd erupted in applause.

"What a show!" Wilbur announced. He and Emily exited the restaurant with the crowd of people and walked back to the truck. "What movie did you decide on?"

"I've been dying to see this fascinating little

documentary," Emily said. "I hope you're going to love it!"

When they pulled up to the theater, Emily led the way to the ticket counter and purchased two tickets. She handed Wilbur his ticket and he followed her to the concession stand where she loaded up on popcorn and chocolate melts.

The documentary centered around an apiary and the inner workings of a bee colony. It was something that Opal would have been delighted to watch. He made a mental note to mention it to her next time he talked to her. He wasn't sure if she still went to movie theaters or not. She and Maude would probably not do well in quiet places. He silently chuckled at the idea of Maude and Opal sitting on the front row reviewing the movie to each other, much to the annoyance of their fellow movie goers. Once the movie ended, Emily turned to him and asked what he thought. "I'm not usually one for documentaries, but that was interesting," he nodded.

"Bees are so fascinating! I hear Ms. Opal is the one to talk to about bees," Emily exclaimed. "Maybe she could help me set up a new hive in the spring."

"I bet she'd be tickled pink," Wilbur agreed as they walked out of the theater. The evening air had grown much colder since they entered the theater two hours earlier.

On the drive back to Rhinestone, they didn't even turn on the radio. They never ran out of anything to talk about. When he pulled into Beulah's driveway, he wasn't sure if he should walk her to the door or not. Emily was a spitfire and already had her hand on the door.

"This has been a lot of fun, Wilbur," Emily smiled. She leaned over and kissed him on the cheek before sliding out of the truck and hopping up the front porch steps. She turned to wave before she opened the front door.

Wilbur was on cloud nine. He dialed Mavis on the way home and breathlessly told her all about his evening. "And she wants to meet the llamas and Clive," he exclaimed.

"Oh Wilbur, you can't talk about me on a date. And you certainly can't talk about livestock and catfish, the animal or the trend," she scolded him. "If you need me to coach you, let me know. I won't even charge you! I know it's been a minute since you've been on the dating scene."

"No way," Wilbur said. It was true that he wasn't very experienced when it came to dating, but he wasn't sure that Mavis' approach to things was the way he should go.

"I'm not saying you need my help," Mavis quickly interjected. "I'm just saying that I'm here if you need me." Before they got off the phone she added, "Just play it cool. Be yourself."

"Thanks Mavis," Wilbur smiled. He wasn't sure that he himself was anywhere near the standard of what was deemed cool, but there was something about him that Emily seemed to like.

He was practically floating as he pulled up to his log cabin a few minutes later. He couldn't wait to see Emily again. They hadn't made definitive plans for the next date, but she had said there would be one for sure. A part of him wanted to call her before bed even though he had just dropped her off, but Mavis had told him to play it cool. He went to sleep that night with a big smile on his face and woke up the next morning with a text message from Emily asking him to lunch that day.

Chapter Five

Still feeling giddy, Wilbur called Emily and said he would love to meet her for lunch. She explained that she had a work function at one o'clock in Junction, but would love to have a quick lunch with him before. To make it easier for her, he said he would met her in Junction at the restaurant of her choice.

"There's this cute little cafe on the corner of Main and First Street. Want to meet there a few minutes after eleven?" Emily suggested.

Wilbur was willing to try anything, especially if it meant more time getting to know Emily. He readily agreed and said he would see her then.

Wilbur rang Mauricio while he got ready. Mauricio laughed and said that he was just about to dial Wilbur's number. "They're being loaded on the truck now. I think the boys will have them at the Manor around three this afternoon. Will you be there?"

"I'll see you all at three," Wilbur agreed. He called Mavis to let her know that the fish truck would be there around three o'clock, and she said she would do her best to be there. He could hear a tone of frustration in her voice, so he asked her what was wrong.

"Wilbur, Maude has done it again!" she swore.

"Is everything ok?" Wilbur gasped.

"No!" Mavis howled. "Listen Wilbur, we need to do something about her," Mavis said. "It's getting serious!"

"What did she do now?" Wilbur asked.

"Where do I begin!" Mavis started.

"Mavis! What's going on?" Wilbur asked calmly.

"She tore up my azaleas! Again!" Mavis grumbled.

"What?" Wilbur asked for clarification.

"Maude drove over my azaleas again last night and I just went out there to check on them and they're tore up to shreds. I can't take this anymore! She hit my trashcan last week!" Mavis continued. She was getting worked up and Wilbur knew it would be best to hear her out.

"Have you noticed how bad her driving has gotten recently?" Mavis asked.

"Recently? It's been terrible for ages," Wilbur said.

"Well, yes, but it's gotten even worse," Mavis said. "She doesn't know how to stop. I swear she doesn't hit the brakes at all! It's like they aren't even a part of her car. I saw the way she parked at the get together the other day."

"You mean my playdate with Emily?" Wilbur smiled.

"Yes. Anyway, did you notice she was all over the curb? If she'd been any closer, she would have run through the restaurant!" Mavis said with far more concern than she normally showed.

"I saw that. I also noticed that she hit the light pole at the Starlight the other day," Wilbur nodded. "But I'm not brave enough to tell her not to drive."

"Me neither, but we need to do something before she drives up on the front porch and through the living room of someone's home," Mavis said.

Wilbur thought for a few minutes. "I'll run over to the lumberyard in Junction tomorrow and pick up some cross ties and make a decorative border in front of the azaleas. It might not stop her, but it should slow her down before she hits the porch."

"You're going to have to do something," Mavis sighed. "It'll probably be my home she runs through!"

"I'll take care of it," Wilbur promised her. "I'll be over a little before three to get the fish taken care of. Emily mentioned that she'd like to see the fish one day, so I'd love for y'all to get together if you want."

"I'd love that!" Mavis gushed in a sudden change of tone. "Bring her with you this afternoon! Oh! Someone's beeping in. I'll see you later!" She hung up before Wilbur could explain that Emily had things to attend to this afternoon, but he was pleased to hear that Mavis was eager to spend more time with Emily.

He finished what he needed to do around the house and got in his truck to drive to Junction. Emily was already seated at one of the tables inside when he pulled up. He felt underdressed when he saw how dressed up she was in her navy-blue pants and matching blazer.

"You look very nice," he told her.

"Thank you," she smiled. "I have a pretty important meeting with a client over in that building across the street at one. Have to look my best!"

The restaurant that Emily picked mainly served a selection of soups, salads, and sandwiches. Emily ordered a Greek salad while Wilbur went with a chicken melt.

"So what kind of meeting is it?" Wilbur asked.

Emily told him about the young startup company that specialized in vegan, gluten-free, and organic snacks. They had been in business for a little over a year and were in the process of making a name for themselves. Their goal was to be statewide within the next two years and have a regional presence within the next five. Her marketing firm was responsible for the massive promotional campaign to launch a new product they were releasing. If it went well, they would sign her firm exclusively.

"Wow! That sounds huge," Wilbur said.

"It's going to be quite an undertaking, but it'll be a challenge and who doesn't like a challenge?" Emily winked at him. "Plus I have an amazing team working on this. They make me look good."

They talked a bit more about the meeting before they changed the subject to Wilbur. "So what are your plans for this afternoon?" she asked.

They spent the next twenty minutes talking

about Wilbur's projects. When the check came, Wilbur instinctively reached for it, but Emily was faster. "Nope. It's my turn," she said.

"But you got the movie last night," he reminded her.

"Yes, and you got dinner. It's my turn," she was firm, but not unkind.

"Yes ma'am," he smiled.

They gave each other a quick hug and kiss on the cheek at the door before Emily turned and marched toward her meeting with a confident stride. He watched her walk away and then slowly walked to his truck smiling wider than he had in a long time.

Wilbur pulled up to the Manor with plenty of time to spare. Mavis was outside in her flower bed covered in dirt mumbling under her breath. She hadn't been lying about the damage Maude had wreaked on her flowers and bushes.

"Oh my," he mused.

"I told you!" Mavis sighed. "I don't know if any of these can be saved." She held up the broken pieces of one of the bushes and shook her head. "Big Mama would have whooped her for sure if she had seen this."

Wilbur chuckled to himself at the thought of Ruby tying up with Maude. Ruby didn't often get upset about things, but when she did, it was best to stay out of her way. She loved her outdoor garden and beds full of her prized flower collections fiercely, which made him think that Mavis was probably right. He helped her rake some of the disheveled greenery and stake what branches could be saved to the healthier ones.

When Mauricio's truck pulled up in front of the magnolia tree, Wilbur brushed off his hands and helped Mavis to her feet. "Go get cleaned up and I'll help them get unloaded."

Mavis waved to Mauricio and his team and scurried inside to wash her hands and change clothes. Wilbur held the door to the Manor open as the men unloaded boxes of tropical fish for the tank. They had brought a few new temperature gauges and pipes and tubes for the tank to install since Clive and his pond scum had damaged the original ones.

Wilbur scanned the paper that Mauricio handed him and smiled appreciatively. "Everything looks good," he nodded.

Mauricio outlined the various kinds of fish he had brought over. "I think she'll be set for a while," Mauricio smiled proudly.

"Look at all the pretty colors!" Mavis squealed as she bounded down the stairs. She pressed her face against the boxes that held the different bags of fish.

"No more catfish," Mauricio joked.

"I swear," Mavis nodded. Her cheeks blushed and she giggled sweetly. "I can't wait to name them!" She watched as the men carefully lifted each bag up to the top of the gigantic tank and gently placed the bags in the water to let the fish acclimate to the water. The brilliant anemones and different corals looked beautiful at the bottom of the tank. The team had brought them in the week before to acclimate to the tank before the fish arrived.

"We're going to let them acclimate for about half an hour before we release them," Mauricio explained. His team checked the levels of the water and made sure the gauges and controls were all in perfect order in the cabinet underneath the tank while they waited. When it was time to release the fish from their individual bags, Mavis could hardly contain her excitement.

"I feel like a little kid again!" she squealed.

Wilbur knew exactly how she felt. He remembered how he felt when Ruby's first order of fish had arrived when he was a kid. The colorful fish brought such a vibrant shock of colors to the pale-yellow walls of the kitchen. It would be nice to see such life in the tank again.

"I bet Clive is hungry," Mavis muttered to herself. She looked out the kitchen window towards the wood line and saw the heavy rain clouds that had moved in. "I didn't see rain on the forecast this morning," she grumbled.

"It's going to be a big storm," Mauricio said. "Might want to tighten up the barn before too long."

"My llamas!" Mavis gasped.

"I'll take care of them," Wilbur said. He shook Mauricio's hand and headed outside to the barn to wrangle the beasts into their stall.

"Don't forget their raincoats! They're on the hooks in their stalls," Mavis told Wilbur. "Each one has a raincoat in their favorite color."

"Raincoats?" Wilbur asked. "I don't think llamas need raincoats."

Mavis looked aghast. "Of course they do Wilbur. These are domesticated llamas, not wild animals."

"Oh, I forgot," Wilbur shook his head and headed to the barn. It didn't take him long to fasten the monogrammed rain jackets onto each llama. They seemed used to Mavis' antics already. When he traipsed back into the house a few minutes later, Mavis turned towards him with a confused look.

"Where's Emily?" Mavis asked. She had suddenly remembered that she had told Wilbur to bring her with him.

"She had a meeting," Wilbur explained. He looked at his watch and saw that it was a few minutes past five o'clock. Surely she was out of her meeting by now. He didn't want to call and interrupt her just in case she was still working, but he decided to send her a picture of the gleaming finished tank for her to look at later. He shook Mauricio's hand again and thanked his team for all of their hard work.

"Thank you so much!" Mavis chirped. She was already head over heels for her new fish.

Wilbur held the door for the men to walk back outside to their truck. The rain had steadily started to come down in the few minutes he had been back inside. He watched the truck drive away and turned back to examine the tank for himself. A few seconds later, Wilbur's phone rang. It was Emily. Wilbur answered on the second ring still out of breath.

"Nice!" Mavis giggled and gave him the

thumbs up sign.

"How did your meeting go?" Wilbur asked Emily, ignoring Mavis in the background. "Tell her I said hi!" Mavis whispered.

"That's great! Oh, I'm fine here. The fish look really good and then I had to make sure that the llamas were dressed in the most fashionable all-weather attire," Wilbur laughed.

"Don't say it like that!" Mavis hissed. "You just don't understand fashion!"

Wilbur could hear Emily laughing.

"Tell her to come over!" Mavis whispered loudly behind him. "Wilbur! Tell her to come see my fish! She can stay for supper."

"Mavis wants to know if you'd like to join us here at the Manor for supper," Wilbur said. He nodded quickly to Mavis who gave a quick cheer. By the time he hung up the phone, Mavis was in the kitchen with several pots on the stove. "It's not cold enough for chili, but spaghetti should be fine," she said as she dropped the noodles in the pot to cook. The wind howled outside and hit the window.

"Sounds good. I'm going to wash up," Wilbur said.

"Hurry up," Mavis said. "You're on garlic bread duty."

"Yes ma'am," Wilbur laughed. He ducked into the small bathroom off the side of the kitchen and rolled up his sleeves and washed his hands. He dried them on the hand towel and hurried back to the kitchen to help Mavis.

"I don't have time to make any homemade

bread since it's last minute, but there's a frozen loaf in the freezer," Mavis directed. "Oh Lord, I'm sure I look a mess! Wilbur, I need you to watch this pasta while I go shower. Don't let it stick!" She flew out of the kitchen and up the stairs.

Wilbur knew how to make spaghetti and garlic bread. He had it ready in no time, complete with the red sauce with chopped up hamburger meat. By the time Mavis came back downstairs, the table had been set and glasses of sweet tea had been poured.

"How could I forget dessert!" she gasped. She threw open cupboard doors and looked around maniacally. "We can't have supper without dessert!"

"It's fine, Mavis," Wilbur assured her. The doorbell rang and Mavis stared at Wilbur. "Go open it!" she encouraged him. "It's your girlfriend."

"She's not my girlfriend," Wilbur hissed. Or was she? He and Emily hadn't exactly defined what they were or weren't yet, but she was coming over to his sister's house for supper, so that had to account for something.

He could hear Mavis still searching for something to serve for dessert in the kitchen while he opened the front door. "You look great!" he exclaimed.

"Thanks, but I'm wearing the same thing from earlier," Emily smiled.

"And it still looks great," Wilbur shrugged. He ushered her inside and out of the rain that was still coming down in sheets. "I'm glad you made it here safely. This storm sure is something."

"This is for dessert," Emily said. She handed Wilbur a lemon loaf that was wrapped in plastic wrap. "My grandmother made it this afternoon and insisted that I bring it with me."

"You don't know how happy you just made Mavis," Wilbur grinned. It made him happy, too. He loved anything with lemons. He led Emily into the kitchen where Mavis was stirring the sauce at the stove.

"Oh Emily!" Mavis beamed as she came around the corner. Wilbur handed Mavis the lemon loaf and repeated what Emily had said. "Oh my! Thank you, Emily! That is so sweet of you to bring us dessert!" She took the lemon loaf and set it on the counter. When Emily turned around to marvel at the tank, Mavis whispered to Wilbur, "Oh my God, I just love her!"

Chapter Six

The three of them had a wonderful time talking over dinner. Emily was able to keep up with Mavis' rapid-fire questions and found her truly genuine. When it was time for dessert, they had already planned a time for Mavis to introduce Emily to Mona so she could join them on one of their yard sale weekends. Mavis wiped down the table while Wilbur rinsed the dishes before putting them in the dishwasher. "So, Emily, what are your plans tomorrow?" Mavis asked slyly.

Tomorrow was Halloween and while Mavis loved a holiday that revolved around candy and themed food, she had already promised Maude that she would come over to her house that evening to hand out candy with her. Opal had put in to turn her own porch into an interactive spooky walk-through event, but Maude refused to help her. Instead she wanted to watch one of the classic black and white films that had terrible graphics and hand out candy when the doorbell rang. Opal reluctantly agreed to put aside her whimsical haunted house, only because Maude had just helped her run a very successful fortune telling booth at the annual county fair earlier in the month.

"I was planning on sitting on the porch of my grandmother's house to hand out candy. Unless you know of something more exciting?" Emily replied.

"I'm not sure what Wilbur has planned, but I'll be at Maude and Opal's making sure they don't scare any of the neighborhood children too badly," Mavis laughed.

"I honestly hadn't thought about Halloween," Wilbur shrugged. "If you need my help over there," he started to say, but Mavis and Emily both said "yes" excitedly.

"They both seem like so much fun!" Emily said.

"That's one way to put it," Wilbur said. He wasn't sure what new and embarrassing things Emily was about to learn about him from Maude and Opal, and even Mavis once she got riled up on candy.

"We're going to have so much fun!" Mavis squealed.

After Mavis showed Emily each of the new fish, they came up with the perfect names for each one. Wilbur ate his second slice of lemon loaf while the women giggled over names like Shakespeare, Othello, Romeo, Juliet, Hamlet, Julius, Puck, and Macbeth. Mavis loved a good theme when it came to naming things, and she had an obsession with Shakespearean works. Emily agreed that it was the perfect theme to name such beautiful regal fish, so she rattled off mores name like Cleopatra, Antonio, Ophelia, and Titania. Wilbur hoped there wouldn't be a quiz at the end of the naming session because some of the fish looked identical to each other and there was no way he could tell them apart.

It was too dark and stormy outside for Emily to get acquainted with the llamas, so Mavis promised to have her over soon so she could meet them properly. Mavis hugged her goodbye and said she couldn't wait to hang out with her again tomorrow night. She went back to straightening up the kitchen while Wilbur grabbed an umbrella and walked Emily out to her car.

"Thanks for coming to dinner, and thanks for bringing that cake. You saved the whole meal," Wilbur smiled.

"I had so much fun! Mavis is great. Are you sure it's ok for me to come crash your Halloween party tomorrow?" Emily asked.

"It's less of a party and more of a small group of potential chaos," Wilbur laughed. "I'd love for you to come. And I know Mavis is excited, too."

The rain hadn't lightened up at all during dinner. The wind whipped through the trees and threatened to tear Wilbur's umbrella from his hands. "You stay on the porch," Emily said. "I don't mind a little rain."

"It's not a little rain," Wilbur countered as a crack of lightning lit up the sky.

"It's fine!" Emily grinned. She jumped off the porch and spun around in the rain like a mad woman. "I love the rain." She laughed out loud as Wilbur shook his head. "See you tomorrow!" She waved and opened her car door and closed it quickly. Wilbur watched her back out of the

Manor's front yard carefully and expertly. Mavis would be thrilled to know that her remaining azaleas were still intact.

Mavis called Maude the next morning and let her know that they had invited Emily to come and spend the evening with them. "I'm glad their playdate went well," she nodded on the phone. "Wilbur can thank me later."

The next afternoon, Mavis and Wilbur arrived at Maude's house around five o'clock. Opal had insisted on making one of her vegan stews made from vegetables from her garden and roots from the tree line behind her house. Maude refused to partake in anything Opal cooked that didn't have at least a pound of meat in it, so she asked Wilbur and Mavis to stop by the Piggly Wiggly and bring a few boxes of fried chicken over. They happily obliged and brought biscuits, mashed potatoes, and green beans as well. Mavis chose two vanilla pound cakes and a container of iced sugar cookies that were shaped like spiders and ghosts.

Emily was set to arrive around six o'clock and Wilbur was getting more nervous as the minutes ticked by. When he arrived at Maude's house with the food, Maude asked if Emily had changed her mind about coming.

"No ma'am," Wilbur said. "She'll be here after work."

"Who will be after work?" Opal asked. She stood on a small stepstool in front of the stove stirring a large pot of thick bubbling liquid.

"Wilbur's girlfriend is coming over," Maude reminded her.

"She's not my girlfriend," Wilbur mumbled.

"You still ain't asked her?" Maude sighed. "Oh Lordy, Opal! We gotta help him again."

"I don't think I need you to arrange another playdate," Wilbur explained. "We're having a great time getting to know each other."

"They've gone on a few dates," Mavis nodded encouragingly. "And she seems to really like him. I'm making sure of that." She patted Wilbur on the arm and then snuck a piece of fried chicken from the box.

"You need to lock her down," Opal added over her shoulder. "Women like Emily don't come around often." Even though Opal hadn't spent any time with Emily, she had a keen way of knowing things about people.

"Lock her down?" Wilbur asked.

"You gotta get down on one knee! I already explained things to you once," Maude said. She slapped him on the back causing him to spill some of this punch.

"He's not proposing!" Mavis shrieked.

"No, no," Opal intervened. "The kids these days do big gestures. You gotta stay hip, Wilbur."

"What's wrong with his hip?" Maude asked. "You need to exercise more?" she asked him.

"You need to exercise more!" Opal rebutted. She turned away from Maude to face Wilbur who was red-faced. "You need a big gesture, but I don't think a ring is the right one just yet. There'll be time for that soon enough. Hmm. Let me think about it for a minute."

"Wilbur just needs to speak from the heart,"

Mavis interjected. "And how do you know about promposals and big gestures?" she asked Maude and Opal. A promposal was the term given to elaborate, and often extravagant, gestures that teenagers used to ask someone on a date or to a dance.

"We are cool," Maude said indignantly.

"We stay abreast of the latest fashion and slang," Opal nodded. "Well, at least I do."

Wilbur nor Mavis wanted to ask any more questions. They weren't sure where the two old ladies were getting their news about standards and trends of the day, but it made for hilarious conversation. Maude and Opal were now arguing over who knew more about modern day teenagers, so Mavis took the opportunity to talk to Wilbur privately. "Just talk to her," she smiled. "She likes you and you like her. Plus, you aren't getting any younger."

"What's that supposed to mean?" he asked.

"According to Maude, you should be on your second wife by now," Mavis laughed. "Oh relax, I'm just kidding. Just talk to Emily and whatever you do, don't take any advice from them without consulting me first."

"Right," Wilbur laughed. "You're the one up to date with the latest trends."

"I've never had a negative review from any client," Mavis shrugged.

"Oh Lord," Wilbur shook his head. The doorbell rang and Maude jumped to attention. "Thanks Mavis, I'll take it from here," Wilbur whispered.

"It's too early for the kids to be out," Maude

said. "Who could that be?"

"Probably Emily," Mavis reminded her, "Wilbur, why don't you check?"

Wilbur nodded and walked to the door. He could see Emily through the window next to the door. She was wearing a bright orange sweater with a black cat embroidered on it, tight black jeans, and a witches hat. He opened the door and she smiled radiantly. "Where's your costume?" she asked him.

"I didn't think to wear one," he replied.

"We can fix that!" Opal chimed in from behind the door. She had donned a set of cat ears and Mavis was drawing whiskers and a nose on her face with a black makeup pencil. "Alright, Maude, you're next!"

"I ain't letting you paint me like one of those girls of the night. No way," Maude shook her head. She was sitting at the kitchen table eating her second bowl of ice cream.

"But it's Halloween!" Mavis protested. She was dressed up like a hippie from the 1970s, complete with large glasses, a beaded vest, bangled bracelets, and smiley face and peace sign fake tattoos on her cheeks.

"I'm fine dressed how I am," Maude replied. She had on a royal blue sweatsuit with a picture of a wild horse on it.

"Yes, she's dressed as an old coot," Opal said. "Same thing she goes as every day."

Emily and Mavis giggled. Maude flicked a spoonful of ice cream towards Opal's head, but missed by two feet and ended up hitting Wilbur in the ear.

"Sorry Wilbur!" Maude croaked.

Emily wiped the ice cream off of him with a paper towel and smiled. "Are you a grump on Halloween, too?" she asked him quietly.

"No," he laughed. "I just haven't dressed up since I was a kid."

"We'll have to make plans sooner next time," she shrugged. Wilbur's heart skipped a beat.

"Alright, time to eat before the kids come rambling over," Maude said. She had the food spread out on the table and handed everyone a paper plate. No sooner had they sat down to eat did the doorbell ring.

"I'll get it," Opal volunteered. She skipped to the door and opened it to reveal a group of tiny children and their parents who yelled "trick or treat!" She oohed and ahhed over them while Maude leaned in closer to Emily and whispered loudly, "Don't eat whatever's in that pot on the stove. It could kill you or either run through your guts so bad that you wish you were dead."

Emily nodded and looked at Wilbur with a slight grin. Opal had already doled her out a bowl of the think gumbo and it smelled delicious. While she was slightly hesitant after Maude's warning, she took a sip form her spoon as Maude stared at her with wide eyes. Emily could feel Mavis and Wilbur looking at her too, so she took the opportunity to be a little silly. She pretended to cough and gag as Opal returned to the table.

"You killed her Opal! All before Wilbur could ask her to be his girl!" Maude howled. She jumped up and whacked Emily on the back just in case she was choking.

"I didn't kill her!" Opal shouted. "She's laughing too hard to be dead."

Emily was indeed laughing at the two women who turned everything into a squabble. Wilbur looked embarrassed and Mavis continued to shovel mashed potatoes into her mouth. "I'm teasing," Emily grinned. "Ms. Opal, the stew is delicious. I can taste the chicory in it which makes it perfect."

"See! She knows good food when she sees it!" Opal cheered.

"Still looks poisonous to me," Maude retorted.

"And what's this about you asking me to be your girl?" Emily turned to Wilbur who groaned.

"He has to ask you to be his girlfriend," Maude explained slowly in between bites of chicken. "He's been out of practice. Wilbur, have you ever had a girlfriend?" Before Wilbur could open his mouth to respond, Maude continued. "He's never had a serious girlfriend before. Mavis has been in a serious relationship once, but that was Earl and he doesn't count."

"He looked like a bird," Opal added. "An ugly bird."

Mavis spit out a bite of her green beans and quickly scrambled to clean up after herself. She had not expected the conversation to turn to Earl.

"There's a lot to unpack here," Emily said. "Wilbur, I like you and I think you like me. We've been on a few dates and talk all day long, so unless this is how you treat all your friends, I think we can go ahead and call a spade a spade."

"He's not good at card games," Opal said solemnly.

Emily smiled warmly at Opal. "I'll have to teach him," she winked. She reached for his hand and held it firmly underneath the table. "And who in the world is this birdlike creature named Earl?"

All eyes turned to Mavis who sat frozen in her seat. "Yes, Mavis, who is Earl?" Wilbur chuckled. He was glad that the attention had been refocused on her because he could feel his heart beating out of his chest. Emily already considered them an item. He was happier than he had ever felt before.

"Well, you see," Mavis stuttered.

"Earl was a crazy son of a gun who near about runed all our lives," Maude interrupted. "He tried to rob us and fight us all."

Emily's eyes widened and Opal jumped in next. "He was Mavis' boyfriend but we got her away from him alright!"

Mavis wanted to hide underneath the table. Thankfully Emily could see that she was mortified, so she leaned over and whispered, "You can tell me later if you want." Then she changed the subject to the documentary that she and Wilbur had seen the other night.

"I heard about that one," Opal nodded. "Remind me later and we can walk over and see all of my hives. Wilbur and Jameson built me those hive boxes back in the eighties."

"I'd love to see them!" Emily smiled.

The doorbell rang again and Mavis offered to clean up the kitchen while Wilbur took Emily and

Opal outside to sit on the porch to hand out candy. Maude stayed behind to help Mavis put away the dinner fixings. Once the leftovers were put away, Maude opened the box of iced sugar cookies and ate one. "What do you think of Emily?" she asked Mavis.

"I really like her!" Mavis said.

"Does she remind you of anyone?" Maude asked warily.

Mavis thought for a second and shook her head. No one was coming to mind. "Why do you ask?"

"Nothing," Maude said. She ate another cookie and looked out the window at the three of them on the porch. "What in the world is going on?"

Wilbur barreled back inside with Opal and Emily on his tail. "What's going on?" Mavis asked.

"My front door camera just went off. Someone just drove past my cabin into the woods," he said.

Maude growled and looked at Opal. "Time to load up!"

"No, y'all stay here and I'll go see what's going on," he frowned. There was no need to expose any of them to any potential danger of trespassers.

Chapter Seven

Wilbur flew out to his truck in a flurry without another word. He had never had to deal with anyone trespassing on his or Mavis' land. What concerned him most was reading about a string of break-ins that had been happening recently. The thieves hadn't taken much during each attempt, but they had caused quite a bit of damage during their time on each property which frazzled him. He drove like Maude all the way to his house. His foot didn't touch the brakes until he pulled into his driveway.

He jogged over to his barn out back near the tree line. He saw fresh tracks and a rut where someone had certainly just been. The footprints in the dirt showed two different boots. The door to his barn was still open, and when he walked inside, he almost swore. Everything that was normally organized and clean was now a wreck. He stepped over busted glass and pushed a discarded box of nails out of the way so he didn't step on them. He could see that he was missing some expensive tools, but what really aggravated him was the fact that someone had been sniffing ⬜ around his prized tractors. The covers had been torn off and there was a fresh scratch across the oldest one. He looked around the barn and didn't see anyone hiding. There were other ways to drive off the land through the woods, which is probably where the bandits had gone. Wilbur knew those woods better than anyone, and though he wanted to go off in search of thieves, he needed to follow proper procedure. He called 911 and then called Harlan who was the sheriff and one of his best friends. Harlan promised to be right over with a slew of other officers.

Once Wilbur got off the phone with Harlan, he called Mavis to let her know that officers were being dispatched to his place and to the Manor to make sure that no one had been there.

"No one's been to the Manor," she said confidently. "My security system is the best money can buy. I know if someone sneezes by the mailbox." She told Wilbur she would have the salesman come out to his house for a demonstration because his current setup didn't seem to be the best. He hurried off the phone with her after asking her to apologize to Emily for leaving so abruptly.

"She's fine," Mavis said. "She and Opal walked over to look at the bees while Maude and I hand out candy."

That revelation made Wilbur feel better, but he was still on high alert. He waited impatiently for Harlan and the other officers to arrive. Once they did, Harlan and another deputy set off into the woods to look for any suspects, but they didn't have much luck. They could see where the truck had driven near the creek and exited through a gap in the fence near the property's edge. Wilbur's camera wasn't able to get a good look at the license plate of the truck, but they could tell that it was an older model Ford.

Meanwhile, Opal showed Emily her extensive network of beehives. She told her how she bottled her own honey and sold it to grocery stores all over the state. Emily was very impressed. There seemed to be little that this older woman could not do. Maude watched Opal walk Emily around her garden about fifty yards away on her land. She was getting more agitated as the minutes ticked by. After a few minutes of sitting on the front porch with Mavis, Maude had had enough. "Why are we just sitting here doing nothing while Wilbur's house has done been robbed?" she demanded.

"Ms. Maude, his house is fine. He just said that everything's ok except for some tools from his barn that can be replaced," Mavis explained.

"That's how they get you," Maude fired back. "They lull you into a false sense of security and then pounce when you least expect it!"

"Who?" Mavis asked.

"The hooligans!" Maude explained tersely.

"Oh, right. Well, Wilbur said that Harlan and the other officers a re g oing t o h andle t hings," □ Mavis said soothingly.

"Back in my day we didn't wait for the police to handle things. We handled things ourselves," Maude said. She stood up and handed Mavis the bowl of candy and stomped down the steps. She took a deep breath and shouted, "OPAL! Get on back in here!"

"Ms. Maude! You're going to give her a heart attack!" Mavis cried. She had near about jumped out of her own skin as it was. "What is the matter?"

"I aim to put an end to this mess here once and for all. Nobody's going to tamper with Wilbur's things on my watch," Maude mumbled. She walked into her house leaving Mavis bewildered. A few more kids came up to trick or treat, but once Mavis gave them their candy, she left the bowl on the chair and walked inside to see Maude still mumbling to herself. Maude had grabbed a plastic shopping bag and piled in the box of cookies, some kitchen shears, and a few dishtowels. Before Mavis could ask about the items she was packing, Maude turned to her and ordered, "Go get those two out there and let's go. I'm driving." Before Mavis could argue, Maude shuffled down the hallway to her room to change clothes.

"Oh dear God," Mavis sighed. She did as she was told and walked out of the back door towards Opal's yard and called for Emily and Opal to come on back. When they returned to Maude's back deck, Mavis explained what she had heard from Wilbur and went over what Maude had said.

"Oh, they've done done it this time," Opal nodded.

"They've done what?" Mavis asked.

"It," Opal replied. She moved past Mavis and grabbed her purse. She began adding random items from the kitchen drawers into her large bag. Mavis swore she saw her slip a lighter, a box of matches, and a ladle into the bag.

"Should we be concerned?" Emily asked. She was grinning from ear to ear.

"With these two, we should always be concerned. Especially since Maude says she's driving," Mavis sighed.

"How about I offer to drive?" Emily said. "We can go ahead and get in my car and get Opal situated, then Maude will have to ride with us."

Mavis knew it wouldn't be that easy, but Emily was too excited about her ideas of helping for Mavis to dash her hopes yet. "Ok, you get Opal settled in the car and I'll go check on Maude. Heaven help me!"

"Deal!" Emily said. She found Opal in the kitchen still packing her bag full of odds and ends that she might need for the adventure.

Mavis turned her back to them and inched down the hallway slowly. She didn't want Maude to mistake her for an assailant and wallop her. She also didn't want to barge in and see something she didn't want to see. "Ms. Maude?" she called out quietly. "Are you ready to go?"

The bedroom door opened and Maude stepped out. She was still wearing her blue sweatsuit, but she had added a backwards baseball cap, tennis shoes, and eye black underneath her eyes. She also carried a hefty backpack on her back. "I'm ready," she said.

"Um, what do you have there?" Mavis asked.

"The less you know," Maude mumbled. She pushed past Mavis and walked towards the front door. Mavis hurried behind her and opened the front door for her so she could squeeze through with her large pack. "I said I was driving!"

"Oh, well, Emily wanted to drive so you didn't have to worry about going through all that mud and standing water on the road," Mavis lied.

Maude groaned, but walked down the porch towards Emily's waiting car. She tossed her backpack into the backseat and glared at Opal who sat happily in the front passenger seat. Mavis wedged herself in the backseat next to the large backpack and held her breath as Maude closed the door sealing them all inside. From the backseat, Maude directed Emily on the best route towards Wilbur's cabin. When they arrived, Emily parked next to a police car. Maude and Opal leapt out of the car with a burst of energy. Wilbur emerged from the barn with Harlan shaking his head.

"I knew y'all couldn't sit still for long," Wilbur chuckled.

"We're here to take over," Maude said. She eyed Harlan up and down and shook her head. "I always said you were too young for the job."

Harlan threw his head back and laughed. He was more than accustomed to the bluntness of Maude Cooper.

"Now Ms. Maude, that's not very nice!" Mavis gasped from behind her.

"Wilbur, we will write up the report and keep you posted," Harlan said, still laughing. "Mavis, everything's fine at the Manor. Wilbur told me all about your security system and I advised him to get one just like it. It's state of the art from what I can tell." He shook Wilbur's hand and patted Maude on the back. "Ms. Cooper, always a pleasure." He got into his car and followed the rest of the officers back to the main road.

Maude and Opal fanned out and began searching the barn for any clues that the detectives missed. Once they were out of earshot, Wilbur turned to Emily and Mavis. "They scratched my tractor," he sighed. "The tools can be replaced, but I can't buff out that scratch." Emily hugged him and walked over to the tractors to see the damage.

Mavis knew how fond he was of those tractors and it aggravated her that someone had upset him so much. It was more than an invasion of privacy. They didn't have to damage something so nice. "Why'd they do that?" Mavis asked. The tractor with the scratch was much older and didn't look near as nice as the shiny one that seemed untouched.

"It looks like they were trying to jumpstart it without the key," Wilbur frowned. "That one's worth a pretty penny, so whoever it was knows their farm machinery."

"Do you think they'll be back?" Emily asked. "If they know what you have here, they could come back and finish the job."

Wilbur nodded and looked at Mavis. "I need the number for your security guy. If he can get out here tomorrow and get me set up, that should help."

"You need to do a stakeout," Emily suggested.

"Exactly!" Maude cheered. They hadn't heard her sneak up on them. Mavis jumped and said, "you've got to quit doing that!"

"Always be on your toes, Mavis," Opal added. She emerged from the pile of hay stacked behind the tractors. "One must always be aware of their surroundings."

"You can't be serious," Wilbur said to Emily.

"It's always an option," she shrugged.

"I'll keep that in mind. Ok, let's get y'all home," Wilbur said to Maude and Opal, but they ignored him and began unpacking the rest of the bags. "Mavis, what in the world did they bring with them?"

Maude unrolled her dark green sleeping bag that she had stuffed in the backpack while Opal set up a ring of stones around a giant flashlight.

Mavis threw her hands up in the air and shook her head. "You know how they are," she sighed. "I don't think they're going anywhere for a while. They even brought snacks."

Wilbur sat down on his tool bench and looked around at the mess in front of him. "I guess I better start cleaning this up. They can fizzle out over there and eat their snacks for a bit."

"We'll help," Mavis nodded. She and Emily began picking up the scraps of wood and swept up the broken glass while Wilbur sorted through the discarded tools that had been thrown around. He reorganized what he could and sanded down the busted wood pieces of the cabinet so no one would get cut. Once they had straightened things up as best as they could, Wilbur walked over to Maude and Opal and thanked them for all of their help. He helped them pack up their spy gear and loaded the large bags into the back of his truck. He told Mavis and Emily that they could head inside his cabin and warm up while he drove Maude and Opal back home.

Mavis took Emily in the cabin and showed her around. She knew Wilbur kept a box of hot chocolate packets on the shelf above the stove. She found three mugs and began making hot chocolate for the three of them. Hopefully Wilbur wouldn't be long.

Emily sat down at one of the barstools and watched as Mavis mixed the hot chocolate powder into the hot water. "So, should I ask who this mysterious Earl was? I liked the description from Ms. Maude and Ms. Opal, but I think there's more to it."

Mavis flinched, but ultimately decided that Emily could be trusted. She joined Emily at the bar and handed her one of the warm mugs. "Earl Boudreaux was a mistake I unfortunately made a few times," Mavis began. She started from the beginning and told Emily everything. She surprised herself at how open and vulnerable she was. Emily listened intently and sipped her hot chocolate while Mavis talked. Once she was finished, Emily said, "Wow. He sounds like a doozy."

"That he was," Mavis nodded. "But he's out of my life and hopefully none of us will ever have to deal with him ever again. He'll be in jail for decades with the way his charges were listed."

"I'm glad you got away," Emily smiled. "You deserve better than Earl Boudreaux." She said his name in a faux Louisiana accent to try and make Mavis laugh.

"Thanks," Mavis smiled.

They heard Wilbur pull up a few minutes later. He hung up his jacket and keys on the hooks by the front door. "I swear those two have more energy than the three of us combined," Wilbur said.

"No lies there," Mavis laughed. She handed Wilbur a mug of hot chocolate. "I was just telling Emily all about your good buddy Earl."

"Another headache in my life," Wilbur chuckled. He glanced at Emily and said, "I hope you never get to meet him. Maybe we should have let Maude and Opal whoop up on him just in case." He told Emily about their last encounter with Earl at the county fair in Junction a few weeks back. Thankfully his own idiocy got him thrown back in jail, hopefully for good this time. He had been a stain on their lives for far too long.

Chapter Eight

A few days later, Wilbur took Emily back over to the Mavis' home to meet the infamous llamas of Magnolia Manor after they had a nice quiet lunch at the Starlight Cafe that had recently reopened under new ownership. The menu was the same, but the inside looked very different. The new owners, two sisters, had replaced the worn booths and sticky tables with newer furniture. The walls were now a crisp eggshell color with dark blue and gray trim. It was strange to not see Harry or Mona behind the counter, but Wilbur knew they were enjoying retirement and finally living the life they deserved.

Emily was so excited to finally get to see and play with the llamas after hearing so much about them. She practically leapt out of the car and met Mavis at the barn before Wilbur could put the truck fully in park.

"Oh, they're so cute!" Emily exclaimed. Mavis was feeding them the pumpkins she had left over from Halloween. She had sliced them into thin strips and giggled as they chomped down on the rind. They were devouring them as fast as she could hand them out. Emily had no idea that llamas loved pumpkins. She really had no experience with llamas ever, so each little thing fascinated her.

Mavis handed her a few slices of the cut-up pumpkin and beamed. "Here, you feed Winnie!" She looked over her shoulder and saw Wilbur walking up. "Be careful though, she likes to bite, according to Wilbur."

"Oh you gorgeous thing, you wouldn't bite me," Emily crooned to the fuzzy llama. She hand fed Winnie the slices and nuzzled her face up against the animal's fuzzy wool. "You're so sweet, aren't you!" She turned to see Wilbur with his mouth agape. "That's the mean one," he whispered.

"You're not mean," Emily continued to say in her sing-song voice to the llama who seemed to be enjoying the attention. Wilbur moved closer to see for himself, but the moment he did, Winnie's ears went back and she hissed. "Wilbur! You're scaring her. She can sense your negativity!" Mavis said.

"Oh dear God," he huffed. He shook his head and stepped back from the fence. "I'm going to get something to drink while you two continue to lose your marbles." He walked off towards the house leaving Emily and Mavis in full conversation about how perfect the llamas were.

"You've met Winifred," Mavis pointed at the llama Emily was feeding. "I like to call her Winnie for short. She and Morgan here look almost identical with their thick white coats, except Winnie has this cute little brown patch by her eye. And this beauty is Clementine, or Clem for short!" She pointed to the regal calico llama that showed its teeth. "Look! She's smiling at you!"

"She is!" Emily gasped. She had never seen a llama smile before, but if one ever did, this was it. Emily reached out and rubbed her hand over Clem's soft fur and grinned at Mavis. "They are seriously cool."

"They really are," Mavis said with an extra pep in her step. "They're so smart, too. They know their names and everything!"

"They have such interesting names," Emily said. "Did they come with names already when you got them?"

"When I rescued them they didn't have names," Mavis sighed. "Can you believe that! These poor defenseless little babies didn't even know what to call each other."

"That is awful," Emily lamented. "So, where did the names come from?"

"Well, I was thinking about it all the way home from Junction that afternoon. Nothing sounded right. Then suddenly, the names hit me like a ton of bricks!" Mavis explained. "Maude and Opal were out here with me when I was bringing them out to the barn, and as you can imagine they were squabbling about something or another, and it hit me! Clementine, Winifred, and Morgan!" Mavis looked so proud of herself, but Emily was still confused. "Are those famous people?" she asked.

"Oh!" Mavis gasped. "I forget that you don't know all the things yet. They're named after the Stone Sisters!"

"The Stone Sisters?" Emily asked. She even more confused than she had been. She had heard of the Rolling Stones and Twisted Sister, but not the Stone Sisters. Maybe that was a band she had somehow missed. Or maybe they were local celebrities that didn't register with her out of town brain. "Who are they?" she asked.

"Oh goodness! Has Wilbur not caught you up yet!" Mavis turned towards the house to see Wilbur walking down the porch steps towards them. "Speak of the devil!"

"What?" Wilbur asked. "What are you going on about now?" He handed them both a bottle of water each and looked confused.

"You haven't told Emily about the Stone Sisters?" Mavis asked.

"Of course I have!" Wilbur argued.

"No, you haven't," Emily explained. She was certain that she would remember something like that.

"Well, I did," Wilbur mumbled. "I just might have forgotten to tell you their nickname."

"I am so lost," Emily laughed. She looked at Mavis and shrugged.

"Honestly Wilbur," Mavis sighed. "Ok, so, Maude and Opal and my Big Mama Ruby were the best of friends. I've never seen a better friend group. That type of closeness only exists in the movies."

"It's true," Wilbur agreed.

"Anyway, they called themselves the Stone Sisters because they grew up in Rhinestone," Mavis continued.

"And Ruby and Opal are stones as well!" Emily gasped. "How perfect."

"I knew she'd get it!" Mavis said. "Exactly!"

"But wait," Emily frowned. "How does Clementine, Morgan, and Winifred add up?"

"Their middle names," Wilbur explained. "Ruby Morgan Montgomery, Opal Clementine Tyler, and Maude Winifred Cooper."

"I love it!" Emily grinned. "Brilliant idea, Mavis!"

"Thanks," Mavis blushed.

"Why don't y'all get washed up and we can dig into some of that key lime pie we brought over," Wilbur offered. He glanced at his watch and said, "It should be good and thawed by now."

"I never say no to key lime pie," Mavis said. She hugged each of the llamas tightly and dumped the bucket of remaining pumpkin pieces into the giant trough. Emily gave each llama a generous pat and followed Mavis and Wilbur to the house.

"Thanks for showing me the llamas, Mavis," Emily smiled.

"Anytime!" Mavis said.

Once they were cleaned up from the llamas, Wilbur cut the pie into thick slices and they all sat down at the kitchen table.

"By the way, thanks for getting in touch with your security guy, Oscar, for me. He came over to the house this morning," Wilbur told Mavis.

"Oh good. He told me he'd take good care of you," Mavis grinned.

"He was telling me that he usually has a three-month backlog," Wilbur said.

"Yes, he's very much in demand," Mavis said. "He's very good at his job."

"Kinda surprised he was able to get me worked in so quickly. What did you tell him?" Wilbur asked.

Mavis blushed, "Oh nothing. I just said I needed a special favor called in."

Emily looked at Mavis and then to Wilbur whose eyebrows were raised.

"He's one of my clients," Mavis smiled sweetly.

Wilbur stared at her for a moment, but didn't ask any questions. Mavis was a certified life coach and had a list of clients that was a mile long.

"He just loves me," Mavis added before turning her attention back to Emily and the llamas.

"I'm sorry I asked," Wilbur mumbled. He listened to Emily and Mavis continue to coo and awe over the llamas.

"And now that we've gotten your house taken care of, don't forget to fix up my yard like you promised," Mavis reminded him.

"I haven't forgotten," Wilbur told her.

"Good, because Maude is getting worse," Mavis said.

"What did she do now?" Wilbur asked. How much damage could one old woman possibly do?

"Well, you know how they have those buggy bins out in the parking lot of the Piggly Wiggly? Apparently she didn't realize it was there and she tried to drive through it," Mavis sighed.

"But?" Wilbur started to ask.

"She wanted to park there?" Emily asked.

"I'm so confused," Wilbur finished.

"I swear, Wilbur, she's either as blind as a bat or she suddenly doesn't know where the brakes are," Mavis said.

"To be fair, she never knew where the brakes were," Wilbur said.

"That's true, but she doesn't need to be driving anymore," Mavis shook her head. "It's really getting dangerous."

Wilbur opened his mouth, but Mavis stopped him. "I know, she's always been dangerous."

"Who's going to tell her to stop?" Wilbur asked. "I'm not that brave or stupid. Nothing good ever came out of getting Maude riled up."

"Neither am I, but you know she's going to drive through a building and I don't want the Manor to have a drive through," Mavis fussed.

"I'll run over to Junction and pick up the ties tomorrow. If she's getting that bad, cross ties might not help though," Wilbur said.

"Anything to save my azaleas," Mavis shook her head. "Stack them up pretty tall so she can't miss them."

"Mavis, she tried to drive through a shopping cart corral. If she can't see a giant blue sign on that thing, I'm not sure she's going to notice some cross ties," Wilbur said.

"It's worth a shot," Emily shrugged.

"I'll call Junior tonight, too," Wilbur said.

"Who's Junior?" Emily asked.

"That's Maude's nephew, Joe Junior, but everybody just calls him Junior so he doesn't get confused with his daddy," Mavis explained. "Even though Joe Senior has been dead for fifteen years."

"How old is Ms. Maude exactly?" Emily asked.

Mavis thought for a minute and said, "Big Mama would have been eighty-four last September, so Maude's right there, too."

"And Opal will turn eighty-four in January," Wilbur added.

"If she's in her eighties, then her nephew has to be, what?" Emily asked.

"Junior's nearing sixty," Wilbur shrugged. "He's not going to be happy about having this conversation."

"Is he local?" Emily wondered.

"He's got a farm just past Junction," Mavis explained. "But he's afraid of Maude, too. I mean, who isn't?"

"Opal," Wilbur laughed. "She's about the only one who can keep Maude in line."

Emily giggled and continued to eat her pie. Ever since getting to know Wilbur and Mavis, her life had been anything but boring. "You know, when I used to visit my grandma as a kid I thought this place was a bit of a drag, but you two seem to know everything that goes on here. Who knew this kind of excitement was in Rhinestone!"

"You have no idea," Wilbur chuckled.

"Maybe Emily could talk to her!" Mavis said suddenly. Wilbur's eyes widened and he shook her head. Mavis turned to Emily and smiled. "She doesn't know you well, so she wouldn't bite your head off," Mavis explained.

"That's never stopped Maude before," Wilbur said.

"No way," Emily laughed. "I love a good thrill chase, but I'd rather keep my head attached."

Wilbur glanced at his watch and said, "Actually, if y'all two want to hang tight, I'll drive over and pick up those ties and get started. Looks like the rain's passed over us, so I might as well get a jump start on things."

"That's a great idea!" Mavis said. "That'll give me time to tell Emily all your deepest and darkest secrets," she teased.

"Oh goodie," Wilbur rolled his eyes. "I won't be gone that long."

"Good thing I can talk fast then," Mavis laughed.

"Do tell," Emily smiled.

"Maybe I should stay around. Sounds like y'all are going to get into trouble," Wilbur said.

"No, go on. We'll be fine," Emily said.

"We can go visit Clive!" Mavis exclaimed. "Oh Emily, you're going to love him!" She jumped up out of her seat and grabbed her picnic basket from on top of the refrigerator.

"Are we packing a picnic?" Emily asked.

"Doubtful," Wilbur laughed as he headed for the front door. "I bet it's for Clive. Be right back. Y'all don't get into too much trouble!"

Emily turned back to Mavis and saw her packing the basket with a package of deli meat, a wheel of cheese, and a box of breakfast pastries. "Clive loves a good snack," Mavis explained.

"All that is for Clive?" Emily asked.

"Yes. Can you believe that Wilbur told me I should put him on a diet? Honestly, sometimes Wilbur gets the craziest ideas. Whoever heard of putting a catfish on a diet?" Mavis asked. "Want to walk down to the pond? The woods are beautiful this time of year!"

"Sure," Emily said. "Should I bring anything?"

"I'll carry the basket if you'll bring us some water bottles," Mavis offered. "It's not a long walk, but we'll definitely get thirsty." She put on her jacket and tossed a few more treats into the basket.

They walked down the path into the tree line. Mavis pointed out the trailer nicknamed the Shangri La and told Emily how she had stayed there while Wilbur was working on some of the renovations to the Manor a few years ago.

"The Shangri La was a gift from Big Daddy to Big Mama one year. She filled it with treasures from all over the world. That's where I got my love of traveling from," Mavis smiled.

"I love to travel!" Emily said. "So much so that I got my pilot's license a few years ago."

"Wow!" Mavis exclaimed. "That's so exciting. I could never do something like that."

"Sure you could" Emily said. "I'll have to take you and Wilbur up in the sky sometime. There's a place in Atlanta that one of my clients owns. He lets me take his planes up whenever I want."

"Opal's been wanting to skydive," Mavis said. "Maybe you could go with her!"

"That would be amazing. I love to skydive," Emily replied.

"Wilbur's always wanted to try it," Mavis lied.

"Really?" Emily said. "That's a little surprising!"

Mavis laughed loudly. "I'm kidding. He says

he likes his feet firmly planted on the ground at all times. He's not a good traveler." They followed the path as it curved down a slight slope heading down toward the lake. It was a clear blue sky overhead and the water shimmered in the light breeze.

"Here we are. Isn't it pretty?" Mavis asked.

"It sure is," Emily smiled.

"Come on, I always talk to Clive up here by the big oak tree. That's why Wilbur put that bench there, so we would have a cozy place to visit," Mavis said.

The two ladies sat down on the bench and Mavis began to pull out some of the goodies from the basket. As she did, she began to call out, "Clive! Oh Clivey! Where's my sweet little boy?"

Emily wasn't exactly sure what she was expecting on this adventure, but she wasn't fully prepared for the enormous head of a fish to emerge from the water. His whiskers hung down on either side of his face.

"There's my sweet little boy!" Mavis cooed. She broke off a large chunk of cheese and tossed it to him. Clive lurched out of the water and caught it easily like a dog performing his best tricks.

"I don't think I've ever seen a fish do that," Emily said.

"He's such a good boy," Mavis said. "Here, you feed him something." Mavis handed Emily the basket.

Emily reached in and grabbed the deli meat. Clive seemed to know exactly what was coming. He watched her greedily as she tossed slices of ham in his direction. He wasted no time diving. They each took turns feeding him the treats from the basket. Emily was amazed that it took less than ten minutes for him to devour everything Mavis had brought him. They enjoyed the peacefulness of the pond for a little while longer before heading back to the Manor to see if Wilbur had returned.

On the walk back, Mavis couldn't contain her question any longer. "Do you really like Wilbur?" she asked abruptly.

Emily didn't seem upset or fazed by her bluntness. "Yes, I do really like him," she smiled.

"Good," Mavis breathed a sigh of relief. "Because he's a really good one and he really seems to like you. I don't want to see him hurt."

"I don't want to see that either," Emily agreed. She put her arm around Mavis' shoulder and together they walked closer to Wilbur who was working on protecting Mavis' beloved flower bed from Maude's recklessness.

Chapter Nine

Emily was off on Veterans Day, which gave Wilbur an idea. He had planned on going bass fishing, an activity he usually enjoyed alone. When Emily casually mentioned on the phone the day before that she didn't have any plans, he surprised himself by asking if she wanted to come with him.

"I've never been fishing before," she admitted.

"You'll be a pro in no time," Wilbur assured her. He said he would pick her up early the next morning and would bring everything they needed for a morning out on the water. Emily invited him to a cookout for lunch at her grandmother's house after their fishing date.

Wilbur drive to Beulah's early the next morning before the sun had come up. Emily hopped in the truck and Wilbur drove her to the river junction where the Duckabush River and Dosewallips River crossed before branching back off. He called this particular spot his honey hole and was thankful that not many people fished it. He backed the boat off the trailer and parked his truck near the bridge. Once he and Emily were ready, he turned on the motor and followed the current to a shady area of the river.

The water was quiet. The wind blew lazily through the trees as Wilbur turned off the motor and let the boat settle its course. For a while they merely listened to the sounds of nature all around them. Wilbur knew that there was a good population of largemouth bass in the area. With the current moving, he knew they would be looking for a meal near the rocks and shaded areas of the river junction. He had brought along enough bait fish to catch the attention of any they came upon. The boat followed the current to a secluded area with a few downed trees from the last big storm. Wilbur knew that would be a good spot to anchor down for a bit.

"Bass like to ambush their prey," Wilbur explained. He tossed a few scraps of minnows into the water and waited. It didn't take long for a few bubbles to appear and the minnows disappeared. Wilbur baited Emily's hook and saw her watch intently. She declared that she wanted to try, so he let her bait his. She watched him cast his line and she promptly followed. She was definitely a natural when it came to fishing, which greatly impressed Wilbur. It came as no surprise when Emily's line was the first one to get interesting. She gasped and jerked at the line the second she felt a tug. "Reel it in!" Wilbur encouraged.

Emily tugged at the line, but whatever was on the other end was putting up a fight. "Help me," she laughed breathlessly. Wilbur leaned around her and helped her pull and reel in the line. "Lord, Emily! You've got a big one!"

After working together for the next few

minutes, Wilbur burst into laughter when the monstrosity emerged from the water. Emily had hooked one of the large trees under the water and together they reeled in one of the moss-covered branches that had broken free.

"I assume this doesn't count," Emily cackled. She was beside herself with laughter after putting in all that work and excitement for a piece of tree.

"Not bad for your first try," Wilbur chuckled. He released the wood and watched as Emily baited her hook and tried again.

Unfortunately the fish just weren't biting today. They had no luck at all. The only thing they hooked all morning was Emily's tree branch and a tin can that someone had tossed into the river ages ago. Wilbur added the litter to the trash bag underneath his seat and cracked open a soda. The sun was high over the water now and he knew that it was pointless to keep fishing in the same spot now that the bright sun was shining overhead. The best time to catch bass was early in the morning before the sun fully rose, or later in the evening near sunset.

Even though they hadn't caught any fish, Wilbur was having a great time. Emily didn't seem to be bothered either. She looked radiant in the early morning sun and didn't shy away from the squiggly worms or fish bait scraps. She was the kind of woman who could work outside in the soil one day and get her hands dirty, then put on a business suit and take on the world the next. The more time he spent with her, the more he started to fall for her. According to Mavis, Emily felt the same way about him.

"Whatcha staring at?" Emily asked. Wilbur hadn't realized he had been staring off into space.

"I'm sorry," he grinned. "What did I miss?"

"Nothing much," she smiled back. "I was just telling you the mysteries of the universe." She flicked some of the condensation from her soda can on him and pulled her baseball cap down further over her eyes. "It's getting really bright out here. Do you think we should call it quits for the day?"

"Are you tired of me already?" Wilbur teased.

"Not at all," Emily replied. "In fact, what would you think if I said that I don't think that's possible."

Wilbur blushed fiercely and set down his reel. "I think that's pretty interesting," he said. "Because I feel the same way about you."

"Good," Emily said. "Because we are both too old for all those games that people play nowadays. I'm a pretty upfront person. It scares people off sometimes, but it's just who I am."

"I like that about you," Wilbur said. "I know we haven't spent a lot of time together, but from what I do know, I like you a lot."

"I've dated guys that have already exhausted me by this point. I think I'll stick around for a while," Emily teased.

"Just a while?" Wilbur asked.

"Depends on if you play your cards right," Emily shrugged. "Even though Opal said you weren't much of a card player."

"I've picked up a few tricks over the years,"

Wilbur smirked.

Later that afternoon, Wilbur and Emily pulled up to Beulah's house for a cookout. Lunch at Beulah's house was rowdier than Wilbur had expected. Beulah had invited her canasta ladies over and Bart sat outside by the pool with the husbands. It was too cold outside to swim, but Bart had built a nice bonfire in the backyard where the men sat and smoked cigars. Wilbur wasn't sure if he should join the men outside or sit around the table while the women played cards after they ate hotdogs and hamburgers and various desserts the ladies had made. There were a lot of good-looking snacks in the kitchen and it was much warmer inside than out. Plus, Wilbur got a kick out of watching the ladies get so animated. After a few rounds, one of Beulah's friends offered to teach the other ladies how to play poker. Wilbur had to hold his breath to keep from laughing as one of them said she had heard of strip poker before, but thankfully Emily talked them into betting pennies instead.

After an hour of listening to the women try to bluff and getting lost on different tangents, Wilbur told Emily that he needed to head home and shower to get ready for a game night at Mavis' house. Mavis had invited Emily, and she promised to be over there by seven thirty. Mavis had originally invited Mona and Harry as well, but Mona had tickets to a concert and Harry already had plans with a friend. Instead of canceling the game night, she asked Maude and Opal if they were busy. She even offered to pick them up, but

Maude had insisted that she could drive Opal and herself over just fine.

An hour later at the table while they were waiting for Maude and Opal to arrive, Mavis remarked how nice it was that Wilbur invited Emily to go fishing with him.

"It was a lot of fun! Do you like to fish?" Emily asked.

"No!" Mavis gasped. "I could never. That's how I ended up with my sweet Clive."

"Oh, that's right!" Emily nodded. "Well, we didn't catch much, but it was fun being on the water and seeing a part of nature I'm not too familiar with. I've never been out fishing on a river before."

Mavis was horrified at the idea of catching a live fish, but she didn't turn up her nose to eating them. Fish tacos were her absolute favorite food in the entire world, but she didn't want to know the fish that went into the delicious lunch. The less she knew about her food, the better.

"He's never invited me or anyone besides Harry or Harlan," Mavis explained. "Maude and Opal go fishing, but never with Wilbur."

"We should invite them next time," Emily suggested.

Wilbur nearly choked on his chocolate chip cookie. "That would be an adventure I'm nowhere near ready for," he said.

"Can you imagine?" Mavis laughed. "I bet all the fish in the river swim as far away as they could!"

"You'd think, but they always come home with

a mess of fish each time," Wilbur said. "It's the craziest thing."

"Opal says she can whisper to the fish," Mavis nodded. "I mean, knowing Opal, it's probably true."

"I could see that," Emily nodded.

"Wilbur, I meant to tell you! You got those ties put up just in time! Maude came over last night to drop off a casserole dish she had borrowed, and I swear I heard her tires screeching from a mile down the road. I don't know how the old magnolia has survived for so long," Mavis said. "She near about rams it each time. Speaking of which, she should be here any minute. Just keep your ears open."

"Big Mama would never forgive her if she hit that tree," Wilbur chuckled.

"She'd never forgive herself," Mavis nodded. "And Opal would never let her forget it. Did you ever talk to Junior about her driving?"

"I called him, but he said there's no way he's getting involved," Wilbur said. "I don't blame him."

Mavis frowned and crossed her arms. "It's not his property that is getting damaged," she sighed.

"Does Ms. Opal drive?" Emily asked.

Mavis and Wilbur both shook their heads. "Not since her strokes," Wilbur explained. He recounted about the time he found her in the woods after her first stroke that nearly killed her. It was right around the same time that Ruby was going through her battle with cancer. It was a hard time for all of them, but Opal recovered well until her next stroke a year later. That one had left her much weaker and had addled her brain for months. They weren't sure that she would ever come back fully, but she had been doing very well lately. Maude and Mavis took turns taking her to her appointments, and doctors were very pleased with her progress. She didn't put up a fuss when everyone agreed that it would be safer for her to stay away from behind the wheel, but they knew that Maude would never give up that freedom.

After a cup of coffee and a few more cookies, they retired to the living room to look at photo albums while they waited. After Mavis and Emily had talked about traveling, Mavis was eager to show Emily her personal photo albums of her travels and Ruby's extensive collection of albums from her decades of adventures.

"Look how young they were!" Mavis exclaimed. She never got tired of perusing the albums that Ruby made with Maude and Opal. This particular album showed their trip to Memphis. "That was before I was born!"

"The stories they could tell," Wilbur chuckled. "Not that I'm sure we'd want to hear all of them, come to think of it."

"I'd love to!" Mavis and Emily said at the same time. "If those pages could talk!" Mavis continued.

They flipped through pages that showed photographs of Graceland and the three women posing in front of the fountain. They saw pictures of the river and the riverboat, and a few of Maude shooting a game of pool with strangers. There was even a picture of Opal standing on top of the bar holding a pool stick.

"This looks like a fun vacation," Emily smiled.

"I've heard Opal ramble about some, well, I'll call them adventures, from this particular trip," Mavis said. "But I'm not sure what all is true or not."

Wilbur nodded. "From Maude's tattoo to them getting arrested, I just don't know."

"Tattoos, huh?" Emily smirked. "Do you have any tattoos I should know about?"

"Wilbur doesn't have any tattoos," Mavis laughed. "Well, not that I know of!"

"I don't have any," Wilbur replied. "Mavis has one though."

"Ooh! Where at?" Emily asked.

"On my foot," Mavis said. "I got it a few months ago, but it's so small. It's a magnolia flower. It hurt so bad I don't think I can ever get another one. What about you?"

"I don't have any, but I'm not opposed to a tattoo," Emily shrugged.

"Maude's got several," Opal chimes in from behind the couch.

"Ahh!" Mavis screamed. "When did y'all get here?"

"About the time you showed the picture of Opal dancing on the table," Maude snickered.

"I didn't hear you come in," Wilbur said.

"We're very sneaky," Opal nodded.

"How did we not hear them drive up?" Mavis whispered.

"Sorry we're late," Maude explained. "Took me a little bit longer at the car place than I thought it would."

"What's wrong with your car?" Wilbur asked.

"Front end damage?" Mavis offered. "Fender fall off?"

Maude cut her eyes at Mavis and shook her head. "There better not be any damage. It's a brand-new car!"

Mavis and Wilbur looked at each other very confused. Maude's car was old, but it certainly wasn't new. "What do you mean?" Wilbur asked.

"We've been at that dang place since early afternoon," Opal yawned.

"I finally talked them down, too!" Maude said knowingly. "No one's taking me for a ride!"

"Did you by chance buy a new car?" Emily asked.

"Sure did!" Maude nodded.

"Oh God," Mavis sighed.

Maude ignored her and launched into the tale. She had taken her car over to the high-end dealership in Junction, but found the salesman condescending and rude. After chewing him out, she asked for the manager and let him know that she would be taking her business elsewhere. There weren't many other high-end dealerships around the area, but she refused to be told that they wouldn't accept her trade in.

"I'm not surprised," Mavis whispered to Emily.

"But you ended up buying a car?" Wilbur asked.

"I already said so," Maude said. "You feeling

ok, Wilbur?"

"She finally fussed enough," Opal explained. "They don't need every detail, Maude. Just show them the Illuminati or whatever it's called."

"It's a Maserati," Maude huffed.

"Oh God," Wilbur and Mavis both gasped.

"Congratulations!" Emily cheered. "Let's go for a spin!"

Chapter Ten

Mavis and Wilbur couldn't believe that she had gone out and bought a brand-new Italian luxury car, and they sure as heck weren't about to ride in it after dark before she learned the ins and outs of it. Emily was the only one brave enough to go with Maude for a spin in her new car.

"You snooze, you lose," Emily shrugged. She kissed Wilbur and looked positively giddy about Maude's new purchase. "You can ride shotgun, Mavis."

Mavis stared at her and shook her head. "Please be careful," Wilbur added.

"See you later, suckers!" Maude sneered from the porch.

"Where'd she learn that phrase?" Wilbur asked as Maude peeled out of the yard barely missing Mavis' mailbox in the process.

"She's been watching old cartoons on those VHS tapes she won't get rid of," Opal said. She had also stayed behind at the Manor saying she'd had enough whiplash for the evening. "You know how old people get."

Wilbur laughed at Opal's explanation. Maude was only four months older than she was, but Opal never let her forget it. Between Maude's birthday in September and Opal's the following January, Opal made as many jokes as she could fit into the conversation.

"And you let her buy that thing!" Mavis said to Opal in a fury. "How could you let her trade one death mobile in for a fancier one!"

"Have you ever tried telling Maude the word no?" Opal shrugged. "It's her money."

"I'm not worried about the money," Mavis countered. "I'm worried about the way she drives a regular car, and now she's upgraded to a space rocket!"

"You only live once," Opal said wisely.

"That's exactly my point!" Mavis snapped. "She's too reckless for a sports car." She turned to Wilbur and shook her head. "And you let Emily go off galivanting with her!"

"I let her?" Wilbur laughed.

"Yes. You should have tried to stop her," Mavis continued.

"Mavis, have any of you women ever asked for permission to do anything in life? She doesn't need my permission to do anything. And neither does Maude." He could see the steam rising from Mavis' ears. "Now hold on, I'm not saying I like the new addition, but she's a grown woman. I'll stake off the magnolia tree and the rest of the garden tomorrow just to be safe." He swore he saw Opal smirk out of the corner of his eye.

Mavis shook her head in disgust and walked upstairs. Wilbur and Opal let her go. Wilbur and Opal knew that it was best to let her blow off steam by herself. They sat together on the couch continuing the discussion over the photo album from Memphis.

"That was the time Maude showed those boys how to play pool," Opal remembered. "She hustled them good."

"And why were you on the bar again?" Wilbur asked.

"Why not?" Opal shrugged.

"Why not," Wilbur agreed, nodding his head sagely.

"You gotta live a little, Wilbur," Opal smiled. Wilbur smiled and nodded as she turned the page. "I remember taking this one. This was right after those two got arrested."

"Now, I just find it hard to believe that Big Mama and Maude were the ones who got arrested," Wilbur said. "Well, at least Big Mama."

"Ruby was quite the rabble rouser when we were younger," Opal said slyly.

"Really?" Wilbur asked. He was astonished to hear such a thing.

"No," Opal laughed. "But they really did get arrested. I had to track them down and bail them out and everything. Maude was as mad as a hornet."

"Seriously?" Wilbur asked. He was still finding it hard to believe. Opal had made comments for years about this alleged event, but Ruby and Maude had always shushed her. Opal had always laughed it off, so no one knew if she was being serious or not.

"Cross my heart," Opal said.

"What did they do to get arrested?" Wilbur

asked.

"Nothing," Opal replied. "At least not that I know of. No, they were simply at the wrong place at the wrong time. Or the wrong street at the wrong time."

"The street?" Wilbur repeated.

"Oh yes," Opal began her story. "They were confused with street walkers. That's very different from a street performer. Well, on second thought, maybe not so different."

"Wait a minute," Wilbur said. He couldn't stop laughing at Opal's storytelling to follow. "They got mixed up with, well, I can't believe I'm saying this word in front of you. They got mixed up with hookers?"

"I think your generation calls them prostitutes," Opal shrugged. I've always admired the entrepreneurial spirit. You do what you gotta do. Or who, for that matter."

"Oh God," Wilbur cackled. "This is too much."

"That's what I said!" Opal agreed. "Who in their right mind would confuse Maude Cooper and Ruby Montgomery with a lady of the night? They weren't even dressed appropriately. We had the hardest time getting Maude out of her sweatpants and baseball cap most nights. Do you think someone is going to pay to spend the evening with that?"

"They actually got arrested?" Wilbur asked.

"I can't make this stuff up, Wilbur," Opal said seriously. "They just disappeared on me. I walked out of the pool hall and didn't see a soul. Thankfully, one of the real ladies told me what had happened. I had to bum my way over to the police station and figure things out. I could hear Maude from a mile away hootin' and hollering." Wilbur had to bury his head in his jacket to try to stop laughing. "Anyway, I used my charms on the sheriff and got them freed," Opal shrugged.

"No wonder Big Mama never let you talk about Memphis," Wilbur howled.

"I'm talking about my womanly charms, not my southern charm," Opal continued. "I don't reckon southern charm would have worked because they're southern, too. And the womanly charm was what got the real ladies locked up in the first place. But that's what happened."

"I bet Maude and Big Mama were fit to be tied," Wilbur chuckled.

"You have no idea," Opal nodded.

"Any other times I should know about?" Wilbur asked.

"I don't recollect Ruby ever getting arrested again. And my records have been clear for forty years," Opal said.

"And Maude?" Wilbur asked.

"What about Maude?" Mavis asked as she walked down the stairs. "Y'all two hens are loud enough for me to hear y'all upstairs."

Wilbur looked at Opal who nodded. She continued to look at the album while Wilbur filled her in on what he and Opal had been talking about. By the time Maude and Emily came back a little over twenty minutes later, Mavis was in her pajamas eating a slice of cheesecake in her recliner feeling much happier after such a tale.

They heard the front door open. Maude shook off her boots and threw her jacket onto the table by the door.

"Opal! This one here's crazier than you!" Maude said. "Lord Almighty, Wilbur, she's a real spark plug!"

"I don't know what that means," Emily cheered. "But ok!"

"What did you two get into?" Wilbur asked carefully.

"Ms. Maude took us down the highway," Emily smiled sweetly.

"I'm just glad you're both back in one piece," Wilbur said. He was relieved that nothing bad had happened to either of them. Emily saw the photo album on the table and asked if they had been looking at it all this time. "We sure have," Wilbur nodded.

Opal winked at Wilbur and closed the book gently. She put it back on the shelf and ushered them all to the table where she had previously dealt the cards for the game. "Alright, jokers are wild," Opal said.

"I thought we were playing a boardgame?" Maude frowned. "Opal cheats at cards."

"I do not," Opal sassed back. "You just don't know the rules of the game."

"No, you don't. You just make them up as you go along," Maude said.

"What exactly are we playing?" Emily asked.

"I think we've had enough poker for the day," Wilbur chuckled.

"I got a new trivia game!" Mavis said. She

pulled the box out of a shopping bag on the counter and placed it on the table.

"I'm lousy at trivia," Wilbur shrugged. "But I'm game." He looked at Emily who nodded.

"Opal's a vat of useless information," Maude pointed out. "She's going to smoke us all in this game."

Mavis opened the box and read the rules. Each person had to be the first to answer a question from each of the five categories correctly to win. Emily set up the board and asked each person what color token they wanted to be. Wilbur picked blue, Maude chose red, Opal chose yellow, Mavis chose orange, and Emily took the green piece. They rolled the numbered die to see who would go first, with Mavis winning with the highest roll. She chose to answer a question from the sport's category to begin. Wilbur chose a card from the deck and read it silently. It was tricky. There was no way that Mavis should know the answer to this question, but she had surprised him many times before with what she knew.

"Alright, Mavis, what do you call it when a bowler makes three strikes in a row?" Wilbur read. He wasn't sure when the last time Mavis had gone bowling was. Mavis scrunched up her face and thought about.

"Where's the timer?" Maude asked. "This could take all night!"

"It's the first question," Wilbur said patiently.

"We still need a timer," Maude said indignantly. "Ten seconds each."

"Ten seconds?" Mavis gasped.

Maude looked at Wilbur and shook her head. "I know that's not right! It's called a chicken."

"What?" Mavis asked.

"Three strikes is a chicken," Maude repeated. "You're wrong. Who's next?"

"I didn't answer yet!" Mavis argued.

"You said ten seconds! And that's not the answer," Maude said.

"I think she was merely saying that ten seconds wasn't long enough," Emily said patiently.

"And it's not a chicken," Opal laughed.

"Oh, whatever!" Maude said. "Then hurry up. I'm ready to win."

All eyes turned back to Mavis who shrugged and said, "I couldn't remember what it was, but when Ms. Maude said chicken, I remembered the term was a member of the poultry family! It's a turkey!"

"That's right!" Wilbur said.

"I know my food, Wilbur," Mavis said. She smiled sweetly at Maude who had turned red. Since she got the question correct, she was able to take another turn. She had no idea who the highest paid actor in the 1980s was, so she shrugged and let Wilbur read off the correct answer.

"Well, now it's my turn!" Maude huffed. She was eager to regain control of the game. She chose to answer a question from the history realm and Opal burst into a fit of laughter. "What's so funny?" Maude demanded.

"Nothing," Opal chuckled.

Emily pulled a card and read the question

eagerly. "Who was the fifteenth president of the United States of America?"

"You should know that one," Opal said. Maude crossed her arms and waited for the punchline that she knew was coming. "Because you were there."

"I wasn't alive then!" Maude bellowed. "But I know it was the man before Lincoln."

"Well, yes," Emily said. "But I think they're looking for a name."

"The white man before Lincoln," Maude said. "That's the answer."

Emily looked at Mavis and Wilbur to see what they wanted to do. "I say we take a vote," Mavis offered. "Yes to accept it, and no for no."

"I vote yes," Maude announced. "Then I'll cancel it out with a no," Opal added.

"I say no," Mavis said gently. Maude frowned at her and turned to Wilbur. "I say yes," he winced.

"Coward!" Mavis hissed.

"Technically she's not wrong," Wilbur whispered.

"I say no," Emily shrugged.

"Hey!" Maude howled. "I thought we were thrill buddies!"

"We are," Emily said gently. "But I have to break the tie."

"You two are just alike," Maude mumbled under her breath.

Opal was next and she chose a science question. She knew instantly that the process by which green plants and some other organisms use sunlight to synthesize foods from carbon dioxide and water was photosynthesis.

"That's not fair!" Maude grumbled. "Opal's practically a plant herself."

Everyone ignored her while Opal deliberated between a history and pop culture question. "I'll take history," she said slowly. She was intense when it came to trivia games.

"What was issued in June 1215 and was the first document to put into writing the principle that the king and his government was not above the law?" Mavis read.

"You should know since you were there," mimicked Maude.

"If I was, then so were you," Opal countered. "You're older than I am. That's how time works."

"I know how time works," Maude pouted.

"Doubtful," Opal said. "That would be the Magna Carta."

"Correct!" Mavis said. "Wow! Great job!"

"Let's do pop culture," Opal continued.

"What animal did Britney Spears famously carry on her shoulders during a performance?" Mavis asked. She knew that Opal had an eclectic taste in music, but she wasn't into television the way that Maude was.

"I don't think I know," Opal frowned. "A bird?"

"No, a snake," Mavis said.

"A snake? Hell no!" Maude shouted. "Ain't no way."

"Your turn, Emily," Mavis laughed.

"Let's see what the literature category is all about," she suggested.

"Which British prime minister was awarded

the Nobel Prize for Literature in 1953?" Maude asked.

"You really were around for that," Mavis said knowingly. She saw Maude shoot her a dagger-like stare. "Well you were!"

"It would have to be Churchill," Emily reasoned.

"That's right," Maude said. "What do you want next?"

"History," Emily said. Maude read the history question and Emily quickly collected her piece for another correct answer. She answered the science and pop culture ones correctly after that, but failed to correctly guess who had won the World Series in 2009, which Maude grumbled about. "I knew that one. I know my baseball."

Wilbur was next and chose sports. He correctly answered the sports and the following history question, but got stumped on the pop culture question about the Kardashian family.

"Maybe we should have played teams," Mavis said after another round of turns. She and Wilbur each had two of the five categories marked off, Maude had zero, and Emily and Opal were tied with one category remaining for each.

"Opal and Emily could run the table," Wilbur laughed. "I want to be on their team."

When it came back to her, Opal answered her question in the last category correctly. Maude pouted and stood up to rummage through the freezer for some ice cream while Emily and Mavis put the game back in its box.

"That was fun!" Emily said. "We should do it

again sometime!"

"Good luck getting Maude to ever play that again," Mavis giggled.

After a brief argument over taking Maude and Opal home since it was so late and dark outside, Wilbur told Mavis to "let it go. They're just as ornery as you are, so let them go."

"Just call me when you get home so we know you made it safely," Mavis said.

"Yes mother," Maude rolled her eyes.

They heard Maude get in her car and back out. She knocked over the large trash can and took out the palm tree Mavis had planted by the mailbox last spring.

"I swear it's like raising teenagers," Mavis sighed.

Chapter Eleven

Over the next two weeks, Maude only got three more scratches on her new car. She was irate, but the dealership refused to take it back, so she was stuck with the gashes from the newspaper stand at the Piggy Wiggly that she claimed hadn't been there seconds before when she backed out of the spot onto the curb. The frantic cashier saw her tire hit the curb and promptly called Mavis who asked if everyone was ok.

"I think so because she's already halfway down the street now," the cashier said. "Honestly, Mavis, something needs to be done about her."

On more than one occasion, Maude had grumbled to Mavis about the people who went grocery shopping. "You wouldn't believe the number of times they've hit my car, my brand-new car, with their buggies. Back in my day we would have at least left a note. Nobody has any home training anymore."

Mavis knew well and good that no one had hit Maude's brand-new car with a buggy. For one thing, Maude left a trail of dents at every establishment she visited. For another, Mavis had never known a buggy that could cause an indention that was perfectly shaped like a light pole. Mavis was able to have her trash cans replaced easily enough and Wilbur staked the palm tree to help prevent any further damage to the young plant, but that did not negate the fact that everything in Rhinestone, living or otherwise, was in grave danger as long as Maude Cooper raced around town in her brand-new hotrod.

To make matters worse, Maude insisted on hosting Thanksgiving this year, but Mavis finally won out. Magnolia Manor had hosted Thanksgiving for the past forty odd years, and Mavis wouldn't hear another word about it.

Emily had invited everyone to her grandmother's house for lunch on Thanksgiving, but only Wilbur accepted the invite. Mavis would be too busy cooking for supper. Opal, Maude, Wilbur, Mona, and Harry would be coming over. Emily was set to come over and meet Harry and Mona as well. When Emily told Wilbur that her parents would be flying in from Chicago, he caught his breath. He wasn't nervous to meet them, but he wanted to make a good first impression.

"Now Wilbur, this is a big deal. It's your first big holiday," Mavis explained. "Don't mess it up."

"I'm not planning on it," Wilbur said. He wasn't sure how one could mess up a day that revolved around turkey, but he didn't want to find out.

"No one ever is, but anything can happen," Mavis continued. "Be on your very best behavior."

Emily said that Wilbur didn't need to bring anything with him, but Mavis wouldn't hear of it. She said that any good guest knew to bring something to an invitation. He stopped by the Piggly Wiggly late Wednesday afternoon and picked up a thirteen-layer chocolate cake. He had never seen so many people in one store at one time. He swore two ladies almost broke out in a fight over the last can of cranberry sauce. He sincerely hoped that Mavis had everything she needed for the dinner, otherwise she might have to do without.

When he arrived at Beulah's house for lunch, Emily was standing on the front porch talking to a man and woman. Wilbur recognized her parents from the pictures she had on her phone. She introduced him to everyone, including her parents who had flown in from Chicago for a few days. Emily's brother wasn't able to attend, but he and his wife and their children sent over a delivery chocolate covered fruit. Emily hoped that Wilbur could meet them one day soon. Emily favored her mother in looks and personality, though she had her father's bright blue eyes. They were so nice and welcoming, which calmed Wilbur's nerves. He shook their hands and asked how their flight was.

"We had a lot of turbulence," her dad, Art, winced. "Emily didn't get her love of flying from me," he chuckled.

"Wilbur! You didn't have to bring anything," Emily said when she saw the cake.

"This looks delicious. Mom will love this," Charlotte took the cake from him and went inside to show Beulah.

They followed her into the kitchen where they could hear Beulah discussing desserts. "Good, we needed another dessert to balance out the table. Move those pies out of the way to make room for it," she instructed Charlotte.

Charlotte walked over to a corner table that was bulging at the seams with sweets of all shapes and sizes. Wilbur walked over and picked up a pie so she could set the cake down.

"Now, where in the world am I going to put that?" Charlotte fretted. She took the pie from him and began to shuffle the other desserts around.

"We're all going to gain fifty pounds from this table alone," Emily laughed. "You didn't have to bring anything fancy like this. You could have simply bought some cranberry sauce or something."

"It was too dangerous to get to the cranberry sauce," Wilbur told her.

A few minutes later, the rolls were out of the oven, the turkey had been carved, and everyone was filling their plates. Wilbur knew that Mavis was preparing a huge meal at the Manor, but he could not resist a second helping of Beulah's homemade potato casserole.

"I got that recipe from Ruby," Beulah told Wilbur. "She used to bring it to every potluck at church. People would fight over it. She put the recipe in our cookbook, you know the one we did when we were building the fellowship hall. Everybody submitted their best dishes for that one. Even Maude. Of course nobody was brave enough to try any of hers, but she put them in there all the same."

"I remember that book. There were some really good ones in there," Charlotte said.

"Of course there were. This town was founded on good cooking," Beulah offered. "We still print a few copies every year and sell them at the school bake sale. Do you have one, Wilbur?"

"Yes ma'am," he nodded. "There are some good ones in there for sure."

Once they were all stuffed, Wilbur helped Emily wash the dishes while Charlotte and Beulah reorganized the refrigerator to accommodate all of the leftovers. Beulah tried to send Wilbur home with enough food to last him a week, but he assured her that he was about to pack his fridge with leftovers from the Manor. Once everything was successfully put away, Wilbur, Emily, Bart, Beulah, Edward, and Charlotte sat around the living room watching football. Most everyone took a nap while the referees blew their whistles and fans cheered on the big screen. Wilbur dozed off while sitting on the couch and was awakened by a text message from Mavis asking him how his lunch was going. He checked the time and gently woke Emily who had fallen asleep next to him. They said goodbye to her family and headed over to the craziness at the Manor.

When they pulled up next to the signature magnolia tree, they could hear the hustle and bustle coming from the kitchen.

"Sounds like there's too many cooks in the kitchen," Wilbur chuckled. He opened the front door and heard Maude and Mavis bickering about how dry the dressing was. Opal was sitting at the kitchen table peeling an orange ignoring the sass between the two arguing women. "What's going on?" Wilbur asked.

"Maude can't keep her fingers out of the dressing, even though she says it's drier than a hot potato at the beach," Opal explained.

"What does that mean?" Emily whispered to Wilbur, but he had no clue.

"What can I help with?" Wilbur asked Mavis.

"Can you set the table in the dining room?" she asked. He could see that she was very stressed. He grabbed the dishes and set off to the dining room to get the table ready.

"Do you like to cook?" Emily asked Maude who was making it a point to chug her glass of sweet tea loudly.

"She likes to eat," Opal chirped.

"Ms. Maude is a fine cook," Mavis said, even though she couldn't really remember many times that Maude had ever prepared a full meal.

"I can cook Thanksgiving. I've done it many times," Maude nodded.

"We started having Thanksgiving over her after Maude almost burned her house down one year," Opal nodded. Emily's eyes widened, but she wasn't sure if Opal was exaggerating or not.

"You always exaggerate. I did not almost burn the house down. It was just a little turkey fire," Maude said. "The fire department put it out. I support the community by keeping those boys and girls employed."

"You burned the turkey?" Emily asked. "I bet

that happens a lot on Thanksgiving. I was reading an article the other day that said Thanksgiving is a very busy week for fire departments across the country, especially now that so many people are using those turkey fryers."

"She didn't so much as burn it as she tried to blow it up," Opal countered.

"Opal, you always tell my business! Emily, if you must know," Maude said. "I stuffed my bird with popcorn kernels."

"Popcorn kernels?" Emily wanted to make sure she had heard correctly.

"They act like an all-natural timer," Maude said.

"The only time Maude does anything natural is when she's trying to blow her house up," Opal added.

Maude shot her a look. "Anyway," she continued, "I buttered the hell out of it, and I'll have you know that I've never served undercooked turkey. Or anything undercooked for that matter."

"It was like a bomb went off," Opal nodded. "She had to get a whole new oven and set of cabinets."

"And kitchen tile," Maude added. "But I needed that anyway. The green linoleum was outdated."

"Big Daddy cooked the turkeys every year after that," Wilbur laughed.

"Ruby wouldn't even let me near the oven on Thanksgiving," Maude shook her head at the injustice of it all. "Next year I'm bringing the dressing."

"The dressing is fine," Mavis sighed.

"Big Mama told us this story every Thanksgiving," Wilbur laughed. "That and Opal's infamous jello salad."

"I'm still dealing with the consequences from that," Maude snapped. "My stomach has never been the same."

"That was the whole point," Opal said. "I was trying to reverse all the abuse you've done to your digestive system over the years. It was a lot."

"There was nothing wrong with my system," Maude said. "At least not until I ate that mess."

"I still have the recipe if you need another refresher," Opal offered.

"Jello salad?" Emily asked.

"It wasn't salad," Maude mumbled. "I don't even think it was jello either."

"It'll cure what ails you," Opal nodded.

"By killing you before any illness can take root," Maude added quickly.

The doorbell rang, interrupting Maude and Opal's bickering. Wilbur opened the door to let Mona and Harry inside. Mona brought a covered dish of sweet potato souffle and Harry brought a few of his famous pies from his days at the Starlight Cafe. Mavis' mouth watered the moment she saw him set them on the counter.

"Happy Thanksgiving," Mona announced. She turned to Emily and said, "And you must be the famous Emily. Mavis has told me so much about you!" Wilbur shot Mavis a look, but she merely smiled innocently at him. Mona and Emily launched into a conversation about the band that Mona had recently seen in concert, while Harry accidentally got caught up in Maude and Opal's tiff about the correct way to pronounce the word pecan.

"I hope y'all are hungry!" Mavis announced, bringing a sudden halt to the bickering between Maude and Opal. She pulled the turkey from the oven and set it on the counter. There were ooohs and aaahs from around the room. Wilber stood off to the side wondering where he was going to put a second full Thanksgiving dinner so quickly after having eaten the first dinner.

"I don't know how much I can eat," Emily whispered to him. "I'm still full from before."

"Me too," Wilbur said. "Maybe Mavis won't notice if we don't get too much."

"Come on everybody. Dig in," Mavis called out. "And there's plenty for seconds when you finish your first plate. And thirds, too."

Thankfully Mavis was too involved in her own plate to worry about what everyone else piled onto theirs. They all gathered around the kitchen table and ate until they couldn't eat anymore. Harry's pies were quickly devoured. Mavis encouraged him yet again to write a cookbook with some of his treasured recipes, which prompted Wilbur to bring up the faded yellow cookbook from the 1980s that the Ladies Auxiliary had published. "Mrs. Beulah made Big Mama's recipe for lunch today," he smiled. "It brought back so many memories."

"I use that cookbook all the time," Mavis said.

Once the kitchen was cleaned up, Wilbur and Harry retired to the living room to watch the remainder of the football game. The women sat around the table and looked through the ads that revealed what specials and sales were going live tomorrow.

"What time do you want me to pick y'all up tomorrow?" Mavis asked Maude and Opal. "Mona's going to meet us for lunch when we're done shopping, so I want to make sure we get everything done that we want to."

"I can drive," Maude offered with a yawn. She had already undone the button on her jeans and was getting comfortable. A few belches helped make some room for another slice of butternut cake that Mavis had made.

"NO!" Mavis replied a little more forcefully than she intended. "I mean, no ma'am. I'll drive. My car is bigger so we can hold more bargains." There was no way that she was going to willingly get in Maude's new car and speed between the different stores trying to catch the best deal.

"Well, we need to get to Junction early to get all the good sales before they're gone," Maude explained. She was adamant that she needed the newest and biggest television that the electronics store advertised. They were advertising an unbeatable deal with a subscription to a streaming service. She wasn't sure what that meant, but if it was free, she wanted it.

"We'll get there early enough. Just tell me what time you want to be there and I'll pick both of you up," Mavis repeated.

"I don't want to get there too crazy early," Opal said. "How about you pick us up about six o'clock?"

"Everything will be gone by then," Maude grumbled. "We won't even have time to stop for breakfast."

"I think that's a good idea. I'll pick y'all up first thing in the morning," Mavis agreed. "We'll grab a bite to eat and then we'll find ourselves some bargains. Sure you don't want to go with us, Emily?"

Emily covered up her laughter with a fake cough. Mavis had been begging her to tag along all evening, but she had plans with her parents before they went back to Chicago.

Maude continued to grumble about the importance of getting there before everyone else, but Opal and Mavis wouldn't budge. "Fine, but if I miss my giant television set I'm going to be upset," she huffed. "Mine's too small."

"Your television screen is huge," Mavis said. "It's way bigger than mine."

"I can hardly see it! I need the new one that's seventy-five inches," Maude said. "I'm telling you, if I miss this deal, I'm going to be very upset."

"Better to be upset than risk life and limb with her driving," Wilbur whispered when Opal started fussing with Maude again.

"Ain't that the truth," Mavis agreed.

"You need to get your eyes checked," Opal said.

"Yes," Mavis agreed emphatically.

Chapter Twelve

Mavis was awake and dressed by five the next morning. She knew she had to be on time or else Maude would drive to Junction without her. She couldn't begin to fathom the amount of damage that that woman would be able to do in the early dark hours of the busiest day of the season.

She chugged down two cups of coffee and ran a brush through her hair. She bundled up in her Christmas reindeer sweater, a scarf, and a new black jacket. She put on her boots by the front door and braced herself for one adventurous day. Anything was possible when Maude and Opal were around.

Even though she arrived at Opal's house with plenty of time to spare, Maude was sitting in her car waiting on Opal to walk out of her house.

"Good morning! What are you doing out here?" Mavis greeted her. Maude lived less than one hundred yards from Opal. Mavis had expected to pull up at Opal's and both of them would jump in and squabble about who got to ride in the front seat.

"Opal and I were about to head over to Junction. I thought you were going to be late," Maude said.

"But I'm twenty minutes early," Mavis replied. She glanced at her watch quickly to be sure. She was actually more than twenty minutes early, but she didn't add that little detail to the conversation. Maude was too easily aggravated when fantastic bargains were on the line, especially if those bargains involved a television set.

"I wasn't sure. You never can tell with you young kids," Maude said. "Sometimes y'all keep strange hours."

"Ms. Maude, I am definitely not a young kid," Mavis said with her hands on her hip.

"Good morning all!" Opal called from her front porch. "Are we caravanning?" she asked as she looked from one vehicle to the next.

"No ma'am," Mavis replied. "Ms. Maude was just getting a little over eager about her new television set."

"Oh good. I didn't want to have to flip a quarter to decide who to ride with," Opal said. "I call shotgun."

"You always call shotgun," Maude grumbled. "One of these days I'm going to beat you to it and ride in the front seat."

"If you snooze you lose," Opal sang. Maude normally beat Opal to the front seat, but this wasn't a time to push the limit.

Once Mavis had them both safely seated in her car, she backed out of the driveway and headed over to Junction. She had already looked to see which restaurants were open this time of morning. She knew it was better to feed Maude first thing off the bat otherwise she'd be hungry and mad the whole day. And nobody wanted to be around a mad and hungry Maude.

Just outside of Junction, Mavis pulled into the parking lot of Danny's Diner, a small restaurant about the size of the Starlight Cafe without the classy atmosphere.

"I hope they have good pancakes," Maude said. "I have a feeling I'm going to need my strength to deal with all the crazy people out and about today."

"You shouldn't eat so many pancakes. You need more fiber in your diet," Opal said.

"I am not about to start eating fiber on today of all days," Maude grumbled.

"I'm just saying it would give you a much sweeter disposition," Opal said.

"I have a very sweet disposition!" Maude said.

"I'm sure they have pancakes," Mavis said. "And Ms. Opal, I'm sure we can find something you'd like to eat as well."

"Oh, I'm easy to please. I just go with the flow. I don't get out of joints like Maude does," Opal said in her whimsical voice.

"I am not out of joint! Honestly Opal, you act like I'm crazy or something," Maude huffed.

"Those are your words not mine, but," Opal raised her palms off the table, "if the shoes fit."

Before Maude could say anything, Mavis spoke. "Nobody is out of sorts and nobody needs any extra fiber today. We're just going to sit here and enjoy our breakfast and then have a great day of shopping adventures." She knew they could not go twenty minutes without bickering about something. It was like traveling with toddlers, except these toddlers could get into Lord knows what.

By the time the waitress set their plates on the table, Mavis had successfully steered the conversation to Christmas dinner. Thankfully that took up the remainder of time they ate breakfast.

"Alright!" Maude said as she threw her napkin down on her empty plate. "I guess it's time to hit the shops."

Mavis finished her third cup of coffee of the morning and paid the bill. They loaded up in the car and headed towards the main part of the shopping district. Maude put in to go to the electronics store first. Mavis knew Maude would never forgive her if they missed the sale on televisions. When they pulled up to the store, they saw a line wrapped around the building.

"I told you we should have got here earlier," Maude fumed.

Mavis pulled up to the front and let Maude out so that she could take her place in the winding line. Mavis and Opal drove around until they found a parking spot. By the time they walked to the store, Maude was already inside. They could hear her before they saw her. Her voice carried over the sounds of the rushing crowd.

"That doesn't sound good," Opal said.

"I don't think Maude's coming home with that television," Mavis sighed.

They found Maude trying to climb into a shopping cart pushed by a teenage boy and his mother. "That was mine!" Maude howled.

"Ma'am, what is wrong with you?" the mother shouted.

"Oh dear God!" Mavis cried. She grabbed Maude around the waist and drug her outside. People all around were staring at them as Maude flailed and Opal waved like she was walking across the stage in a pageant.

"What were you thinking?" Mavis asked.

"I wanted that tv," Maude huffed. "That youngster beat me to it!"

"Dear God!" Mavis sighed. "You can't act like that in public. Some people are dangerous. You pull up on the wrong person and they're liable to shoot you!"

"Mavis, I could have beat up that nerd and his mother," Maude rolled her eyes.

"It's true," Opal nodded.

"You cannot beat people over a TV," Mavis tried to explain.

"Well, technically you can as long as you don't mind going to jail afterwards," Opal reasoned.

"Opal!" Mavis said.

"It's true. And since Maude is a hardened criminal, she could survive a little time in the cooler," Opal continued.

"Please, Opal," Mavis said again, this time pleading slightly in her voice.

Opal nudged her on the arm. "Cooler is slang for jail. Maude could probably handle it, but she wouldn't like the food."

"I'm too old for this mess," Mavis sighed. "Can we please get out of here? Everyone is still staring!"

Maude, in all her aggravation, decided that her anger would best be calmed down by walking next door to the home goods store. Mavis and Opal followed behind her listening to her curse under her breath the entire way. Her not-so-quiet whisper caused several parents to cover their children's ears.

Maude grabbed a shopping cart and set off on her way leaving Mavis and Opal to fend for themselves. Mavis hadn't seen anything in the advertisement that she wanted from this store, but it didn't hurt to look around. She didn't end up finding anything worthwhile, so she and Opal walked outside and sat on the bench to wait for Maude. A few minutes later, they heard her voice at the door.

"Y'all didn't find anything?" she asked.

"Looks like you bought it all before we could," Opal said.

"What in the world did you find?" Mavis asked. Maude's shopping cart was loaded down with shopping bags of various sizes.

"Deals," Maude said. "I found some good deals."

Mavis opened the trunk and helped Maude stuff the bags in semi neatly. "What all did you end up with?"

"I found a great deal on a mixing bowl set, a fruit basket, some beach towels, a new comforter set, a lemonade pitcher, and a bunch of wrapping paper. You can't go wrong with wrapping paper," Maude explained.

"Do you really need eleven tubes of wrapping

paper?" Mavis asked.

"They don't go bad," Maude reasoned. Mavis couldn't argue with that logic. She shut the trunk and drove to the mall down the road. As expected, it was crawling with people. Mavis found a parking spot and helped Maude and Opal out of the car. She didn't trust them enough to drop them off at the front of the building after Maude's antics at the electronic store.

"What are we looking for in here?" Mavis asked.

"We'll know when we see it," Maude said. She had a crazed look in her eye as she scanned the terrain before her.

"That's what I'm afraid of," Mavis sighed.

Maude liked to touch every item they passed. She said she needed to inspect the quality to make sure that it was worth the price. Somehow they survived the glassware and porcelain housewares without any broken pieces. When they passed the maternity section, Opal asked Maude if she saw anything she might like.

"I don't shop in the paternity section," Maude howled.

"What about maternity?" Opal asked.

"Oh shut up," Maude snapped. "I don't need those stretchy clothes. Well, on second thought." She meandered around the clothing racks and held up a few pairs of the jeans with the soft elastic waist panel that allowed for stretching. "There would have been perfect for yesterday. I think I may get me some for next year."

Even though Mavis tried to explain to her that

she didn't need to buy maternity pants, Maude ignored her and stood in line to pay for her new jeans. Mavis and Opal walked around the shoe racks across the aisle while Maude checked out at the register. Mavis couldn't even look the cashier in the eye. It probably wasn't every day that a women in her eighties purchased maternity pants for herself.

Maude was proud of her new jeans and decided to reward herself with popcorn and a lemonade. "Aren't you still full from breakfast?" Opal asked.

"I've already walked ten miles today," Maude said.

Neither Mavis nor Opal wanted any snacks, but Mavis didn't think it would be a good idea for Maude to go alone. She asked her to wait a few minutes so she could test the new perfume that the perfume counter had on display, but when she turned around, both Maude and Opal were nowhere in sight.

"Where in the world did they go?" Mavis asked aloud.

"What was that?" the saleswoman asked. She had spritzed the perfume sample on a white card and wafted it in front of Mavis' nose to smell. It made Mavis gag and cough. "Oh, this is not good. No thanks!" Mavis said. She needed to find the two women quickly. The food court would be the best place to look, so she hurried to the center of the mall as fast as she could. She found Maude at the condiment counter stuffing napkins into her □ purse.

"There you are!" Mavis cried.

"Where's Opal?" Maude asked. Mavis looked around and didn't see the small old woman anywhere. "What do you mean?" Mavis asked. "I thought she was with you!"

"Why would she be with me?" Maude asked. "I went and got popcorn."

"This isn't happening," Mavis sighed. Maude and Opal were double trouble. She hurried back into the store she had just left with Maude hot on her heels.

"You better find her," Maude said. "You know how she gets into things." She wiped her greasy hands on one of the folded tea towels on the shelf. "Nice of them to put towels out for the shoppers."

"No, that's not, never mind," Mavis said. She knew it wouldn't do any good to explain that that was a towel available for purchase. She tossed the Christmas themed tea towel into her basket and followed Maude around the store as she called out for Opal.

"There she is!" Maude said. She pointed over a few dress racks to where Opal was talking to a man holding measuring tape and a notepad.

Mavis breathed a sigh of relief and walked quickly over to the salesman and Opal who were engaged in a lively discussion. "I hope she's been behaving," Mavis said sweetly. There was no telling what all Opal had gotten into without any supervision.

"She's the sweetest lady," the salesman said. His name tag said that he was one of the stylists at the department store. His name was Jacob. "Is she your grandmother?"

"More like a kooky aunt," Mavis said. There was no need to get into things with a stranger. "Ok, Opal, time to go."

"I think I'm going to buy this one," Opal said. She pointed to the olive-green pantsuit on the rack.

"Why do you need something fancy?" Maude asked. She had already eaten half of her popcorn and was ready to head to lunch.

"I'm going to marry Wilbur," Opal announced.

"Do what?" Maude choked on her soda. Mavis had to whack her on the back to help her.

"You're marrying who?" Mavis asked.

"Wilbur," Opal repeated.

"Who's Wilbur?" Jacob asked.

"My brother!" Mavis gasped.

"Oh my," he squealed. "So that makes her your aunt and sister-in-law?" He scratched his head and looked between the three women waiting for an explanation.

"What?" Mavis gasped. "No, Opal, you aren't getting married to Wilbur. What in the world?" She turned to Maude and asked, "Is she having another stroke?"

"I don't think so," Maude said. "I think she's just lost her mind."

"You can't get married to Wilbur," Mavis repeated.

"I'm not marrying Wilbur," Opal said. She looked at Mavis like she had two heads.

"You just said you were!" Mavis shrieked. Maude nodded and asked, "Did your mind forget already?"

"I'm not the one with memory problems," Opal said.

"You just said you were getting married!" Maude said.

Opal shook her head and said, "You're crazy. I'm going to perform the ceremony." She looked at the salesman who was still utterly confused.

"What ceremony?" Maude asked.

"Wilbur's wedding," Opal explained patiently.

"Wilbur's getting married?" Mavis asked. Opal nodded. "To whom?" Mavis gasped.

"To her?" Jacob squealed. "Wait, or not. I've lost track. Huh?"

"Wilbur's getting married and didn't tell me!" Maude scowled. She looked at Mavis and demanded to know why she hadn't shared the news.

"I didn't know!" Mavis countered. "He apparently didn't tell me either!"

"He didn't tell anyone," Opal said. "Not even himself."

"What's going on?" Jacob asked. His head was about to explode from the noise and confusion.

"Wilbur doesn't know he's getting married?" Maude asked. "That ain't legal. Not anymore. We can't betroth him to anyone. He's too grown."

Jacob leaned closer to Mavis and asked her if he needed to call someone. "Is Wilbur ok? How old is he?"

"He's a grown man," Mavis sighed. "This is insane. Everything is fine. Everyone is fine. Well, they're crazy, but sheesh."

"We've heard that time and again," Maude

shrugged.

Jacob still looked confused. Mavis thanked him for his time and said she would handle things from here. As he walked off muttering to himself, Maude stopped him. "Hold your horses! Opal wants that fancy pants thing there."

"Oh, ok, right," Jacob said. He took the pantsuit and brought it to the counter and rang it up. Opal paid for it and he placed it in a nice dress bag for her to carry out.

"Good luck at your wedding. I mean, congratulations. Or, well, I don't know," Jacob sighed.

Mavis ushered Maude and Opal through the rest of the store back outside to the parking lot. She was beyond exhausted and it was only eleven o'clock, but she was ready to call it a day.

"Is it time to meet Mona for lunch?" Maude asked. She didn't wait for a response before saying, "Tell her to meet us at this sub sandwich shop over here."

"Yes ma'am," Mavis sighed. She sent Mona a text message telling her where Maude had picked for lunch. Mona said she would be there right at noon, so Mavis had to find something to occupy Maude and Opal in the meantime.

There was a bookstore across the street that didn't look too crowded. Both Mavis and Opal loved to read. Maude wasn't interested in literature, unless it involved a good bit of action. The problem with most the books these days was that the good action books also came with a fair amount of modern-day romance which Maude said she could do without. Hopefully, they could find something relatively tame to keep Maude occupied.

Chapter Thirteen

Wilbur had made the same chili recipe for more than twenty years. It was one he had worked to perfect since he started cooking for himself. There was a lot of trial and error involved in the process, but he was pretty happy with the finished product. On more than one occasion, he had been asked for the recipe, but he never entertained these requests. To do so would have meant sharing his secret ingredient, and he never divulged that tidbit of information. Ruby Montgomery was the only soul who had ever known that secret ingredient, even though Mavis pestered them both to find out over the years.

He lined up his ingredients on the counter and made sure that he had everything he needed. First he browned the ground beef. Then in a large stock pot on the stove, he added water, beef stock, and a few splashes of red wine. He didn't want to distract from the bold flavors of the peppers he was going to put in, but the sweetness of the wine elevated the chili as a whole. Once the liquid was simmering, he added his cooked ground beef. He then stirred in the garlic, chili powder, salt, black pepper, red pepper, and tomato paste. It wasn't conventional, but he liked doing things his own way in his own order.

Once he was happy with the way the beef was incorporated with the spices and liquid, he added a tablespoon of brown sugar and a dash of cocoa powder. The sweetness of the sugar and sharp bite of the cocoa helped tame the spice from the peppers that came next. He stirred in the juice from the jar of jalapeños and blended the peppers in the blender with a few chunks of fresh tomatoes. Once that mixture was added to the pot, he turned the stove down to let it simmer.

He roughly chopped a large yellow onion on his cutting board and added the pieces to the simmering pot. The thick tomatoes and pieces of beef were going to be plenty filling once the chili simmered for another hour or so, but the addition of yellow onion made it much better. He checked his watch and noted that it was around the time that Emily should be saying goodbye to her parents in Montgomery. They had had lunch before their flight back home to Chicago. It had been nice to meet them at Beulah's house. He looked forward to seeing them again and hopefully spending more time with the rest of the family in the future.

He hadn't heard anything from Mavis or anyone else all day, but he hoped they were having the time of their lives shopping and snagging some good deals. He had told Mavis that Emily was coming over for an early dinner and that she should come over for dessert afterwards and they could all hang out after she dropped off Maude and Opal. He knew that Mavis would probably have a few stories to tell them once she arrived. Maude and Opal knew how to keep things interesting.

Wilbur vacuumed the rugs and swept the floors while the chili finished on the stove. He set the table and added a candle in the middle of the table for an added effect. He started a fire in the living room fireplace and popped the loaf of bread into the oven. The aroma of baking bread made his whole cabin smell amazing. When Emily arrived on his front porch, his heart nearly skipped a beat. He opened the front door and she handed him a large glass mason jar sealed tight.

"What's this?" he asked.

"My grandma insisted that I bring this over," Emily laughed. "She said it's the best apple cranberry jam to date. Oh, I didn't see this last time I was here." Emily pointed to the mounted catfish above the fireplace.

"That's almost forty years old," Wilbur chuckled. He told Emily about the first time he had ever been fishing with Jameson Montgomery. It had been the first time he had ever been fishing in his entire life. A few weeks later during Christmas, Jameson had pulled out one last present for Wilbur to open. It was one of the catfish he had caught that Jameson had mounted professionally. It would always be one of his most prized possessions.

"It's beautiful," Emily smiled. "Jameson and Ruby sound amazing. My grandmother says they were the best people she ever knew."

"They were truly wonderful," Wilbur smiled. He missed them both every day. He couldn't imagine what his life would have looked like if it weren't for them taking him in when he was eleven years old. They quickly became his forever family with Mavis who was a little kid at the time. He grew up never wanting or needing anything ever again. Maude and Opal had become a part of his life back then, too. It was Opal who found him hiding in the woods early one morning while she looked for ingredients for her natural hair dye line. He never could have imagined that his chance encounter with Opal Tyler would have changed his life for the better. Opal would always be one of his personal heroes.

While Emily looked at the pictures Wilbur had framed on the mantle, Wilbur took the bread out of the oven and sliced it. As soon as the chili was ready, Wilbur ladled the thick stew into their bowls and they sat down at the table to eat. They talked throughout the meal and ate the entire loaf of bread with Mrs. Beulah's jam. Emily told Wilbur that Nadine's house officially went on the ☐ market today. Wilbur cringed slightly. He knew that Maude wasn't going to take the news well, even if she knew it was coming sooner than later.

"It's a nice house," Emily said. "I may go look at it tomorrow."

"You're interested in buying it?" Wilbur asked.

"Maybe," Emily nodded. "I can't live with my grandparents forever, and it has a beautiful garden."

"It sure does," Wilbur nodded. Once they were finished eating, he told Emily some of the stories involving Nadine and Maude from over the years. He had a feeling that the dump truck full of manure that Maude had ordered and paid to be spread over Nadine's yard years ago had something to do with the excellence of the garden.

There was a sudden commotion on the porch and Wilbur pulled out his phone to check the cameras. He hoped it wasn't the tractor bandits coming back for round two. Emily watched as he opened up the app and chuckled to himself. Before Wilbur could get up to answer the door, he saw Maude push her face against the camera. He and Emily could see up her nose. "Oh Lord," he laughed. He raced over to the door and opened it to see Maude and Opal pushed against the door fighting for the doorbell.

"We thought you'd never open up," Maude said. She walked past Wilbur and set her purse on the bar. Opal hugged Wilbur and waved over her shoulder at Mavis who was just now walking up the front steps. "Y'all already ate supper? We had us some chicken."

"I'm exhausted," Mavis mouthed.

"She needs more fiber," Opal added. "I have a tea for that."

"No!" Maude shouted from the kitchen. She had already poured herself a glass of wine from the wine bottle on Wilbur's counter. "What are y'all up to?"

"We were just about to pick a board game," Emily smiled.

Maude groaned and poured herself more wine. She was not interested in playing the trivia game from the other day. Who cared about the medieval era or what dinosaur had the smallest brain. She should've looked more at the board games the bookstore had to offer when they were there earlier.

"I tried to scoot out without them," Mavis whispered to Wilbur. "But once they heard I was coming here, they hopped back in the car."

"It's fine," Wilbur said. "We just finished eating. Emily was looking at the board games while I cut the apple pie."

Mavis looked past Wilbur and saw a warm apple pie on the counter next to a tub of vanilla ice cream. Wilbur knew she could never pass up a thick slice of pie topped with ice cream.

While Emily and Opal talked about the various games Wilbur had available, Wilbur gave each person a slice of pie topped with ice cream. He joined Maude and Mavis at the table and waited for the other two to select a game.

"This is perfect," Emily agreed. She brought the worn red box over to the table and smiled at Wilbur.

"I hate that game," Maude frowned.

"I love this one!" Mavis cheered at the same time.

The object of this particular game was to earn the most points by making a list of words that all began with the same letter based on a series of category cards. There was a multi-sided die with different letters on it that they could each take turns rolling. Once the game was set up and lists were distributed, Maude rolled first.

"A," she sighed. "That shouldn't be too hard."

"That's a good letter," Emily agreed.

Wilbur set the timer and they all got to work on their lists. Opal finished first, followed by Emily. Mavis and Wilbur barely scraped by and Maude rolled her eyes once the timer went off. "I want a do-over," she grumbled.

"Alright, a boy's name?" Emily began. "I put Adam."

"So did I," Mavis giggled.

"I put Abner," Wilbur said. They all turned to Maude and Opal to see what they had come up with.

"Apollo," Opal smiled. "What a strong Greek name." They all stared at Maude who continued to frown.

"Allan," Maude said. She eyed Opal who smiled back sweetly. Allan was the name of one of Maude's ex-husbands. Opal once told Wilbur that she was sure that Allan had never gotten over Maude, even after he moved to the Midwest.

"Great!" Mavis said. "Everyone gets a point except for me and Emily. "Number two, name something you'd find in a zoo."

"Antelope," Opal said.

"Anteater," Mavis nodded. "They're so cute! I'd like to have one."

Wilbur shook his head and said, "Alligator. What did you write down, Emily?"

"Alpaca," she smiled. "I thought Mavis might put that."

"How did I not think of that!" Mavis gasped.

"What did you put?" Opal asked Maude.

"Animals," Maude said dryly. She'd already

given herself a point for that answer.

"Number three, tropical travel destination," Mavis continued. "I put Aruba."

"So did I," Wilbur and Emily said.

"I put Antigua," Opal smiled.

"Atlanta," Maude said. Before she could give herself a point for that, Mavis and Opal both interrupted.

"Atlanta?" Opal laughed.

"I don't think that's very tropical," Mavis said.

"Sure it is," Maude countered. "It has all kinds of plants and people there. I've been there on vacation many times."

"Just let her have it," Wilbur whispered quietly.

Mavis rolled her eyes but moved on to the next category. "Things you collect."

"Albums," Opal said. "Vinyl and picture books."

Wilbur patted her hand and smiled gently at Opal. She had the best vinyl collection, and looking through Ruby's photograph albums was still everyone's favorite pastime.

"Animals," Mavis grinned.

"That's the truth!" Wilbur agreed. "I didn't get this one."

"I said antiques," Emily revealed.

"Another great answer!" Mavis said. As usual, Maude was the last one to answer. "Acorns," she said sharply.

"Acorns?" Mavis repeated, as if she hadn't heard her correctly.

"Yes," Maude nodded.

"You could've said autographs or arrowheads

or alarm clocks," Opal laughed. "Acorns?"

"Squirrels collect them," Maude shrugged.

"Well, they do," Emily agreed.

Mavis shook her head and sighed inwardly. "Last one is holiday things."

"Angels," Emily said.

"Apples," Mavis announced. She loved to go bobbing for apples in the fall, not to mention the sweet caramel apples the local bakery sold.

"I said America," Wilbur shrugged.

"April Fool's Day," Opal smiled. "Maude?"

"Ass," Maude said plainly.

"That's a holiday?" Mavis gasped.

"There's an ass on every holiday," Maude yawned. "Holidays bring out the worst in people."

"That's every day for some folks," Opal mumbled.

Wilbur laughed until Maude and Mavis both shot him a look. He drank the rest of his glass of water and got up to refill it. It was always an adventure with Maude and Opal.

"Are we done yet? This is boring," Maude said. "I brought over this pound cake and it needs to be cut. Mavis, you cut it. Opal makes the slices too small."

"Yes ma'am," Mavis replied. While she cut the cake, Emily boxed up the game and winked at Wilbur who merely shrugged.

Maude dug around in her purse until she found the envelope that she was looking for. "I just had these developed!" she announced.

"I'm afraid to ask what's on that roll," Mavis whispered.

"No one wants to see those," Opal grimaced.

"Yes, they do," Maude frowned and stuck her tongue out at Opal. "It's from the fair a few weeks ago."

"Why are you still using a disposable camera?" Mavis asked.

"Because I want to," Maude answered. She dumped the photographs onto the table and picked the one on top up. "Damn't Opal, why you gotta make that face every time?"

"Because I want to," Opal mimicked. In several of the photographs, Opal had scrunched up her face and stuck out her tongue behind Maude who liked to pose in front of the gigantic carnival rides.

"Oh heavens!" Mavis sighed. "Did you really have to take pictures of him?"

"Is this the infamous Earl?" Emily wondered.

"Unfortunately," Mavis sighed.

"Oh goodness," Wilbur chuckled. "If we never see him again, it'll be too soon."

"The birdman," Opal nodded.

"And there's Opal taking a whack at him," Maude admired. "Made him think twice about ever coming 'round these parts again."

"He didn't want your parts," Opal gagged.

"Oh God," Wilbur said.

"You really got him good," Emily said appreciatively.

"Sure did," Maude said. "And here's one of us four all dressed up. Wilbur wouldn't wear the wig Opal got him."

"This is amazing," Emily grinned. "Mavis, is that you with a crystal ball?"

Emily held up a photograph of Mavis wearing a long-bedazzled cloak with her hands over an ornate crystal ball, but Mavis didn't respond. She was engrossed in something on her phone. "Are you ok?" Wilbur asked. "Earth to Mavis."

"Mavis?" Opal asked gently. She put her hand on Mavis' back which startled her.

"Are you ok?" Wilbur asked again.

Mavis nodded and brushed a tear away from her cheek. "My DNA results came back in," she whispered.

Emily put the photograph back down on the table and sat down next to Mavis. Maude and Opal both walked closer and waited with bated breath.

"And?" Wilbur asked.

"I have a sister," she breathed.

Chapter Fourteen

Mavis was generally quite impulsive when it came to near about everything, which usually caused Wilbur great concern. He was the one who was more thoughtful and careful when it came to making decisions, which is why this sister situation perplexed him greatly. After they had all gathered around Mavis at the announcement of her sister, Mavis had sat frozen for many minutes. Maude and Opal huddled together near the couch and spoke in low tones where the rest of them could not overhear. Emily glanced back and forth between Mavis who kept staring at the ancestral chart and Wilbur who had sat down next to Mavis with his arm around her.

"What do you want to do?" Wilbur asked Mavis gently.

"I don't know," Mavis whispered. She handed Wilbur her phone and he quickly scanned the information. The results were crystal clear. There was a woman who shared almost twenty-six percent of Mavis' DNA, thus making them half siblings.

"Mavis, it says you have a sister and a host of relatives out there. Wow," Wilbur breathed. He saw a plethora of distantly related cousins that went pretty far back on both sides. Mavis nodded and looked up at Emily who was still standing nearby. "You don't have to do anything right now," Emily said softly. "Right, Wilbur?"

"Right," Wilbur nodded. "Or ever if you don't want to. This is your decision to know more about your family."

"You all are my family," Mavis whispered.

"We'll always be your family, Mavis," Wilbur replied. He hugged Mavis tightly and gestured over to Maude and Opal. "Including Bonnie and Clyde over there."

"Speaking of those two, what exactly are they doing over there?" Emily asked.

"There's no telling," Wilbur said.

Emily quietly walked over behind the two older women and heard their chatter go radio silent. They both turned in unison to look up at her. "Yes?" Maude asked.

"Everything ok over there?" Wilbur called out.

Opal opened her purse and took out a nail file while Maude rustled around her bag for some candy or gum. "Fine as wine," Opal smiled.

"Yea, fine," Maude nodded.

"What are you two conspiring about?" Wilbur asked directly.

Maude looked over at Mavis who had set her phone down on the table and was staring back at them. "Do you know anything about this?" Mavis asked timidly.

"Maybe," Opal shrugged.

"It's possible," Maude offered.

Wilbur hid a smile behind his hand while

Mavis raised her eyebrows.

"We don't know everything," Maude shook her head.

"We know very little," Opal added.

Maude and Opal made room for Mavis to join them on the couch. "Come on you two," she gestured to Wilbur and Emily. Wilbur took a seat in his recliner and Emily sat on the arm of the couch next to Mavis.

"We don't know much," Opal warned.

"Somehow I doubt that," Wilbur whispered.

"We're just two kooky old ladies," Opal smiled back at him.

Wilbur shook his head. As kooky as these two were, they were also brilliant. Opal may have had two strokes that almost killed her, but she rarely missed a beat. He still trusted her with his life.

"Can you tell me what you know, or what you think you know?" Mavis asked.

"Are you sure you're ready, Mavis?" Wilbur asked. "We can give you privacy on this matter."

"We're all family here," Mavis said.

"Well, it all started long ago," Maude said.

Opal rolled her eyes and elbowed her in the gut. "This isn't a medieval tale."

"Who's telling this story?" Maude rebutted. "Like I was saying, it was a long time ago."

Opal rolled her eyes again and smiled slightly at Mavis who was waiting on pins and needles. "I've never asked you guys about my mother," Mavis said quietly. "Any time I asked about her or when I was born, Big Mama and Big Daddy would tell me about her, but I've never asked about it all from your point of view."

"I remember it like it was yesterday," Maude nodded.

"Sure you do," Opal cackled.

"I knew Melanie since before she was born, you old coot!" Maude howled.

"So did I," Opal smiled. "Melanie was beautiful, Mavis. Just like you."

"Thank you, Mavis smiled. She held Opal's outstretched hand while Maude continued. "Melanie left for Hollywood the minute she could. It was right after she graduated high school. Ruby didn't want to talk much about it. We all thought she'd get it all out of her system and be back soon enough, but she stayed put. Near about broke Ruby and Jameson."

"There wasn't much contact until, well," Opal shrugged softly.

"Until Melanie came back home late one night in labor," Maude said. "She was all alone."

Mavis nodded. "Big Mama nor Big Daddy had any idea who my father could be. I know it doesn't matter, but what if he's out there?"

It dawned on Wilbur that the revelation of a sister must mean that the identity of Mavis' father could be finally known. As far as anyone knew, Melanie had only given birth to Mavis. The fact that Mavis had a sibling indicated that they shared a direct line from one man.

"You two don't know anything about him, do you?" Mavis asked.

"Well," Opal started to say, but Maude cut her off and said, "Now don't go thinking that Ruby or Jameson kept anything from you, because they didn't."

"Never!" Opal agreed.

"They just didn't know all the things," Maude finished.

"How do you both always know everything?" Wilbur chuckled.

"We don't know everything," Opal smiled. "Maybe nothing at all."

"I'm trying to tell y'all," Maude said. "Back when Mavis was born, well, we didn't know Melanie was pregnant. Ruby and them didn't either. It wasn't like it is today with all the news and things online. Melly didn't tell anyone. She showed up back home and then Mavis girl was born right here in Rhinestone. That was back when Rhinestone had a hospital. But Melanie was very sick, so you were both sent over to Junction to the bigger hospital that same night."

"My mother was an addict," Mavis said to Emily.

"I'm so sorry," Emily said.

"Came as a shock for all of us," Maude nodded. "Ruby called us in the dead of night and asked us to feed the dogs and keep an eye on her house. We knew something was up. When me and Opal got to the hospital, we could hardly recognize Melanie in the bed. We were plum shocked to see you, Mavis. You were so tiny and cute!"

"Ruby loved you from the moment she saw you. We all did," Opal said. Mavis smiled and felt Emily's hand rub her shoulder. "Still do," Opal smiled.

"Jameson told us that Melanie had showed up at the Manor in labor. She named you Mavis Elaine Montgomery while we were standing outside the room," Maude continued.

"Big Mama said she had no idea where my name came from," Mavis frowned.

Maude and Opal both shrugged.

"Jameson said that Melanie wasn't able to take care of Mavis right then, so she was going to go home with them to the Manor and get her strength back," Maude explained. "Ruby spent every second of the next few weeks taking care of Melanie and Mavis, but," Maude sighed.

"Melanie left and went back to California by herself," Opal finished.

"Mavis stayed at the Manor with Ruby and Jameson. Melanie came back to see her, but she ended up passing away two years later from an overdose," Maude continued.

"An accidental overdose," Opal corrected.

"Jameson went out there and got her stuff from her little apartment. He told us once how it looked. He said there were broken bottles and needles all over the counters on the floor. It was dirty with bugs and rats everywhere," Maude said. "He didn't want Ruby to know. He was always trying to protect her."

"Ruby was stronger than any of us gave her credit for," Opal said. "You both know that," she said to Wilbur and Mavis.

"We were the lucky ones," Mavis agreed. "We sure are," Wilbur nodded.

"Blessed for sure," Maude said.

"But what does that have to do with my father?" Mavis asked.

"I'm getting around to it," Maude said. "Kids these days are so impatient."

Mavis was nearing her mid-forties, but to a woman in her eighties, she might as well have been a child.

"No one knew who your dad was. Melanie had been seeing a guy off and on for the past few months, but he swore up and down that Melanie was already pregnant when he met her. He even did a paternity test and he was telling the truth. Wasn't any help after that," Maude explained.

"But we had other ways," Opal interjected when she saw Mavis start to ask another question.

"We're nosy as hell," Maude shrugged. "When Jameson brought home a few boxes of Melanie's stuff, he asked to store it at my house. He was beside himself in grief, and Ruby couldn't bear to go through any of it, and she didn't need to. We said we'd handle it."

"It wasn't much to go on," Opal winced. "But we sifted through it all."

"What was in the boxes?" breathed Emily. She was very invested in this story already. Maude and Opal knew how to drag it out for suspense.

"Do you still have any of it?" Mavis asked.

Maude looked at Opal and waited for her to speak. "Most of the stuff wasn't salvageable," Opal began.

"There were a few t-shirts that Ruby made into a quilt for you," Maude told Mavis who nodded. That quilt had been on her bed for as long as she could remember. "There were a few random photographs that were not able to be restored and some costume jewelry. Jameson said there wasn't much in the house that could be kept."

"There was a stack of mail," Opal added.

"But most of it was bills," Maude explained.

"But there was a letter," Opal said.

"From someone named Jack," Maude said. "It was torn and faded, but it was dated March 1980. Mavis was born in September of that same year, which could mean that whoever this mysterious Jack man was."

"Could be my father," Mavis finished.

"He could be, but he could also not be," Opal said wisely.

"What did the letter say?" Wilbur asked.

"It was so faded, we couldn't make out much," Maude frowned. "Best we could tell it was a breakup note."

"But Melanie kept it, so it had to be important," Opal said.

"You never told Big Mama?" Mavis asked.

"We never wanted to hurt her. Knowing a random person's name wouldn't bring Melly back," Maude said.

"She did see it technically," Opal said.

"When she was ready to go through the box of stuff, the letter was in there, but she never even glanced at it. It wasn't Melly's handwriting, so she skipped over it. Tossed it into the trashcan," Maude explained.

"Oh," Mavis sighed.

Wilbur watched Opal out of the corner of

his eye and knew without a second thought that Opal had recovered the letter. He wondered if she would say something, but she let Mavis ask questions instead. He didn't want to put her on the spot in case he was wrong. If Opal had retrieved the faded letter, he was sure she had a good reason for keeping it hidden all this time.

"Do you know anything else about him, the Jack person?" Mavis asked, but Opal shook her head. "We looked all over the place for him, but we didn't have a last name."

"Mavis, the results say a woman named Brandy Stevenson is your sibling. She could have the answers. Is there a way to contact her?" Wilbur asked. Mavis handed him her phone and he studied the screen again. "It says you can send her a message."

Mavis studied the tiny profile picture of the woman that shared her DNA. She couldn't make out any distinguishing pictures in the small, pixelated photo, but she could see that she had dark hair that was shoulder length. She could not tell if the woman was tall or short. She could not tell if they shared the same nose or cheekbones or shape of the eyes. She had an innate desire to know more, but she was afraid that it could potentially change everything. Not that change was necessarily bad, but this was something that Mavis had never thought to explore before. She never knew that it was possible.

"Should I contact her?" Mavis asked the group.

"Only if you want to," Emily nodded.

Mavis looked around at the four faces who were all staring back at her. Maude and Opal had been there since the day she was born. She had never known a life without them. Wilbur hadn't entered her life until a few weeks after her sixth birthday, but she could hardly remember a time without him either. Even though Emily had only been her friend for a short time, Mavis adored her and hoped she would be in her life forever.

"You could always sleep on it," Wilbur suggested.

"Or eat another piece of cake," Maude offered. "We all think best on a full stomach."

Mavis turned to Opal who had remained quiet on the matter. "What do you think?" Mavis asked the sage like woman.

"Follow your heart," Opal said after a moment. "Your heart always knows the right thing to do."

"I don't know about that," Maude frowned. "That's how she got mixed up with that old alligator fool."

"That wasn't my heart," Mavis sputtered. "I don't even know what that was."

"We all make mistakes," Emily said with a smile.

"Follow your heart," Opal repeated. She stood up without another word and began to peel the orange from her purse over the trashcan.

"She's going to turn into an orange one of these days," Maude shrugged. "Anyway, what does your heart say to do, Mavis?"

Mavis took a deep breath and clicked on the name of her sister. It showed that she hadn't logged into her account in the past three months, so she must not know the details of such a revelation just yet. Mavis was about to potentially change this stranger's life as well. What if she didn't want to know her? What if this revelation ruined her relationship with her parents or siblings? Mavis suddenly felt a weight the size of Texas fall upon her chest.

Opal turned towards her and met her gaze immediately and smiled.

Somehow Opal always knew the right thing to do in a moment of crisis. Mavis was going to contact the woman on the other end of the test results. She typed up a short message and hit the send button before she could change her mind. "There. I did it," she whispered. "I sent my sister a message."

"Now we wait," Emily said.

"Now we wait," Mavis nodded.

Chapter Fifteen

Mavis anxiously checked her phone over the next few days. She had half expected her new sister to have responded by the next morning, but the message was still unread days later. Rather than let feelings of self-doubt and fear set in, she called Mona on the third day of waiting and asked if she wanted to have lunch and go look at antiques. Mona could tell that Mavis was chomping at the bit to tell her something. She readily agreed to pick Mavis up a few minutes after noon in her new car.

Mavis hurried to get ready and threw a load of towels into the washing machine. She heard Mona pull up into the driveway underneath the signature magnolia tree right on time. Mavis ran down the porch steps and marveled at how beautiful the bright red car shone in the sunlight. "Where we headed?" Mona asked. She put on her oversized sunglasses and revved the engine as soon as Mavis climbed inside. "Pick anywhere in Junction. My treat!"

Mavis had a hankering for fried chicken, and there was only one place in Junction that had the best homemade fried chicken. "Let's go to Gil's," Mavis grinned. They had an all-you-can-eat buffet that Mavis knew all too well. As soon as they pulled into the parking lot, they could smell the crispy fried paradise that awaited them. There weren't any lines in the parking lot to designate actual parking spaces. It was more like a free for all in a slightly paved open field. Mona found a rather tight place between two pickup trucks near the front door and hopped out. The cafeteria style line held many delicious items. Mona and Mavis each piled their plate high with fried chicken, green beans, mashed potatoes, and a thick slice of cornbread. Once they got to the dessert portion of the line, Mavis couldn't decide between banana pudding or strawberry shortcake, so she got them both. Mona had her heart set on peach cobbler and took a big bite of the hot syrupy peach dessert as soon as they found seats at one of the long wooden tables full of other customers.

Gil's Southern Shack was always lively. It was impossible to find a minute during their open hours when they weren't busy. Mavis kept glancing at her phone while they ate. Mona waited for Mavis to bring up what was on her mind, but she continued to eat and sigh intermittently. Finally Mona put her fork down and looked at Mavis. "Are you ok?" she asked.

"Yes, I'm fine," Mavis nodded. "Do you remember when I ordered that DNA test thingy?"

Mona nodded. "You sent it back to the lab, right?"

Mavis took a bite of her chicken and nodded. "I got the results back. I found out I have a sister.

I think," Mavis explained.

"Mavis! That's wonderful!" Mona smiled.

Mavis nodded again. "I think it could be." She explained how she had taken the test and mailed off her results. The app showed that she had relatives, including a half sibling in another state. Mavis was very excited at the prospect of having more family, but she was on pins and needles waiting for a response. It concerned her that she hadn't heard back from Brandy yet.

"Don't be nervous," Mona said. "She wouldn't have done the same test if she wasn't wanting to find out more. Maybe she knew she had a long-lost sister out there! Mavis! This means you'll finally find out who your dad is. He's probably still alive. Maybe he's been looking for you!"

"I have always wondered," Mavis said. "I just wish Brandy, that's my sister's name, would respond. Every second that goes by I get more nervous."

"Maybe she's on vacation," Mona offered. "You love to go on vacation! Maybe she does, too! How fun!" Conversation quickly turned to planning for their next vacation and whether or not Emily might want to go with them. The three of them could get into some serious adventures! When Mavis and Mona were finished eating, they decided to visit the large antique store where Mavis once worked. She loved being an antiquities dealer. Those adventures took her all over the country. She had an eye for finding the best deal!

"Are you looking for anything in particular?"

Mona asked.

"I'll know when I see it," Mavis winked. She stopped at every booth they came to and admired the stacks of magazines and dusty books. There was something special about opening an old magazine and inhaling the smell of age and time. Mona found an older model record player that reminded her of her grandfather. She purchased it and a few Glen Miller records, but Mavis didn't find anything she just had to have.

Later that afternoon, Mona dropped Mavis back home at the Manor and made Mavis promise to keep her posted on the messages. "She'll be in touch soon, I just know it," Mona smiled. "Who wouldn't want to know you!"

Mavis hugged her goodbye and checked the pansies growing in her flower bed. Maude hadn't gotten close to them yet thankfully. It was too early to start supper, but too late to make any real plans. It was one of those early December days where Mavis really missed Ruby. Her grandmother would have known exactly what to do in this situation. She would have been thrilled for Mavis to discover more about her heritage.

After she swept the kitchen and put away the clean dishes from this morning, Mavis called Wilbur to see what he was doing. She remembered that Emily was out of town, which meant that he was surely bored and needed some company. He answered out of breath after a few rings which alarmed Mavis.

"What's wrong?" she asked quickly.

"Nothing," he frowned. "I just can't seem to

get this new camera aligned correctly." He had been so happy with the security system that had been installed that he purchased an extra camera for the backside of his barn that videoed all the way to the wood line behind his house and barn.

"I'll come over and help you," Mavis assured him. "I'm an expert when it comes to that sort of thing. If you're not doing anything, I can order pizza and we can hang out like old times."

"I'd love that," Wilbur said. "See you soon."

Emily was away for the weekend on a work trip. She had called Wilbur earlier when she checked into the hotel before dinner with her team and their new clients, a hotel tycoon from Atlanta. Wilbur had spent the day installing new cabinet doors in his workshop and organizing the new tools he had replaced. An hour later, Mavis arrived at his house with a batch of homemade chocolate chip cookies and said the pizza would be delivered soon. Once it arrived, they ate at the kitchen table and Mavis told him about the different antiques she saw today. There was a new booth at the antique mall that he might like to visit. It had antique fishing rods and tackle boxes stacked to the ceiling.

Wilbur nodded and said he would definitely check it out. He handed Mavis his phone and she showed him how to adjust the settings on the new camera in the barn. The thieves hadn't been back around his neck of the woods since the break-in. As far as Wilbur knew, they hadn't been caught either. He couldn't shake the feeling that they would be back once the fuss died down for his prized tractors.

Wilbur put the leftover pizza in the refrigerator and settled down in his recliner to catch up on the basketball scores from the evening. He wasn't an avid fan, but he enjoyed sports of all kinds. Mavis lounged on the couch and scrolled through her social media pages. "Oh my God," Mavis gasped after a few minutes. The message bubble on her phone pinged twice. It was from Brandy, her previously unknown sister. "Wilbur! It's her!"

Wilbur smiled encouragingly and waited for Mavis to pick up her phone that she had thrown next to her. "Are you going to read what she said?" he asked.

"Of course I am," Mavis said staring back at Wilbur. She didn't make a move towards her phone.

"Ok," Wilbur smiled. "Do you want to maybe wait a bit and maybe have some ice cream while you wait?" Mavis nodded. The way she wasn't blinking freaked Wilbur out a little. He was hoping that the ice cream would snap her back into reality.

After he scooped out large scoops in two bowls, he handed Mavis her bowl and sat back down in the chair. He watched her out of the corner of his eye scarf down the ice cream. "I can't do it," she whispered suddenly. "What if she doesn't like me? What if she hates me, Wilbur?"

"No one could ever hate you, Mavis," Wilbur shook his head.

"Can you look?" she whined.

"Yes, hand it here," he said. He braced himself

for the off chance that the woman on the other end of the message portal didn't want to know more about Mavis. He wondered if she knew about Mavis already or if this was the shock of a lifetime for her, too. Mavis handed Wilbur her phone and stared at him as he put on his reading glasses from his pocket and took the phone from her outstretched hand.

Wilbur opened the message and saw that it was a long reply. That had to be a good sign. He read through the two paragraphs and smiled. Mavis had nothing to worry about. Brandy seemed genuinely excited at this new find and couldn't wait to learn more about Mavis. "All good things," Wilbur grinned. "She wants to talk on the phone and get to know you better."

"Really? Oh, Wilbur!" Mavis dove for her phone. Wilbur barely had time to brace himself and the empty bowl of ice cream as Mavis burst into happy tears and hugged him tightly. She took the phone and read the message out loud. "Brandy is forty years old and she's married with two kids. Oh my God! I'm an aunt! Wilbur! She lives in Colorado. She gave me her phone number!"

Mavis suddenly had the energy of a woman on a sugar bender. Wilbur was over the moon excited for her. He checked his watch and saw that it was nearing eight o'clock in the evening, but Colorado was two hours behind them. He watched as Mavis' fingers typed up a storm.

"I can't believe this!" Mavis squealed. "Oh, she's writing back!"

After a few messages back and forth, they

agreed to call the next morning and speak on the phone. Mavis was nervously excited. "I wonder what she sounds like. I wonder what she looks like? Oh, Wilbur, this is incredible."

"Yes, it is," Wilbur said. "You might want to have a notebook or something close by to take notes tomorrow. You've got quite a few people following this story."

"You're right," Mavis nodded.

"I'm going over to Harlan's tomorrow to help him build a ramp for his mother, but I want to hear all about it when I get home," Wilbur said.

"Of course!" Mavis smiled. "She can be your sister, too, you know. You're the best big brother anyone could ever have."

Wilbur blushed and playfully tossed the pillow at her. "Don't go getting all sentimental now," he grinned.

They decided to watch one of Jameson's favorite movies while eating some more cookies. Wilbur and Mavis both had such fond memories of sitting around together watching old black-and-white films with Jameson and Ruby. The holidays were always a time where their presence was missed the most.

After the movie ended, Mavis hugged Wilbur goodbye and headed back to the Manor. She was giddy with excitement for the next day. She took a quick shower, climbed into bed, and fell asleep instantly.

Early the next morning she got dressed and headed downstairs to make an entire pot of coffee. She drank half the pot in one sitting while she jotted down a list of questions she wanted to ask Brandy. When the bread slices popped out of the toaster, she jumped in her seat. "Slow down on the coffee," she laughed to herself as she buttered the thick slices of bread. She fried two eggs and added them to the top of the toast. It was a simple breakfast, but she wasn't sure that she'd be able to eat much this morning. There was so much that she wanted to know and she hoped that talking with Brandy would be able to heal parts of her that she had long since hidden away. She watched the clock above the table as it slowly ticked each minute away. Mavis was supposed to call Brandy at ten o'clock, which was still an hour away. She tossed a load of laundry into the washing machine and did the crossword puzzle in the newspaper. There was still plenty of time before her scheduled meeting, so she went ahead and prepped a casserole for dinner and made a grocery list for the coming week. There wasn't anything to clean or tidy, so she sat back down at the table and waited. Her phone suddenly rang and Mavis wondered for a second if she had got the time wrong, but it was Opal calling instead.

"Hello?" Mavis answered.

"Hey Mavis," Opal smiled.

"Is everything ok?" Mavis asked.

"It surely will be," Opal replied.

Mavis glanced at the clock and saw that it was five minutes until ten. "Where are you?" Mavis asked.

"At home," Opal explained. "I just had a feeling you needed some encouragement."

"Oh," Mavis gasped. "Did Wilbur call you?"

"No," Opal said. "Just be yourself." She hung up before Mavis could respond. Opal always had a funny way of naturally knowing things. It was equal parts amazing and creepy. There was no one else like Opal Tyler in all the world. Mavis was sure of that. Two minutes ticked by and Mavis knew it was now or never.

"Ok, here goes," Mavis whispered as she clicked on Brandy's name. The phone rang twice before the woman on the other end of the line answered.

"Hello? Is this Mavis?" Brandy squealed happily.

"Yes," Mavis replied just as excited.

"Oh my God, how are you?" Brandy asked. She sounded out of breath.

"I'm good. You?" Mavis echoed.

"So good. I can't believe this is happening," Brandy said.

"Me either," Mavis said. "It almost doesn't feel real."

"I know," Brandy agreed. "Oh, tell me everything about you. I want to know everything. We have so much lost time to make up for."

"I have so many questions," Mavis said at the same time.

"I'm sure you do!" Brandy nodded. "Well, ask away. I'll do my best to answer."

Mavis took a deep breath and asked the number one question on her mind. "What's my father like?"

Chapter Sixteen

Mavis and Brandy spoke on the phone for three hours before they hung up. They had both laughed and cried and laughed some more while on the phone. Mavis felt an instant connection with her. Before they hung up, Brandy invited Mavis to come visit as soon as she was able to. Mavis asked when Brandy would be available and Brandy had said, "the sooner, the better. We are all dying to meet you."

Mavis said she would check her calendar and get with Wilbur to make sure he could look after the Manor and her animals, but she would be in touch and hopefully on a plane in the next few days. She wanted to hop on an airplane and fly there immediately, but she had to make plans for her home and the llamas first.

She hung up the phone feeling completely overwhelmed in the best of ways. She had taken three pages of notes to share with Wilbur and Mona. She knew that Maude and Opal would be waiting as well. She felt so loved and genuinely appreciated the family that she had around her on a daily basis now and forever. Discovering her family by blood would never change any of that. She hoped they knew that.

As Mavis reviewed her notes, things finally began to sink in. Brandy had unloaded a lot of information during their three-hour call. Mavis' head was spinning as she read over her notes. Brandy had a younger sister named Sarah who lived in California with her husband and daughter. Brandy and Sarah were full siblings with the same father and mother, which made Sarah Mavis' half-sister as well. Brandy's parents had divorced when she and Sarah were in elementary school, and her mother had gotten remarried a few years later to an investment banker in Colorado. One simple test had revealed not one, but two sisters. Brandy told Mavis that she had already called Sarah the night before and told her everything she knew from their messaging. Sarah was ecstatic and couldn't wait to meet Mavis. She promised to be at Brandy's house when Mavis scheduled her trip out there.

Mavis instinctively walked to the hall closet and pulled out her nice set of luggage. Hopefully she would be meeting her sisters face to face this week. She hesitated to call them long lost sisters because they had never been lost. She merely did not know that they existed prior to the test results. While she wanted to celebrate the fact that she had two sisters, she still couldn't help but feel an aching pain for the man who was her father. Brandy had taken a deep breath before she revealed to Mavis that their father, Jack Phillips, had passed away twenty years earlier. As far as Brandy knew, Jack had never known that Mavis existed. If he had, he certainly never shared that fact with anyone or in any of his personal effects he had left behind.

Brandy and Sarah had been mainly raised by their mother, Terri, and their stepfather, Charles. Jack had stayed in California and traveled up and down the coast as a drummer in a band until he passed away from lung cancer decades ago. He had never remarried or fathered any other children as far as they knew. Brandy had plenty of pictures of him and couldn't wait to show Mavis when she arrived in Colorado. Talk had soon turned to Mavis' mother and whether or not Brandy remembered Jack ever mentioning someone named Melanie. That name didn't sound familiar to Brandy, but she offered for Mavis to sort through a large plastic bin of pictures and tokens that she had of their father. It was worth a shot. Everyone had always told Mavis how much she favored her mother when she was growing up. Melanie had passed away when Mavis was a toddler, so she didn't have any personal memories of her, but there were plenty of pictures of the beautiful raven-haired woman up until her high school graduation. After that point in time, there weren't any photographs as Melanie had hightailed it out of Rhinestone in search of a new and exciting life among the stars. Instead of becoming a celebrity, Melanie had found a life of drugs and alcohol. She succumbed to her addiction a few short years later.

Mavis took her luggage upstairs and looked out the window in her bedroom that overlooked the wide-open grounds of the backside of

Magnolia Manor. Even after all of her travels, she knew that her home was the most beautiful piece of land there ever was. There was so much history within these acres and soil. She had been to Colorado before, but this time would be different. This time she had a more concrete plan that was life-altering.

There was so much to tell Wilbur. The clock on her nightstand read fifteen minutes until two in the afternoon. She had talked her way through lunch. Now that she thought about it, she was hungry. She wasn't sure how long it would take Wilbur and Harlan to complete Mrs. Patsy's home renovation projects, but she doubted they would be done before supper time. Emily wasn't scheduled to return from her work trip until late tomorrow afternoon, and Mona had driven down to Mobile to tour the USS Alabama battleship, so they were both unavailable. She knew that Maude and Opal would be sitting on pins and needles if they knew that she had just spoken to Brandy for the last few hours. Yet somehow she knew that they must already know. Maybe Opal sensed the vibrations or whatever she liked to say. She was a wildcard, and as long as Mavis had known her, she had never been wrong.

Mavis walked back downstairs to her cell phone that was still on the breakfast table. She chuckled to herself to see two missed calls from Maude. Usually that many missed calls in succession would make her nervous, but she had a feeling that Opal had told Maude what was going on. She knew she better call her back before the old woman showed up on her front porch.

"Hello," Mavis said when Maude picked up.

"Mavis? It's about time. We been waiting for hours," Maude said gruffly.

"Waiting for what?" Mavis asked.

"Opal, do you hear her? She acts like we don't know anything," Maude grumbled. Of course Opal was right next to her. Where one was, the other wasn't usually far behind.

"Where are you?" Mavis asked.

"Sitting on your front porch," Maude said matter-of-factly.

Mavis rushed to the front door, and as sure as she had said, there they both were in the porch swing. Opal wore canary yellow overalls over a cream-colored sweater. Her brown boots looked pristine in the afternoon sunshine, even though Mavis knew she had worn that same pair of boots for the past twenty or so years. It amazed her how that spunky woman could still frolic through the woods and mud at her age and yet never look out of place. Maude, on the other hand, wore an all-black wind suit and a brand-new pair of white tennis shoes that were clearly meant for athletes. They both certainly had their own style.

"Are you gonna let us in or do I need to use my key?" Maude asked directly. Mavis rolled her eyes and hung up the phone. Through the door she could hear Maude gasp and turn to Opal. "She hung up on me!"

Mavis quickly opened the door and ushered them both inside. "How long have y'all been out there?" Mavis asked.

"Felt like an hour," Maude huffed. She picked up a plastic bin from underneath the swing that Mavis hadn't noticed and walked past Mavis into the Manor. "Only ten or so minutes," Opal corrected. She smiled up at Mavis before following Maude into the house. Mavis shut the door behind them and found them both in the kitchen sitting at the table. Maude rummaged through her purse and pulled out a piece of cake wrapped in tinfoil and began to eat it. "I'm starving," she mumbled.

"We ate lunch two hours ago," Opal pointed out.

"I couldn't eat much on a nervous stomach," Maude replied.

"What were you nervous about?" Mavis asked.

Maude rolled her eyes and finished the last bite of cake. "How'd your telephone call go this morning?" she asked.

"Y'all are too much!" Mavis laughed. Opal smiled brilliantly and took a few sips from her thermos she had brought with her. "How do you already know everything before it even happens?"

"Opal knows it all. It's creepy and obnoxious, but I'm nosy so hurry it up," Maude interrupted.

Mavis showed them the notebook where she had written down different things. Maude and Opal had been correct after all. The mysterious man named Jack was indeed Mavis' biological father. Maude frowned when Mavis told her that he had unfortunately already passed away.

Opal opened the bin in front of her and pulled out a plastic bag that contained an envelope that looked like it had lived through ten different wars. It was faded and had stains that Mavis hoped had once been coffee or tea. "Is this the letter?" Mavis gasped. She carefully opened the plastic bag and pulled out the envelope. There was nothing written on the outside. Inside the envelope was a small piece of lined paper that was faded and stained with the same light brown hue. She could clearly see the name Jack signed near the bottom in faded black ink. The rest of the letter was splotchy and had a few rips and tears to where she couldn't fully make out what was written. Like Maude and Opal had surmised forty years ago, it looked to be a breakup letter from Jack to Melanie.

"We haven't opened it since that day. Opal put it in that bag and we left it alone," Maude said.

There were a few obvious words that could be read clearly, but the letter was mostly an enigma. Mavis could see the word band a few different times which made sense. Brandy had said their father was in a band and traveled frequently. Near the end of the letter before his signature, Jack apologized to Melanie and said he hoped that she could forgive him for choosing the band over her. It was as simple as that. There was no way to know whether or not Jack or even Melanie knew that she was pregnant at the time.

Mavis turned the letter over to see if there was anything written on the back, but there didn't appear to be any words. She placed the letter and envelope back in the plastic bag and sealed it shut. Opal pushed the bin towards her and patted her on the back.

"We threw out the old box ages ago. It was falling apart and stunk to high heaven," Maude said. "But this was what was in it." She handed Mavis an old ball cap that had some sort of sticky residue on it, a few pens that had long since dried up, some coins that resembled laundry tokens, a pack of cigarettes, a stack of unpaid bills, and a stuffed animal that at one time might have been some sort of bear. "Only other stuff was the stack of shirts and some empty pill bottles."

"Thank you both," Mavis said. She put the items back in the plastic box and hugged them both.

"When are you leaving?" Opal asked.

"Leaving? Leaving where?" Maude asked.

"I'm going to visit my sister in Colorado. Sarah lives in California, but she said she would fly out to Denver and we could all meet up," Mavis explained.

"We'll watch over the Manor," Maude said. "We've been keeping an eye on things here and over yonder at Wilbur's ever since those hooligans messed up his barn."

"You have?" Mavis asked.

"Of course," Maude nodded.

Mavis hadn't seen either of them on any of her security cameras. She was sure that Wilbur hadn't either. She pulled up the app on her phone and reviewed the footage from earlier when Maude and Opal had arrived. The camera showed Maude's car skidding into place underneath the ancient magnolia tree. Maude and Opal both walked up the porch steps. Before Maude could use her key, Opal guided her to the swing. Mavis didn't turn up the volume to hear what they were saying, but she could tell that Maude was frustrated.

"When you say you've been keeping an eye on things, what do you mean?" Mavis asked.

"You ain't gonna see us on that thing," Maude said pointedly. Mavis looked at her and then to Opal. "Mavis, we helped build this place. We've been a part of these grounds since before that magnolia ever sprouted."

If Maude and Opal could sneak around the cameras, Mavis wondered if the thieves could figure it out. She would have to talk to Wilbur about this once he finished with Harlan. Her stomach rumbled audibly and she figured that she might as well eat some lunch. She had some ripe tomatoes from Slocomb that would make the perfect tomato and mayonnaise sandwich. She asked the two women if they wanted anything and they both said a sandwich sounded perfect.

Mavis whipped up a stack of sandwiches and poured them each a glass of iced tea she had made earlier. There was something comforting and familiar about a tomato and mayonnaise sandwich. Once they polished off the platter, they walked to the barn together to check on the llamas. The three llamas were all in the pasture eating grass and seemingly enjoying the cool breeze that blew through the nearby trees. Mavis had made sure that they each had on their insulated color-coded blankets that she referred to as jackets. As soon as they saw Mavis approaching, they hurried over to the fence to greet her. They knew she kept treats in her coat pockets.

Mavis handed Opal a handful of the llama treats, but Maude refused. She still did not understand the fascination for these big-toothed animals. She was sure that they were dangerous, even if Mavis and Opal were downright giddy as the beasts ate from their hands. Instead of watching them get closer to losing their limbs from one of the llama's severe underbites, Maude walked back to the porch and plopped down in one of the wooden rocking chairs.

Her phone buzzed and she casually glanced down at it. It was Wilbur. "Hello?" Maude said.

"Hey," Wilbur said. "Are you at home?"

"I'm at the Manor watching Opal and Mavis acting a fool with those llamas," she huffed.

"Ok," he sighed. "I'm headed to the Manor. Y'all hang tight. How'd Mavis' call go?"

"I reckon it went great because she's headed out there to visit soon," Maude explained. "You ok?"

"Yes ma'am," Wilbur said. "I'll be right there directly."

Chapter Seventeen

Wilbur arrived at the Manor in time to see Opal showing Mavis some new stretches she had learned in one of her physical therapy sessions. Maude was still sitting in the rocking chair on the porch watching the two crazy women in the yard.

"You gonna learn some new stretches?" Maude asked.

"I think I'm a little too tired for that," Wilbur said. "Harlan and I built Mrs. Patsy a ramp today for a porch. Then she had a good size list of other things around the house she needed done."

"You're a good boy," Maude said. She patted Wilbur on his knee and continued to watch Mavis and Opal twist and rotate their bodies in the late afternoon sunlight. "They're crazy, I swear."

Wilbur smiled and watched as Mavis and Opal began to do what he thought might at one time have been yoga.

"What's on your mind?" Maude asked seriously.

"There's no easy way to say this," Wilbur began. "But I need to tell you something."

Maude heard the sincerity in his tone. She turned to see him take a deep breath. "Teddy Butler passed away last night."

Maude's heart sank. She hadn't dated Teddy Butler since the late eighties, but he would always be the one she let get away. They had parted as friends when he took a promotion near Atlanta decades ago. They had kept in touch until the past few years for whatever reason. Wilbur knew that she would be devastated, but he wanted her to hear the news from him before she found out from someone else. "The department is sending a representative over to his funeral service. His daughter said Rhinestone was always his favorite. I was thinking we could all ride over there if you wanted to."

Teddy had been an important fixture in all of their lives, especially when Wilbur first came to know the Montgomery family. As one of Jameson Montgomery's closest friends, he had been a part of holiday celebrations, birthday parties, fishing trips, and farm chores. He had been the first deputy to respond when Wilbur's father, Pete Reynolds, broke into the Manor on the night of the worst storm of Rhinestone's history. Teddy had been the first to inspect Pete's body when he died underneath the magnolia tree. When Teddy accepted a promotion at a station in Atlanta a few years later, everyone felt the loss of his presence in Rhinestone.

"I'll drive you and whoever else wants to go," Wilbur offered. Maude nodded and rocked slowly in the wooden chair. "He was a good man," she sighed. Wilbur stood up and nodded. He figured he'd better tell Opal and Mavis before the news spread. He was a little surprised that Opal hadn't already heard. She kept in touch with any and everybody who had ever lived in Rhinestone.

He walked down the porch towards Mavis and Opal who were sitting in the grass with their arms high above their heads. "Care to join us?" Mavis asked.

"No thanks," Wilbur shook his head. "Y'all about ready to head back inside? Looks like some rain's about to come through."

"Sure is," Opal nodded. She studied Wilbur's face as he leaned down to help her stand. "Is Maude ok?" she whispered.

Wilbur turned to look back at Maude and sighed. "I just had to tell her that Teddy Butler passed away last night."

"Oh no!" Mavis gasped. She knew how special Teddy was to Maude. "What happened?"

"I don't know any details yet. The funeral home in Atlanta requested that Harlan send over a deputy or two for the service on Thursday. Said Teddy always talked so highly about his time in Rhinestone. Harlan told me and I said I better get on back here to talk to y'all," Wilbur explained.

"What time is the service?" Mavis asked.

"It's right after lunch on Thursday," Wilbur said. "I already said I'd drive whoever wanted to go over."

"Thank you," Opal smiled. She brushed off her pants and walked towards Maude on the porch.

Wilbur and Mavis let the two of them talk on the porch while they washed up inside. It dawned on Wilbur that he hadn't checked in with Mavis all day. "Mavis, I'm so sorry! I haven't asked about your phone call this morning!"

"It went well," Mavis smiled. "How about we ride into town and have supper. We'll invite Maude and Opal, too. They already know most of it, but I think they need to be with us. Teddy Butler, who didn't love that man!"

Mavis ran upstairs to change clothes while Wilbur went outside to invite the women out to dinner. He found them sitting next to each other on the porch swing. "Mavis and I were thinking about going into town for some supper. We would love for you both to come along."

Opal nodded. "I was thinking that Maude needed some food."

"Where are y'all going?" Maude asked.

"We haven't narrowed down a place just yet. Any ideas?" Wilbur asked.

"Somewhere that has brisket," Maude said. "In honor of Teddy, let's have brisket."

"That sounds wonderful," Wilbur agreed.

"You know that was the recipe he submitted for the cookbook we did all those years ago," Maude explained. "Thanks to Nadine."

"Nadine sure was feisty about that recipe book," Opal smiled.

"She badgered him for weeks until he finally gave in," Maude nodded. "Crazy to think that they're both gone now."

It had been a rough few months for Maude and Opal. Wilbur couldn't imagine what it must be like to attend the funerals of your lifelong friends. The older he got, the more he found himself saying goodbye to the men and women of Rhinestone who had helped mold him into the man that he was today.

Mavis came down the stairs and asked if they were all ready to go to dinner. Wilbur told her about Maude's suggestion and she wholeheartedly agreed. They all loaded up in Mavis' vehicle and drove to their favorite barbecue place. They were seated immediately at a booth near the salad bar. Once they gave the server their orders and Opal piled her plate full of leafy greens, Maude again thanked Wilbur for offering to drive them to Atlanta.

"Of course," Wilbur nodded. "Big Mama and Big a Daddy considered him family." Mavis added.

"He sure was," Wilbur agreed. "Never once made me feel like I was a bother."

"He loved you, Wilbur," Maude smiled. "He agonized over leaving Rhinestone when it came down to it. He was leaving his lifelong friends and his home. He moved to Rhinestone when he was twenty-five. It had been his home for twenty years, but he couldn't pass up a promotion like that though. And it all worked out in the end."

About a year after he moved to Atlanta, Teddy started dating someone and they got married a couple of years later. The woman had two teenagers, a boy and a girl, who absolutely adored him. Once Teddy retired from the police force, he got to be a full-time grandfather, which seemed to make him very happy. The last time any of them saw him was at Jameson's funeral over a decade ago.

"You know, when Teddy accepted a promotion

in Atlanta back in the late eighties, he asked me to move with him," Maude said quietly.

"He asked you to marry him," Opal said gently.

Maude nodded. Mavis nor Wilbur had ever heard that part of the story. "I couldn't leave Rhinestone," Maude explained. "He knew that."

"Do you wish you had?" Mavis asked suddenly.

Maude thought about it for a second and shook her head. "No, I made the right choice." She picked up the basket of corn fritters and buttered one before she popped it into her mouth. "Never stopped thinking about him though."

"He was the one who got away," Opal nodded, and Maude didn't correct her.

"He was a lovely man," Mavis said again.

"He really was," Opal agreed. She put her arm around Maude who smiled ruefully. "Mavis, do you remember that blasted cat thing you gave Ruby for Christmas? That awful ugly one Opal helped you buy?"

Mavis and Wilbur both laughed at the memory of the ceramic ginger colored cat that doubled as a tissue box. Once the tissue box was inserted underneath, the tissues poked out of the rear end of the cat. It was a gaudy gift that had made everyone who ever saw it in the Manor's living room cackle. "How could anyone forget that cat!" Wilbur laughed.

"Jameson sent it with Teddy when he moved," Maude smiled. "Packed it in a bag and shoved it in his trunk without him knowing. Teddy called me later that night howling in laughter. I figured he'd keep it, but he brought it back to Rhinestone a few weeks later and slipped it onto Ruby's shelf in the pantry after supper one night. Didn't tell a soul. Ruby near about had a heart attack seeing that thing the next morning."

"That poor cat," Mavis shook her head. She was pretty sure the ceramic cat was in the trailer. If she could find a few minutes to herself, she planned to go look for it and hide it at Wilbur's as a harmless practical joke. As far as she knew, Emily hadn't heard of the infamous Christmas gift yet. Mavis knew she would love it just as much as she always had.

"Here you are," the server smiled. "Three brisket dinners." He handed Mavis, Wilbur, and Maude three plates of thick sliced brisket and fries.

"To Teddy Butler," Wilbur smiled.

"To Teddy," Mavis and Opal cheered.

"To Teddy," Maude held up her iced tea glass and smiled softly. They finished dinner and headed back to the car. "Sure you don't want me to drop y'all off at home?" Wilbur asked Maude and Opal.

"My car's at the Manor," Maude reminded him.

"We can bring it to you tomorrow," Mavis offered.

"No, I'll drive it home," Maude said. "You can pick me up Thursday morning though," she told Wilbur.

"Yes ma'am," he smiled.

Once they were all back at the Manor, Maude and Opal drove off into the night leaving Wilbur and Mavis sitting on the porch. Mavis held her breath as Maude backed out of the driveway and took off down the highway.

"No damage," Wilbur chuckled.

"This time," Mavis pointed out.

"You ready to book your flight?" Wilbur asked.

"If you're sure you can hold the fort down while I'm gone," Mavis nodded.

"I think I can handle it. Won't be my first rodeo," Wilbur smiled. "I promise to look after the llamas."

"And Clive!" Mavis added.

"Of course," Wilbur nodded.

Later that evening, Mavis took the plunge and booked her flight to Denver. She was set to fly out early Wednesday morning and Brandy promised to pick her up at the airport. Even though they had added one another on social media, Mavis still wasn't sure that she'd recognize her right away in a crowd of people, but she was too excited to care.

On Tuesday morning, Maude set out to go shopping for clothes for Teddy's service. She dropped Opal off at the Manor with Mavis. Even though Mavis loved any excuse to go shopping, she had elected to stay at the Manor as she had booked her trip to Colorado for the following day and needed to pack. Opal stayed behind as well because she already had the perfect outfit, according to her. She also confided to Mavis that she thought Maude could use a little alone time to process her feelings. "Plus, Maude said I needed to keep an eye on you," she laughed as Mavis stood in the laundry room and haphazardly tossed random clothing items into her largest suitcase. "Now that she's gone," Opal said as Maude turned down the highway. "There's something I need your help with."

"What is it?" Mavis asked. She folded the last of her shirts and smushed the pile of clothes down as far as she could. "Can you sit on top of this while I try to zip it up?"

"Do you really need all of that for a five-day trip?" Opal asked.

"You never know what we'll get into," Mavis replied. "I like to be prepared."

"We raised you right," Opal nodded. She tried to push all of her weight down on the vibrantly purple suitcase while Mavis zippered it shut. Once it finally closed, Mavis helped Opal up and they sat down at the table in the kitchen together.

"I want to get ordained," Opal said.

"I thought you already had that thing from the internet?" Mavis asked. She knew Opal had performed a few different wedding ceremonies over the years.

"I have that one," Opal said. "But I'm talking about something else."

"You've been talking an awful lot about weddings recently," Mavis pointed out. To her knowledge, Opal hadn't been dating anyone, but that didn't mean anything. "Are you getting married?"

"Heavens no," Opal said with gusto.

Opal had never had any desire to get married. Not that she had never been asked. Over the years Opal had probably been proposed to at least two dozen times by different men, but she always politely let them down, as only Opal could.

"Why did you never get married?" Mavis asked.

"Why on earth would I?" Opal smiled.

Mavis was satisfied with that answer. It was probably because Opal had never met anyone who could keep up with her. She was the happiest person Mavis had ever known. If there was something she wanted to do, she went out and did it. There's really nothing that woman couldn't do. She had inspired Mavis from the time she was a little girl and still did.

"I thought about getting married once," Opal said suddenly.

"Really?" Mavis gasped.

"Well, not really. There was only one man I might would have said yes to, but he never asked," Opal shrugged. "Even then maybe I wouldn't have."

"Who was it?" Mavis asked. She had no clear idea of who it could be. She mentally went over the list of names that came to mind that Opal had dated over the years that she knew of. It could have been a myriad of them. As far as she knew, Opal had never split with any of the men in her life on bad terms. In fact, she had regularly kept up with each one of them until they either passed away or moved. She was sure there had to be a laundry list of people when Opal was younger. She had heard stories of men falling in love with Opal from all over the world. There wasn't anyone in all the world who didn't like Opal Tyler.

"That's a story for another day," Opal smiled. "So, will you help me?"

"You haven't said what exactly you need help with," Mavis frowned.

"I need to update my officiant license at the courthouse," Opal explained. "I need to be ready."

"Ready for what?" Mavis asked.

"I'll know when it happens," Opal said confidently.

Mavis had no idea what that meant. She was more confused now than she had been when Opal first began the conversation.

"Ok," Mavis shrugged. "Let's get you to the courthouse. Then I need to pick up a few things for my trip."

"Look at us moving mountains!" Opal cheered.

.

Chapter Eighteen

Mavis had not arrived this early to the airport in ages. She was usually the traveler that was seen dashing through security on her way to the terminal. She was usually the last one aboard the plane, except when she traveled with Wilbur who insisted on being there hours before takeoff. He was the planner in the family.

Mavis had been lucky to find a flight at this time of year straight to Denver. Airlines always hiked the cost of flights around the holiday season. She was thankful that she had probably snagged some traveler's last-minute cancellation. She took it as a good sign. Once she boarded the plane, she took out her book and began reading. It was all about sites to see in Denver and the surrounding area. She didn't think that she would be skiing or hiking the Rocky Mountains anytime soon, but it made for an interesting read. She would be perfectly content sitting in Brandy's living room catching up on the last forty years of their lives. Plus, she couldn't wait to meet Sarah! She and Sarah had not been able to connect on the phone yet, but that was fine. It was going to make their face-to-face meeting even sweeter. On the phone last night, Brandy had let Mavis know that she had sent her husband and kids to her mother-in-law's house for the next few days so that she could have Mavis all to herself. When Mavis told Maude that, she found it highly suspicious. Mavis overheard her telling Opal that she hoped that Brandy and Sarah weren't secret serial killers. Opal assured her that everything was going to be alright, but Mavis wouldn't be surprised if they somehow popped up in Brandy's neighborhood if she forgot to check in.

The flight to Denver was one of the easiest flights she had ever taken. There was hardly any turbulence. Her seatmate had fallen asleep as soon as the plane took off and didn't wake up until the wheels touched down in Colorado. The line to exit the plane took forever, but Mavis finally disembarked and made her way to the baggage area. She found her set of luggage and looked around for Brandy in the mass of people. At first she didn't see anyone who resembled the pictures on Brandy's social media account, but then she heard her name called from the abyss and her heart swelled. She knew immediately that it was Brandy. When she turned around, the woman half rugby tackled her in the crowd. Both women immediately burst into tears and jumped for joy. They did not care that everyone in the baggage terminal was staring at them.

Brandy wore a pair of black sweatpants and a matching black sweatshirt. She kept her coat unbuttoned while Mavis pulled her own jacket and scarf tighter around her. Brandy must have been used to the cold weather, which was something Mavis would never understand. She was a sunshine kind of girl through and through.

Brandy took Mavis 's largest piece of luggage and wheeled it to her car with Mavis following behind her. Brandy told her that Sarah would be flying in later that afternoon and asked if Mavis was hungry. She knew the perfect spot to take her for lunch. It was near a large outdoor mall where they could kill time catching up and do a little bit of shopping while they waited for Sarah's flight to arrive. Mavis could not get over Brandy. She was so kind and friendly. She was drawn to her and felt so close to her already.

Brandy and Mavis looked nothing alike. While Mavis had always had dark black hair, Brandy had a reddish tint to her brown hair. The only similarity they shared was their eyes. They had the exact same eye color and shape. Where Mavis was big boned with wide shoulders, Brandy was short and much thinner. There was something about Brandy though that made Mavis feel instantly at home. They were definitely kindred spirits and they both loved to eat. Brandy pulled up in front of an all-you-could eat sushi buffet which delighted Mavis. She had an inkling that Brandy also knew where to find the best deal in town. That was something that could not be taught.

Over lunch, Mavis told Brandy all about Wilbur, the llamas, and her beloved Magnolia Manor. Brandy listened in awe and said she couldn't wait to come visit. She took a particular interest in Opal and Maude and laughed hysterically at some of their adventures that Mavis shared. "You should write a book!" Brandy howled. She couldn't wait to make the cross-country trek down south to meet this cast of characters in Mavis' life. Though she was a little hesitant about meeting Clive. It wasn't every day that someone learned about the existence of whale-sized catfish.

As it got closer for Sarah's flight to land, Mavis and Brandy packed up their shopping bags in Brandy 's SUV and drove back to the airport to find a parking spot. Sarah was the youngest of their newly formed trio, and from what Brandy said about her, she was fancy. She was the epitome of a Los Angeles businesswoman. Brandy said she was the life of every party and would absolutely adore Mavis. They found a table in one of the airport coffeeshops and waited for her plane to land. When Brandy's phone rang, it was Sarah saying that she was headed to the baggage terminal.

"I can't wait!" Brandy cheered. "The three of us will finally be together!"

Brandy and Mavis huddled together and waited for Sarah to appear. When she did, Brandy grabbed Mavis by the arm and wheeled her around to face Sarah. Sarah was indeed glamorous in her floral white pantsuit and pink high heels. Her long reddish tinted hair was pulled up in a bun and her oversized sunglasses were perched on the top of her head. She hugged Brandy and squealed when she saw Mavis. "Mavis! Oh my God! Mavis!" She enveloped Mavis in a hug and the three of them squealed like little guinea pigs in a huddle.

Once Sarah's luggage was loaded into

Brandy's vehicle, Brandy got on the interstate to head to her house. Mavis stared out the window at the beautiful snowcapped mountains. The scenery was unlike anything she had ever seen before. She snapped pictures on her cell phone and couldn't wait to show her friends and family back in Rhinestone. As Brandy pulled into her neighborhood, Mavis held her breath. Brandy lived in a beautiful two-story house that looked like it had been featured in magazines. The front yard was blanketed in a perfectly untouched layer of snow. The eaves of the home were decorated in Christmas lights. Mavis felt like she was in the middle of a winter wonderland.

"Let's get you both settled and figure out where we want to go to dinner tonight," Brandy smiled. She showed Mavis to the guest room on the first floor and Sarah put her bags in the den off the kitchen. Mavis said she didn't mind sleeping on the pull-out couch in the den, but Brandy and Sarah wouldn't hear of it. Once Mavis changed into nicer clothes, she met Brandy and Sarah in the kitchen and they decided on a restaurant for dinner. Mavis was game for anything. Sarah had a craving for Italian, which suited Brandy and Mavis just fine. They piled back into Brandy's SUV and drove downtown to the restaurant district where they had a lovely dinner. Sarah told Mavis all about her job, her husband, and her daughter. She loved living in Los Angeles where she was an accountant for a film editing production company.

"The three of us couldn't be any more different," Brandy smiled. "How cool is that!"

After a delicious dinner, Brandy drove them back to her house. "I was thinking we could look at some photo albums and introduce you to dad," Brandy said. "Sarah, did you bring that thing I asked you to?"

"I sure did," Sarah smiled. She leaned forward from the back seat and handed Mavis a VHS tape. "It's an old video of dad singing at one of our birthday parties. I haven't watched it in years. Want to see it?"

"I'd love to," Mavis smiled.

When they pulled back into Brandy's neighborhood, Mavis could see all of the twinkling Christmas lights that lit up the homes in the darkness. She had always loved the Christmas season. That was something she had inherited from her grandmother, Ruby. Mavis made a mental note to purchase a few Christmas ornaments while she was in town. She had a tradition of putting ornaments on one of the Christmas trees in her home from each of her travel destinations. She normally put up four different Christmas trees at the Manor, which Wilbur often teased her about. He was content with his one tree in his living room. She would be sure to buy him an ornament, too. One could never have too many Christmas ornaments.

"Let's get into our pajamas and I'll bust out the wine and cheesecake," Brandy offered.

Once they were all settled in the living room, Brandy made a fire in the fireplace while Sarah opened the lid of the medium-sized plastic bin that contained loose photographs, coins, slips of paper, posters, arm bands, and other band paraphernalia from the early eighties and nineties.

"The Salty Pelicans?" Mavis held up a piece of faded neon pink paper. The black ink ran down the page announcing the next show for Jack's rock-n-roll cover band back in 1985.

"There's a few more of those posters in there," Brandy chuckled. "Here's dad when he had long hair." She handed Mavis a picture of Jack with his arm around some woman. Only half of her face was showing, but Mavis gasped the moment her eyes took in the photograph.

"That's my mother," said Mavis. Even though she didn't have many pictures of Melanie from that time in her life, she was absolutely certain that the woman in the picture with Jack was Melanie. This might be the only picture that existed of her parents together. Looking at the two of them in the aged photograph was an experience she never thought she'd have. She was finally looking at the two people who were responsible for her being born. She couldn't help but wonder how different her life would have been had Jack and Melanie stayed together. There was no way to know for sure if things would've turned out differently. Mavis had always been thankful that her grandparents had raised her. They had given her everything she had ever needed or wanted. Never once in her life did she wish that things could've been different. But there was something about seeing her two biological parents in a photograph together that made her wonder about things she had never thought about before. Mavis, Brandy, and Sarah poured through the rest of the box, but there weren't any other photographs of Melanie to be found. Mavis put the picture of Melanie and Jack in her purse and spent the rest of the evening listening to stories about Jack and the two daughters he had known and loved.

Meanwhile back in Rhinestone, Wilbur had his hands full. While he was out to dinner with Emily, his phone started going crazy. "Oh no!" he gasped. He pulled up the camera app and frowned. Something was setting off his alerts, but he couldn't see anyone on the various cameras.

"Is everything ok?" Emily asked.

Wilbur showed her the alerts in his notification bar on his cell phone. Emily flagged down the waiter and asked him to box up their food. "We've got a tractor thief to catch!" she explained.

Wilbur drove a little faster than he normally did. He didn't realize he passed Maude and Opal on the road until Maude called him in a panic. "Where are you flying off to?" she demanded to know. Wilbur quickly explained to her what was going on and she hung up after saying, "We'll handle it!" Wilbur wasn't sure what that meant, but he didn't waste any time trying to figure it out. He drove past his front gates down to his barn and saw fresh tire tracks, but the barn door was still locked. They drove through the woods carefully but didn't see anything out of sorts. By the time they drove back to his cabin, Maude and Opal were waiting on Wilbur's porch with camouflage bags slung over their shoulders.

"What in the world?" Wilbur asked.

"We're ready for the stakeout," Maude said.

"What stakeout?" Wilbur asked.

"I'm in!" Emily agreed.

"Emily," Wilbur's eyes widened.

"I think it's a great idea," Emily said. "We can set up a tent and keep an eye on things."

"A tent?" Wilbur asked.

"Got one right here," Maude nodded.

"Oh, Wilbur, this is going to be so much fun!" Emily smiled.

"Oh, not a chance," Wilbur chuckled. "I'm not sleeping on the ground when I have a perfectly good bed right in there. Y'all don't have to do this either."

"We won't be sleeping," Maude said. "We have thieves to catch."

"Are y'all serious?" Wilbur asked.

"Never been more serious," Maude said. "Turn off all the lights on the porch and barn."

"How will you see anything?" Wilbur asked.

"We have our own equipment," Maude replied. She couldn't believe that Wilbur was slow to catch on. She was an expert shopper and had all of the necessary spy equipment they would ever need.

"We'll get them, Wilbur," Opal said pensively. She and Maude began to walk to the barn with the heavy packs before Wilbur could offer to help. "We brought enough for you, too, Emily!" Maude shouted over her shoulder.

"This is amazing!" Emily said. She kissed Wilbur goodbye and hurried off behind Maude and Opal who were almost to the barn. Wilbur thought about following them, but he figured the less he knew, the better. The thieves were probably not even in the area anyway, as Maude's erratic driving and screeching tires had probably blown their cover. Wilbur was almost certain that nothing too crazy would happen tonight. Once they got this stakeout mess out of their system, Wilbur would find another way to catch the bandits. There was no way the three of them could be quiet enough for a stakeout. He pulled his truck behind the cabin and walked inside his house and turned off all the porch lights like Maude had instructed. There would be no use in watching the cameras tonight because the three of them would probably set the various cameras off every few minutes. After a quick shower, Wilbur settled into his recliner to doze off while the newscasters predicted heavy snowfall in the northeast regions of the country.

Chapter Nineteen

"The key is being quiet," Maude whispered loudly.

"Like animals in nature," Opal echoed.

"Right before you shoot them!" Maude nodded.

"Oh my God," Emily gasped. She had been assured that neither Maude nor Opal had a gun, but she wouldn't put it past either of them to bust out some sort of surprise.

They had turned out all of the lights in the barn. Thankfully Maude had thought ahead and brought snacks and bottles of water. Though in the dark Emily was pretty sure that Maude was sipping from a bottle that contained more muscadine wine than water.

"Did you hear that?" Emily asked after a few minutes.

"Shh," Maude suddenly hissed. "I think I hear something." She pressed her ear against the barn door and held her finger up to her lips. "Something's out there." She beckoned Opal to come closer. Opal walked closer and pushed her ear against the same door. "Is it friend or foe?" Maude asked her.

Opal closed her eyes and thought for a

moment. "Two men, one about six feet tall, dirty blonde hair," Opal nodded.

"How does she do that?" Emily gasped.

"She's an expert," Maude nodded. "Now get into position."

Emily, Maude, and Opal assumed their positions around the barn door. Opal held firmly to her baseball bat that Wilbur had hidden from her a few weeks before. He was never the best at hide-and-seek. Maude grasped the binoculars and peered out the tiny hole she had drilled through the wall. Wilbur wouldn't be too happy about that, but he'd be able to repair it easily once the bandits were apprehended. Emily watched as the two women crouched down and waited. Sure enough, there were two distinct voices a few feet away. The two men must have walked from wherever they had stashed their vehicle. As they crept closer to the barn door, the voices got louder. They couldn't seem to agree on the best way to load up the tractors.

"Idiots," Maude snickered.

Emily hoped the men weren't dangerous. Maude had given her a gigantic fish net to use, but she wasn't sure what she was supposed to do with it when the time came. She honestly had not thought that the bandits would be back that night. She had volunteered to hangout out with Maude and Opal because she genuinely enjoyed spending time with them. She found them hilarious and figured a night of camping in the barnyard would be fun. This was turning into an adventure she hadn't planned on, but it was still enjoyable. Once they were planted in the barn, Maude had quickly changed her mind about the tent and instead said they would hide in the hayloft to keep watch.

The barn door rattled and one of the men kicked at it to see how sturdy it was. Wilbur had reinforced the wood from the last time they had successfully broken in. Emily wondered for a split second whether or not she should call the police, but she wasn't sure if she would have cell service this far out. Even if she did, talking that loud into the phone might scare the men off.

A loud clanging noise rattled the building and the wood on the door cracked. "Here they come," Maude hissed. She buried herself in a mound of hay while Opal wedged herself behind the stack of barrels Wilbur kept rainwater he collected to use in his gardens.

Emily stood frozen by the door. They hadn't gotten around to the part of the plan where hiding places were established. The two men pried open the barn doors and looked around. "Where's the light switch?" the heavier one asked. The women couldn't see the other man shrug in the darkness. A beam of light suddenly radiated from the flashlights they carried. Emily pressed herself against the wall and Wilbur's giant toolbox as best she could. Thankfully the two men were too preoccupied with the thought of the prized tractors to pay her any attention. "Which one should we wire first?"

"Let's get the smaller one rolled out. If we have time we'll come back for the bigger one," the heavier man replied. He climbed into the seat and pulled out a screwdriver from his shirt pocket.

Out of nowhere, Maude's voice pierced the stillness. "Get them!"

Opal jumped out from behind the barrels and took a swing at the closest man who was still standing by the tractor's front wheel. She missed, but the man hit his head on a stack of wooden beams when Maude rushed him from the other side of the barn.

The man who had been sitting on the tractor jumped down, but Emily swung into action and miraculously nabbed him in her net. Opal flipped on the barn lights to see Maude covered in hay straw and Emily sitting on top of one of the men who was dressed in all black. He looked like a deer caught in the headlights, or rather a gangly fish caught in a net.

"Hurry! The other one's getting away!" Maude yelled. The man who hadn't been caught ran into the night as fast as he could. They heard a truck crank about two hundred yards away. "Damn't!" She jumped on top of the captive man's legs and began to tie them together.

Once Emily was sure the man was not an immediate flight risk, she stood up and pulled out her phone to call the police. As soon as they said they were sending someone out, Emily hung up and called Wilbur. She could tell that she had woken him up from a deep sleep. She told him that they had captured one of the tractor bandits, but one of them had gotten away.

"Oh Lord!" he yelled. He ran outside and stood on the porch looking around. He heard a commotion in the barn and hustled over there. Maude and Opal were hog-tying one man who was wrapped in a giant fishing net.

"What is going on?" Wilbur hollered.

"We got him!" Maude yelled.

"Y'all, what is going on here?" Wilbur asked.

"No time to explain!" Opal said. She and Maude scurried past Wilbur and Emily out the barn door.

"The police are on their way," Emily said. "I better go watch after them."

"Where are they going?" he asked.

"To catch the other one!" Emily said. She kissed Wilbur on the cheek and dashed out into the night. "Wilbur, you stay here and make sure he doesn't get away." She pointed at the man struggling in the barn. Wilbur had turned to follow her, but she was insistent.

"Shouldn't we wait for the police?" Emily called after Maude and Opal.

"There's no time. And don't worry about that hoodlum back there," Maude said. "We made sure he ain't getting loose from that one."

"I don't think your car is going to make it through the woods out back," Emily pointed out.

"We ain't taking my car," Maude explained. "We're taking Wilbur's truck."

Emily wasn't sure how she had gotten the keys to his truck, but Maude found the correct key on her massive key ring and threw the truck into drive. Emily jumped into the bed of the truck before Maude peeled through the back gate into the wide pastureland without bothering to turn on the headlights, and crossed the open field in a matter of seconds. As they entered the woods, Opal stuck her head out the window like a dog on a joyride. They listened for any sound of the truck that had fled a few minutes before. Opal suggested that they try down by the creek because there was a slight gap in the fence that might have been made big enough for the truck to slide through.

They drove on a ways and found the truck stuck in mud near the creek bed. Opal and Maude got out their flashlights and searched like two bloodhounds on a trail. They found the shivering man huddled underneath the truck flat on the ground with his arms spread eagle.

"Please don't hurt me!" he cried.

"Get on out from there," Maude ordered. The man slowly crawled out from underneath the truck and Maude promptly whacked him with a stick she had picked up off the ground. He howled in pain and called her a few different names which only aggravated her further. She told Opal that she should have brought her bat.

"Don't worry! I brought it with me!" Opal said. She got it out of Wilbur's truck and stood over the man menacingly. Wilbur pulled up in the John Deere Gator a few seconds later with Harlan. Two sheriff's deputies were with them. They asked if everyone was alright and handcuffed the man that was on the ground. Emily could see that he had a few bumps on his head from Maude and the wooden beams back in the barn. "Did you find the other one in the barn?" Maude asked.

Harlan nodded. "I've got Bill and Curtis with him. Wilbur, I don't know how in the world these two do it. And it looks like they've recruited another one to join their band."

"Harlan, this is Emily," Wilbur chuckled.

"So this is the famous Emily?" Harlan smiled. He shook her hand and nodded to Wilbur.

"I'm famous, am I?" Emily drawled.

The officers loaded up the man into the Gator ▯ and Wilbur drove his truck back to the cabin with Maude, Opal, and Emily. When they got back to the barn, they could hear the two men putting up a fuss.

"Those old bats are crazy!"'

"They need serious help!"

"Near about killed me!"

"Keep them away from me!"

Maude threatened them again with the stick she still clutched in her hand. "I'll show you crazy! Opal, where's your bat?"

Wilbur turned around and realized that Opal was clutching the baseball bat that he had hidden from her after the Earl incident at the county fair.

"Where did you get that?" he asked her. She merely smiled at him and refused to answer the question.

"Alrighty then," Harlan said. "We'll take care of these two while y'all get settled. Thanks for all your help. We'll keep you posted, Wilbur."

Once the barn was cleaned up from the remnants of their stakeout, Wilbur loaded up Maude's car while Emily took the two women inside to warm up with some hot chocolate. He came back inside to a steaming cup of cocoa with tiny marshmallows on top. Maude added extra whipped cream to her cup and then shot a dollop straight into her mouth.

"You heard from Mavis?" Maude asked.

"Yes ma'am, she landed around lunchtime. She sent a few pictures of the scenery. She's having a blast," Wilbur nodded.

"Good," 'Maude nodded.

"Are y'all out of your minds?" Wilbur asked. He couldn't help but laugh at the three women who sat at the table in front of him.

"Excuse me?" Maude asked.

"Y'all could have been seriously hurt out there tonight. What if they had a weapon or ran you over? That was dangerous," Wilbur said. "Even for you two." He pointed at Maude and Opal on the last beat before turning to Emily. "You're just as bad as they are," he grinned.

"She fits in real well," Opal nodded.

"Sure does," Maude nodded. "A little slow on following directions, but she nabbed him real good!"

"I don't even know why I try," Wilbur laughed. "Y'all are too much."

"You wouldn't have it any other way," Maude shrugged.

You know what? You're right," Wilbur agreed. "But promise me you will all slow down on the adventures though. I need time to catch up before the next one."

"You have a little less than a month," Opal said.

"What does that mean?" Wilbur asked.

"We're going skydiving," Opal said.

"The hell we are!" Maude howled.

"Who is we?" Wilbur asked.

"Me and Emily," Opal shrugged. "And you're invited, too."

"No thanks," Wilbur and Maude quickly said.

"Mavis can come, too!" Emily said.

"Ha!" Maude sneered. "Mavis is crazy like y'all, but even she knows your feet should stay on the ground."

"Mavis won't jump out of a perfectly good place," Wilbur agreed.

"More open sky for us," Emily smiled at Opal.

"And when is this blessed event taking place?" Wilbur asked.

"For Opal's birthday," Emily answered.

"It'll be her last if she falls out of that durn plane," Maude mumbled.

"I'll take care of everything," Emily assured Wilbur and Maude. "We'll make a whole day out of it and celebrate Opal!"

"You've made it this far in life and you want to jump out of an airplane?" Maude turned towards Opal. "In the air?"

"Well, yes, that's the point," Emily pointed out.

"She could jump to the ground from one standing still," Maude shrugged.

"I think I could handle that one," Wilbur said.

"I know what we'll be doing come February then," Emily grinned.

"Good job, Wilbur, you've got her in for the

long haul," Maude encouraged. "Birthdays are big deals."

"Christmas," Opal whispered.

"That's true," Maude nodded. "What's he getting her for Christmas? Lordy, he probably needs our help." She turned to Wilbur unaware that he had heard everything she had just said. "We got Christmas taken care of."

"I've already got it covered," Wilbur smiled. "Thank you though."

"We'll see," Maude huffed.

"I can't believe Christmas is only ten or so days away," Emily changed the subject.

"What are your plans for Christmas?" Opal asked Emily.

"I'll be spending my first Christmas here in Rhinestone since I was a teenager," she smiled. "My parents are going to visit my brother since they were with me for Thanksgiving. They invited me out there, but I think I'm going to hang out here if y'all don't mind."

"Don't mind at all," Opal smiled sweetly. "We don't mind at all."

"When's Mavis coming back?" Maude asked.

"Late Saturday night," Wilbur said. "If y'all can manage to stay off national news, we'll wait to tell her about your little adventure tonight. I don't want anything to ruin her time with her family."

"I'm sure she's having the time of her life," Emily agreed. "Just like we're going to in January!"

Wilbur and Maude both groaned. "It'll be fine," Emily said. "I know the perfect company out of Atlanta. They provide everything and do same-day training. I'll make sure Opal only jumps with the very best."

"I'll bring my own chute," Opal nodded.

"I don't think that's allowed," Emily explained.

"Why not?" Maude asked. "She doesn't know this place. She'll bring her own. I'm sure she's got one or two in the attic."

"Just let it go," Wilbur mumbled underneath his breath to Emily. He drank the rest of his hot chocolate and then yawned deeply.

"It' my bedtime," Opal said.

"Y'all are welcome to stay here," Wilbur said. It was close to two o'clock in the morning by this point.

"No, we're fine to drive home," Maude countered. "Now that we took care of things like we always do."

"We'll see you both tomorrow morning," Emily smiled.

"In a few hours," Maude nodded.

Chapter Twenty

Wilbur and Emily picked up Maude and Opal a few hours later. They ran through the drive-through at one of the local donut shops and loaded up on coffee and breakfast pastries for the long ride. Wilbur could tell that Maude wasn't herself. She only ate one of her donuts and barely finished her coffee on the drive to Atlanta. She didn't even bicker about sitting in the backseat with Opal. There wasn't much said on the journey other than small talk between Emily and Wilbur in the front seat about what had happened to Teddy. Wilbur had found out that Teddy had passed away from an aneurysm in the middle of the night. It was sudden, but doctors assured everyone that he went quickly and didn't feel a thing. That provided a bit of comfort to those who loved him most.

When they arrived at the chapel, Maude stepped out of the backseat of the truck and clutched her purse. Wilbur could see a small photo album sticking out of the top of her deep bag. There was already a line of people waiting to enter the chapel to pay their respects.

Maude, Opal, Emily, and Wilbur took their place in line to enter the chapel for the visitation before the funeral service. Sheila, Teddy's widow, stood in front of the casket with her family. Wilbur remembered Sheila from Jameson's funeral back in Rhinestone. She had been so kind to Ruby, Wilbur, and Mavis. When Teddy introduced her to Maude and Opal, she had hugged them both tightly. As far as Wilbur knew, they had all kept in touch. When Ruby passed away, Teddy and Sheila had been in New York and couldn't make the funeral, but they had sent flowers and platters of food to the Manor.

As they wove their way closer to the casket, Wilbur watched Maude out of the corner of his eye. She was holding up well. When they got to the front of the line, Wilbur hugged Sheila and introduced her to Emily. While Opal hugged Sheila next, Wilbur and Emily stood off to the side to give them a chance to talk. "I'm so sorry," Maude whispered to Sheila. The two women hugged and made small talk while holding onto each other.

Opal patted Sheila on the arm and left Maude and Sheila to talk privately. Emily took Opal's arm and Wilbur followed behind them to the fifth row of pews in the adjoining chapel. Maude joined them a few minutes later and wedged herself between Opal and Emily. Wilbur noticed that the album was no longer in her purse.

A few minutes later, the pianist began to play and Teddy's family took their seats. Teddy's adopted son spoke first, followed by his daughter, and a few friends. The slideshow of pictures that played behind the casket was full of moments from Teddy's long life. There were even a few from his time in Rhinestone. The preacher closed

the service as the police officers in attendance []
carried the heavy casket outside to the hearse.
Maude elected to not go to the graveside, and no
one sought to change her mind.

The drive back to Rhinestone was somber, but
sweet. They ate at a soul food restaurant right
before they crossed the state line. Maude and
Wilbur had fried pork chops and enough collard
greens to feed an army. Emily and Opal ordered
the vegetarian plate that came with rice, black-
eyed peas, collards, and thick pieces of cornbread.
They all walked back to the car with full bellies.

Wilbur dropped Maude and Opal off at their
respective homes and drove by the Manor to
check on the llamas. While Emily fed them treats,
Wilbur gathered Mavis' mail from the mailbox
and put it on her table. He fed the exotic fish and
locked the front door. He found Emily in the barn
talking to the llamas like he had heard Mavis
countless times before.

"I think I need to get some llamas," Emily
grinned.

"Oh Lordy," Wilbur laughed. When Emily was
finished saying goodbye to the llamas, they got
back in Wilbur's truck and he drove through the
woods towards his cabin. They shared the last
piece of apple pie and hot apple cider before
sitting around the living room.

"That was a beautiful service," Emily said.
"I wish I could have met him. He sounded so
wonderful."

"He really was," Wilbur nodded. "I wish you
could have met all of them."

The next few days passed uneventfully. Mavis arrived late Saturday evening and Wilbur found her in the barn with the llamas talking up a storm. "Hey! How was your flight?" Wilbur asked.

"It was fine," Mavis smiled. She wrapped him in a giant hug and started telling him all about her trip as they walked towards the Manor. Mavis made some sweet tea while Wilbur opened the gift bag she had brought him.

"Thanks, Mavis!" he grinned. She had found him a nice cowboy hat with a red-tailed hawk feather in the band. "And I really like the shirt."

"Great!" Mavis beamed. "I got Emily a matching one."

"She'll love it," he agreed. "I'm headed to pick her up in a few for dinner. Care to join us?"

"Maybe next time," Mavis said. "I've got laundry to do and I'm exhausted. I had the best time! Brandy and Sarah are already planning their trip here in the next few months. They can't wait to meet you!"

"Looking forward to meeting them, too," Wilbur nodded.

"I almost forgot! Look at this!" Mavis shrieked. She walked over to her purse on the counter and pulled out a faded photograph. Wilbur took the photograph from her and looked it over. He could see that the woman in the photograph was Melanie, Mavis 's mother. "Is this?" he started to ask.

"Yep," Mavis nodded. "My parents."

"Wow," Wilbur said.

"It's weird," Mavis said. "I never felt like I was

missing anything until I saw this picture. I reckon it's the only one of both of them."

"You look so much like your mother," Wilbur smiled.

"They look happy in this picture. Weird that I never knew either of them," Mavis said. "Is it terrible of me to be almost glad that I didn't know them?"

"What do you mean?" Wilbur asked.

"I had a wonderful life," Mavis smiled. "Just from what I know, I don't think my life would have been as wonderful as it's been had I known them. I'm so thankful they got together and had me, but Big Mama and Big Daddy, Opal, Maude, and you, y'all are who made me who I am today."

"Yea," Wilbur nodded. "I understand that. I'm glad you have a picture though. I'm grateful for the pictures I have of my parents, even though they don't look happy or anything like that. I can't imagine not growing up here at the Manor after my parents passed. We both could have had very different lives."

"Ain't that the truth," Mavis agreed.

"Maude took some photos to the funeral," Wilbur said. "I didn't ask her about it, but I do wonder what they were."

"I bet she had some good ones of Teddy," Mavis said. "Probably a few none of them had ever seen before." She emptied her suitcase full of dirty laundry into the washing machine and jotted down items on a pad of paper so she could make a quick run to the grocery store. "Need anything from the Pig?"

"I think I'm good," Wilbur said. "Well, if you're sure about dinner, I better head on out to Mrs. Beulah's. Emily should be about ready. I know she'll be tickled pink to hear about your trip when y'all get together next."

"We need to talk about Christmas," Mavis said. "Let me know what y'all decide to do and I'll make a big meal here like always. It doesn't matter if it's lunch or dinner, just let me know what Emily's plans are."

"I'll let you know later tonight for sure," Wilbur nodded. "I may need your help with something Christmas related." He hugged Mavis goodbye and walked outside to his truck.

Beulah was sitting on the porch when he pulled up. "Howdy Wilbur!" Beulah called out. "Emily's nearly ready."

Wilbur sat down in the swing next to her and asked about her plans for Christmas. "Didn't Emily tell you? We're flying out to Chicago on the twenty-third. I'm sure she would've told you!" Beulah frowned.

"Oh, um, maybe she did," Wilbur nodded. He tried to hide his confusion and hurt that he would not be spending Christmas with Emily after all.

Emily walked outside a few seconds later and smiled broadly. "You ready?"

Wilbur nodded and waved goodbye to Beulah. "Have a wonderful trip," he smiled.

"Yes, yes," Beulah smiled. "Merry Christmas, Wilbur."

"She is so ready to hop on that airplane," Emily chuckled. "She's never been to Chicago before. I think she's going to have a blast!"

Wilbur smiled and backed his truck out of the driveway. He turned onto the highway and headed downtown to the Mexican restaurant.

"What's got you so quiet?" Emily asked.

"Oh, nothing," Wilbur said quickly.

Emily raised her eyebrows and pursed her lips. "I'm a woman," she explained. "I know the code words. Fine, nothing, ok. All of those words mean the opposite. What's up?"

"It's nothing, really. I just didn't know everything about the Chicago trip, that's all," Wilbur sighed.

"Oh," Emily said. "Are you upset I didn't tell you?"

Wilbur nodded, but then shrugged. "It's fine, I mean it's ok. What's the word I can use that's not code?"

"I didn't think you'd be upset that I didn't tell you my grandparents were going on the trip. I'm sorry, Wilbur," Emily said soothingly. "They're going to Chicago to see my parents and brother and to see real snow for the first time."

"Aren't you going with them?" Wilbur asked hesitantly.

"Goodness no!" Emily laughed. "I've had enough snow to last me a lifetime. I love my family, but I figured I had something worth staying here for this Christmas. We talked about that, remember?"

"Oh," Wilbur said. Suddenly he felt one hundred percent better about the situation.

"Is that why you were upset? Emily asked.

"When I was talking to Miss Beulah, she said y'all were flying to Chicago a few days before Christmas," Wilbur explained. "When she said we're flying out, I thought she meant you, too."

"She and Bart are," Emily nodded. "I thought that I might hang out in Rhinestone and see what all we can get into. What do you think?"

"I think that sounds perfect," Wilbur smiled as he pulled into the busy parking lot of the restaurant. This Christmas was shaping up to be one for the memory books.

After dinner, Wilbur dropped Emily back off at Beulah's house. Emily had an early morning meeting near Montgomery that she said would last all day. She rarely had to work on the weekend, but that would give Wilbur plenty of time to wrap up Emily's pre-Christmas gift. He was going to need Mavis' help with this surprise, which Mavis was already ecstatic about.

Wilbur had been working on the best route to take Emily for a night of looking at Christmas lights. He had planned the entire evening with hot chocolate, gingerbread cookies, and a playlist of some of Emily's favorite Christmas songs. Mavis and Mona had planned to go to the movies on Christmas Eve while Maude and Opal did their own thing. Wilbur wasn't sure what that exactly meant, but he figured the less he knew the better.

Christmas was on Sunday this year, which meant that Christmas Eve was on Saturday, just a few days away. It would be the perfect time to look at lights while half the town finished their last-minute Christmas shopping. He only needed to keep the adventure a secret for a few more days.

Over the next few days, Wilbur stayed busy getting ready for Christmas. He finished the gifts he was handmaking and made time to help Mavis with her last-minute projects. Wilbur stood on a ladder late Wednesday afternoon helping Mavis add more to her already tacky Christmas decor. She badgered him relentlessly with questions about Christmas gifts. Mavis wanted Wilbur to propose to Emily, but he shook his head and tried to curb that conversation. "We aren't there," he said.

"Maybe not yet," Mavis squealed. "But it's coming!"

"You are too much," Wilbur replied. "Now help me string these lights." Mavis had bought twelve more boxes of Christmas lights from the hardware store earlier that morning. Never one to pass up a good deal, she had called Wilbur and begged him to come over as quickly as possible to put them up so anyone who drove by would be able to enjoy them.

"Between you and Maude, I swear," Wilbur sighed. Not to be outdone, Maude made it her life's mission every holiday season to cram more blowups and gaudy decorations in her front yard. It was well known that Maude Cooper's yard was the place to see all kinds of Christmas decorations and lights.

She had not always been so into Christmas. Her love of tacky yard displays was more of a recent phenomenon over the past ten years.

There wasn't a flea market or store in town that could get in a shipment without Maude being the first customer. One would have thought that Opal would have been the one to go all out at Christmas time, but she was content with her antique reindeer display and large Christmas tree that lit up her front yard for miles around.

Wilbur was sure Maude did it mainly to annoy Nadine when she was alive. Those two were always in some sort of competition with each other. Now that Nadine had passed away, Wilbur wasn't sure that Maude would decorate so vigorously this year, but he was glad when she hired the same company she always did to dig out her decorations from her giant storage shed out back. It normally took them two days to get everything to her liking, but it had taken an extra day this season because Maude added three giant snowmen and a light up stocking that needed a commercial crane to help set them up.

"You aren't turning into Maude, are you?" Wilbur asked.

"I don't think I have the room for all that," Mavis said.

"Mavis, the Manor can be seen from space," Wilbur pointed out. With all the lights on and around Magnolia Manor, he was certain any spaceships would clearly be able to see it. "I'm surprised you didn't think the llamas needed decorations."

As soon as he said it, he knew he had given her an idea. "Oh, I didn't mean that!" Wilbur howled.

"Brilliant idea!" Mavis said. "I know just the

thing! I'm going to run into town real quick and I'll be right back!"

Two hours later, Mavis returned with a trunkful of lights and three small artificial Christmas trees. She had somehow found ornaments in the shape of llamas, donuts, coffee mugs, palm trees, and kittens.

"Mavis, they'll eat those durned trees," Wilbur pointed out. He helped her carry the load of boxes into the barn.

"Oh, hold your horses! I'm not going to put the trees in their pen," Mavis replied indignantly. "If you'll string up the lights all around their stall, I'll decorate each of their little trees and put them on the counter by the door. That way they can see the trees at night. I won't have to plug in their nightlights anymore."

"You got enough lights to go around their stall and the outside of the barn," Wilbur mumbled.

Chapter Twenty-One

Emily had heard many legends about Opal Tyler on the stage throughout the years, but she never thought she would be able to see her perform live in person. Opal had long since retired from her days of singing and dancing in various community theatres and churches across the tri-county area.

They had all planned to see the annual Christmas pageant at the church, but now they had an even bigger reason to be excited. When the lead actress came down with a stomach virus the night before the Christmas recital at Beaver Crossing Holy Church for the Faithful, Maude quickly volunteered Opal to fill in as the angel. Opal had played the role of the angel many times when she was younger, so it would be old hat for her.

The only person who was nervous about it was Reverend Ezekiel Simmons. While the church had performed the Christmas pageant for decades before he became the preacher, he had not been brave enough to re-institute the annual program until this year. It had been a big undertaking to find the perfect cast, but thankfully the Gonzalez couple had twin boys a week before Thanksgiving.

Their little family would make the perfect Mary, Joseph, baby Jesus, and backup baby Jesus if the need arose. Everything had been going well until Kathleen Crockett came down with the dreaded stomach bug. Thankfully it didn't hit anyone else in the cast. That would have been the ultimate disaster. Opal only had one night of rehearsal, but she seemed ready to go. The costume fit perfectly, which Reverend Simmons took as a sign from above. The tiny woman looked radiant in the all-white choir robe and metallic halo that crowned her white hair like a tiara.

"This is going to be great!" Mavis said from the third pew. "Remember when we went every year to the Christmas and spring shows to see Opal? She was a star!"

"Of course," Wilbur nodded. He was looking forward to this show. It had been too long since Opal had graced the stage.

"I just hope she behaves," Maude grumbled. She sat down next to Wilbur on the end of the pew and shook her head.

"Aren't you the one who volunteered her?" Mavis leaned over and asked.

"Yes," Maude snapped. "But you know how fame goes to her head. She gets crazy when she hears people cheering."

"I don't think people are going to cheer at the Christmas story," Wilbur said. "It's a pretty quiet story usually."

"Not when Opal Tyler is involved," Maude mumbled.

The church was filled to the gills with

people. It was standing room only that Friday evening by the time that Reverend Simmons took to the pulpit. He no longer stuttered when he was nervous, but seeing the crowd this size was certainly intimidating. If only he could pull a crowd like this on Sunday mornings. Maybe live performances could be a game changer. He made a mental note to add more theatrics and interpretive dance to his sermons.

"Welcome everyone," he shouted into the microphone behind the podium. "I'm honored for you all to be here this evening." He asked the crowd to bow their heads and he prayed a very long and spirited prayer for the actors to do their best and present the message of the Christmas story to the many people who waited in anticipation.

When the lights dimmed and Reverend Simmons scurried offstage, the pianist began to play softly. A teenage boy walked up to the podium and began to read from the Bible. As he spoke, the actors began to take their places on the stage and acted out his words. The woman playing Mary wasn't a teenager, but she did look rather young for her mid-thirties. Her real-life husband played the stoic carpenter, Joseph, and looked the part with his wrench set that he carried with him. When it was time for Opal to give her speech to the virgin Mary, she decided to deliver the good news in an Australian accent. To her credit, the woman who played Mary managed to not burst into a fit of laughter, unlike the audience and a few kids who were playing sheep. Wilbur could

see the color draining from Reverend Simmons'
face on the pew in front of him, but the crowd
seemed to love it.

"I just love her," Emily giggled quietly.

"That's because you're just like her when she
was younger," Maude mumbled.

Wilbur looked at Maude and asked what she
meant. "Geez, Wilbur, they're practically the
same kind of crazy," Maude rolled her eyes.

When baby Jesus was born and placed in the
manger, the real-life baby let out an intense wail.
"Oh goodness," one of the shepherds gagged. He
held his nose and passed the baby off to someone
backstage. The replacement baby Jesus was
swiftly brought out and placed in the makeshift
manger instead. This one was quiet and slept
through the rest of the narration. As the story
wound down, Opal descended from her steps
near the baptismal and quoted the final passage
of the night in her impeccable Australian accent.

"Luke, chapter two, verse twenty-one says,
'On the eighth day when it was time to circumcise
the child, he was named Jesus, the name I had
given him before he was conceived.' Good day,
mates!" Opal winked.

Mary picked up the sleeping baby and held
him close. The lights dimmed and the actors all
came center stage to show that the play was over.
Everyone in the audience stood up and clapped
and cheered. Opal bowed when it was her turn
and waved at her friends in the crowd. She was
obviously the most popular performer of the
night. She posed for many pictures and talked to

everyone who came by the front of the stage to speak to her. Maude and Mavis stayed glued to their seats while Emily jumped up and had Wilbur take a few pictures with her once the line died down.

After Opal changed back into her regular clothes, she found Maude, Wilbur, Emily, and Mavis waiting for her outside near the front steps of the church.

"I told you to behave," Maude grumbled.

"I did behave," Opal shrugged.

"I don't think the archangel had an Australian accent," Maude corrected.

"But you don't know for sure," Opal replied. "No one knows for sure."

"Australia wasn't discovered yet," Maude frowned.

"That doesn't mean anything," Opal said.

"Australia definitely existed back then," Emily agreed.

"You see what I mean," Maude whispered to Wilbur. "Two peas in a pod full of crazy."

"Alright, where to for supper?" Wilbur asked. He didn't want the argument to escalate any further regarding the status of Australia during Biblical times.

They decided to let the star performer decide where she would like to eat her celebratory meal. She chose the Mediterranean place between Rhinestone and Junction that had just opened a few weeks before. None of them had ever been, so they piled into Mavis 's SUV and headed that way.

"Ain't that place big on meat?" Maude asked. "What are you going to eat there?"

"They'll have plenty of options," Emily assured her. She pulled up the menu on her phone and drooled over the beautiful pictures the restaurant shared. "The spanakopita pinwheels look heavenly."

"The what? That can't be a real word," Maude said.

"It is," Mavis nodded. "Brandy made some while I was in Colorado. She said our grandmother was part Greek. She gave me some recipes to try. You should try it."

"I don't even know what it is," Maude said.

"Spinach and feta cheese," Emily read. "They also have baklava for dessert."

"If I can't pronounce it, I ain't eating it," Maude said.

"Baklava is a type of sweet pastry with nuts," Emily explained.

"I can always make an exception," Maude countered. She had a significant sweet tooth and rarely passed up a chance at dessert.

When they pulled up to the restaurant, they saw a line had formed out the door. Mavis dropped Wilbur off at the front while she went to find a parking space. There was a thirty-minute wait. Wilbur put his name down on the list and gave the host his cell phone number to text once their table was ready. When he got back inside the car, Mavis was on the phone.

"It's her sister," Emily whispered.

"Seriously? That's amazing! I can't wait!"

Mavis squealed into the phone. "I'll call you tomorrow and we can talk about it more. Yes, yes. Merry Christmas!"

Once Mavis hung up the phone, she squealed some more. Once she calmed down, she told them all that Brandy and Sarah had purchased round trip plane tickets to fly into Atlanta at the end of January. She was so excited to pick them up and bring them to the Manor. She couldn't wait to show them around Rhinestone and for them to meet everyone.

"How exciting!" Emily and Wilbur agreed.

"We'll get to vet them properly," Maude nodded towards Opal. "We'll sort them out. About time, too."

Mavis looked at Wilbur. She seemed quite alarmed by Maude's veiled threats against her newfound sisters. "It'll be fine," Wilbur assured her.

While they waited for their table, they finalized what items they were all bringing to the Manor for Christmas lunch on Sunday. Mavis was making the traditional ham and garlic mashed potatoes. Emily volunteered to bring a sweet potato casserole and macaroni and cheese. Wilbur had been tasked with bringing the rolls and various drinks. Opal made the best green bean casserole and also offered to bring a wine and cheeseboard for them to graze on throughout the morning while the ham finished baking.

"And I'm handling dessert," Maude said. She had already placed her order at the best bakery in Junction for two pecan pies, a hummingbird cake, and a tray of iced sugar cookies. She was set to pick them up in the morning.

"There it is," Wilbur said as his phone buzzed. "Our table is ready."

"It's about time," Maude said. It had only been twenty minutes, but she was practically starving. She hurried into the restaurant and was already seated by the time the rest of the group walked inside.

Opal ordered a round of spanakopita for the table. Maude reluctantly tried one of the pinwheels and was pleasantly surprised. "Took eighty years, but she's finally expanding her palette," Opal laughed.

Opal ordered a large Greek salad with extra olives. Wilbur ordered a traditional Greek moussaka while Mavis surprised them by choosing a lemon and Parmesan pasta dish. She usually went for the meatier dishes, but she said she had also tried this dish at Brandy's and wanted to see how it compared. Emily, who sat closest to Maude, helped her peruse the menu until something caught her eye.

"Anything fried?" Maude asked. She looked disappointed when Emily shook her head.

"Why don't you try the chicken and lamb kebabs?" Emily suggested.

"Yea, I can do that," Maude agreed. "And some rice. But don't put any of that spicy stuff on it."

Once Maude's order was placed, Emily ordered a salad with blistered tomatoes. Maude leaned across Emily and glared at Wilbur. Opal and Emily had practically ordered identical items which only furthered Maude's earlier point.

Dinner was a hit. All five of them enjoyed their particular meal. They all agreed that the baklava was some of the best they had ever had.

"What did you think?" Emily asked Maude.

"I'll admit when I'm wrong," she nodded. "It was a good choice."

"Wow," Opal grinned. "Hell must have frozen over."

"What does that mean?" Maude demanded.

"You never admit when you're wrong," Opal shrugged.

"I do!" Maude snapped. "I'm just never wrong."

Mavis drove them all back to their respective homes. The closer they got to Maude's house, they could see that her automatic timers had turned on. They weren't sure how her neighbors did not hate her. The lights lit up her home and the surrounding homes like an airport runway.

"How do you sleep at night?" Mavis gasped.

"Like a baby," Maude shrugged.

"Those lights have to shine through to your bedroom," Wilbur said to Opal. Her house was next door to Maude's. The bright blinking lights bounced off the crisp white paint of Opal's house.

"I had blackout curtains installed years ago," Opal said. "Not even those eyesores can pierce through."

"They sure are something," Wilbur nodded.

"Say what y'all want, but Ruby would have loved it all," Maude said.

"Now that I can agree with," Mavis smiled.

Ruby Montgomery loved all things Christmas. The bigger, the better. Christmas had always been her favorite time of the year. She would have been just as invested in all of the new life-sized decor as Maude was.

Mavis dropped Emily off next. "See you Sunday!" Mavis called out the window of her vehicle.

Wilbur walked Emily up the porch steps and waited for her to unlock the front door. "And I'll see you tomorrow evening," Wilbur grinned.

"You still won't tell me where we're going?" Emily batted her eyes.

"Not a chance," Wilbur laughed. "I'll pick you up at eight o'clock."

"See you then!" Emily smiled. She still had presents to wrap and deadlines to meet for work, but she was confident that she could get it all done tomorrow during the day. She was excited to see what surprise Wilbur had planned for them tomorrow evening.

Once Wilbur got back to the SUV, Mavis hummed the "Wedding March" by Felix Mendelssohn.

"Cut it out," Wilbur laughed.

"I'm just saying," Mavis giggled. "We all really like her, Wilbur. Don't mess this up. You aren't getting any younger."

"I don't plan on it," he winked. "Speaking of old age, you're not far behind me in years."

"I've sown my wild seeds," Mavis shrugged. "I haven't found anyone who thrills me."

"I understand. No need to settle for anything

less than wonderful," Wilbur said.

"You sound just like Big Daddy," Mavis smiled.

Jameson Montgomery was known for his beautifully wise sayings that he had passed down to both Wilbur and Mavis.

"Need any more help for tomorrow?" Mavis asked as she pulled up to his cabin.

"I think I'm ready," he said. "Thanks for making those cookies. I don't know how you do it, but no one can beat you in the kitchen when it comes to baking."

"Besides Big Mama," Mavis smiled. "You know, Wilbur, she would have loved Emily, too. They both would have."

"You're right," he nodded. "I really think they would have."

"I know they would have," Mavis smiled. "I'm just glad I'm around to keep you focused. Whatever would you do without me?" she giggled.

"Merry Christmas, Mavis," Wilbur smiled. He walked up to his porch and turned and waved once more. He couldn't help but feel like he was the luckiest man in the world.

Chapter Twenty-Two

Wilbur was excited about the evening ahead. He had made a homemade batch of hot chocolate. He dutifully ladled the hot chocolate into two brand new large, insulated cups and topped the hot liquid with fresh whipped cream and small star-shaped marshmallows. He had mapped out the perfect route to look at the best Christmas lights between Rhinestone and Junction. As soon as Emily said she was ready, Wilbur told her to dress in her warmest pajamas and that he would be over to pick her up soon. When he pulled into the driveway, Emily was sitting on the front porch wearing thick footed pajamas. She had the hood pulled up over her ears. Wilbur doubled over laughing. She was dressed like a Christmas reindeer. She hopped up in his truck and smiled. "We could get matching ones," she added.

Wilbur said he would like that. He made a mental note to never tell Maude about this because she would double down on the fact that Emily was just like Opal. Wilbur was running out of reasons to prove her wrong. "You ready to go look at Christmas lights?" he asked.

"Absolutely!" Emily smiled. Wilbur handed her a cup of hot chocolate and took his matching cup in his other hand. "Cheers," he grinned. He then opened up the container of Christmas cookies and the smell of warm gingerbread filled the truck's cabin. "Mavis out did herself with these," he explained.

"Mavis really is the best baker," Emily agreed.

It was shaping up to be a perfect night. To begin the adventure, they headed down the highway to see Maude's display. Even though they had seen it before, Wilbur felt that it was the perfect starting place. He told Emily how Nadine had always had beautifully elegant lights strung up on the eaves of her roof complete with a manger scene in her front yard. Her empty house had sold already, but the new owners had not moved in yet and decorated. That made Maude's ornate display look even more magnanimous. Wilbur turned left on the highway and headed towards Junction. There were beautiful farmlands with acres of Christmas lights on the rolling hills. Once they got to the town center, the fountain in the middle of the park sparkled with colorful lights. He turned the truck's radio to a certain station where the lights played in tune with the songs. Junction's Chamber of Commerce had done a wonderful job of revitalizing the town center. Rhinestone once had a thriving downtown area like Junction. Wilbur hoped that one day Rhinestone would grow back to its previous glory. They drove up and down the streets of downtown where Wilbur told her how The Comb Over, Opal's old salon in Rhinestone, used to have the prettiest window displays of anyone in town.

They ate some of the cookies and drank their hot chocolate on the drive around town and pointed out their favorite displays. "Next year we'll have to head south towards Enterprise. They have an amazing setup in town where you can drive through a neighborhood full of lights and interactive displays. I've never seen anything like it!" Wilbur said.

"That sounds amazing! I think Maude's well on her way to becoming that," Emily giggled.

"I think you're right," Wilbur agreed.

"I can't wait to have Christmas with everyone," Emily announced. "I'm really looking forward to it."

"They feel the same way," Wilbur assured her. "They really seem to love you."

Emily looked at Wilbur and smiled. "They do, huh?"

"Of course!" Wilbur said. "What's not to love?"

"Wilbur Reynolds! Are you finally confessing your love for me or is it just the family?" Emily teased.

Wilbur felt his cheeks blush. He flipped up his blinker to turn back towards Rhinestone. He could see Emily smiling in the seat next to him.

"I'm just saying," Emily continued. "We're both adults here. I'm pretty stuck on you and I'd say you're pretty stuck on me. Who else gets their sister to bake homemade cookies?"

"I'd say you're right again," Wilbur nodded.

"Good, glad we got that figured out," Emily said. She put her hand on his leg and turned up the radio and sang along to the Christmas tunes from old country crooners that came out of the speakers.

Wilbur was on cloud nine for the rest of the night. When he skipped into the Manor the next afternoon, Mavis smiled at him while stirring the pot of simmering stew on the stove. "I take it last night went well?"

"Only due to your gingerbread cookies," Wilbur replied.

"Yea, yea," Mavis rolled her eyes. "Oh, look what came in this morning." She pointed to the table where Wilbur saw a stack packages addressed to Mavis.

"What did you get?" he asked.

"Oh, they're not for me," she blushed. "It's Christmas gifts for the llamas. And something for Clive, too!"

"Of course," Wilbur chuckled.

"Do you mind opening the boxes for me? I want to make sure I get them all situated before tonight," Mavis said.

Wilbur opened the four packages on the table and couldn't help but laugh. The first package contained three ornaments. Each ornament was shaped like a llama that looked exactly like the real-life llama in the barn complete with their name stenciled on the front. "I knew you'd be adding Morgan, Winifred, and Clementine to your Christmas tree at some point," Wilbur said.

"I couldn't leave them out!" Mavis declared. She had numerous trees put up throughout the Manor. The largest one in the living room had ornaments for all of their pets over the years.

The next package was considerably larger. Wilbur took out his pocketknife to cut the packaging tape on the box and Mavis squealed in delight. "The llamas are going to love these!"

"What in the world is it?" Wilbur asked.

"Holiday themed treats," Mavis explained. "They're grain based, so nothing sugary. It won't hurt them a bit! I can't wait to see their cute little teeth chew on these!" The treats came in a large container. Wilbur opened the container and saw treats in the shape of Christmas trees, wreaths, snowflakes, and snowmen. "Aren't they adorable?" Mavis buzzed about the kitchen.

"I never thought I'd think treats for livestock were adorable, but here we are," Wilbur laughed.

The last two packages had enough dog treats to feed a few dozen litters. "What in the world is all this?" Wilbur asked.

"Those are for Clive," Mavis explained. "They don't exactly make fish treats, but I'm sure he'll love these just the same." She hadn't found anything that Clive wouldn't eat.

"Is Emily coming by later?" Mavis asked. "I bet she'd love to help me feed Clive and the llamas!"

"She's doing Christmas with her family tonight on the computer. That way she can see her niece and nephew open the gifts she sent. She said she had something to do afterwards, too. I don't know what, so it will just be me and you tonight. I've still got to wrap all my gifts. What about you?" Wilbur asked. He swore he saw Mavis smile when he mentioned that Emily had some last-minute plans to take care of, but he couldn't be sure.

"I've got some of them wrapped, but you know how it is. This is such a busy time of year. Oh! Let me show you what Mona gave me earlier. Great minds think alike! I gave her a gift certificate for a spa day and she gave me the exact same thing. Isn't that funny!" Mavis recalled. She showed Wilbur the gift certificate for a fancy salon and spa in junction. "We're going to plan a whole day together. It'll be nice to relax and be pampered."

Wilbur nodded and asked if she needed any help finishing supper. She said she didn't, so he cleared for the table and stacked the llama and fish treats by the back door for her. He threw away the used tape and flattened the cardboard boxes so Mavis could add them to her recycling bin. "I'm going to get the gifts out of my truck and take them to the living room to wrap. I'll go ahead and wrap yours so don't come in there sneaking around."

"Yes sir," Mavis teased. She added some more spices to the stew in the pot and checked the bread in the oven. Her homemade garlic bread was already filling the kitchen with an amazing aroma.

Mavis and Wilbur both looked forward to their Christmas Eve tradition of wrapping gifts and eating French onion soup. They often turned on old Christmas movies in the background, but this year Mavis had suggested they watch old home videos instead. She pulled out an old VHS tape from 1990 for their viewing. Once Wilbur announced that it was ok for her to enter the living room, she brought in the two-fold up trays and set them up. She and Wilbur both ladled the bubbling soup into bowls and ripped up pieces of the thick bread. Mavis poured them each a large glass of sweet tea and they settled into the living room to eat and watch the old video. Neither of them had ever watched that particular one, but they both remembered that Christmas vividly.

Wilbur was fifteen at the time and Mavis was ten years old. Jameson and Ruby bought Mavis a puppy for Christmas and she was elated. Wilbur had helped pick it out. She knew she had had her eye on a litter of chihuahua puppies that had been born a few weeks before Thanksgiving. That Christmas Wilbur received a vintage chess set. It was made from ebony and had come from Spain. Wilbur still had it to this very day. That Christmas, like all the ones they had spent together, was perfect. The Montgomery family knew how to make even the smallest moments count. Wilbur had never celebrated Christmas or any other holiday before moving in with them when he was eleven years old.

"That was the cutest puppy ever," Mavis smiled as she dipped a piece of bread in her soup.

"Maude didn't think so," Wilbur pointed out. "It bit her, what? Two or three times before she stopped messing with it."

"Cassie really didn't like her, did she?" Mavis grimaced. "Oh well, she was still the sweetest little dog there ever was." Cassie had lived for twelve years and really only let Mavis near her. She was the most finicky dog Wilbur had ever seen. Most everyone gave the small beast a wide berth.

"Sometimes I miss having a dog around," Mavis volunteered. "What about you?"

"Yea," Wilbur said after a minute. "I guess I do, too. It's been awhile since I've had one." His last dog was a rescue he adopted from one of the local animal rescues. It was part of their senior program where they find farms for old working dogs to live out the rest of their days in peace. Cookie had been a sweet old hound that passed away a few months after Wilbur adopted her. He hadn't looked for another dog since, and that had been a few years ago. "Hard to imagine you lonely with three llamas and a whale out in the pond," Wilbur added.

"Oh, I'm far from lonely," Mavis laughed. "Just been thinking about a dog, maybe a puppy, recently."

"Should have put one on your Christmas list like you did that year," Wilbur smiled and pointed at the television. They both looked up just in time to see Jameson open up a gift box with a new bow tie in it. "I remember that tie!" Mavis smiled. "I bought it at the market at school. It had fish and worms embroidered all over it. I can't believe he ever wore it in public."

"It matched the apron you had made for Big Mama," Wilbur chuckled.

"It sure did! They were both such good sports," Mavis agreed. "Oh! Before we start to wrap gifts, can we go look out in the trailer for the ceramic cat? I'd love to display it for our gathering tomorrow."

"Yes!" Wilbur said jubilantly. "I think the cat definitely deserves to make an appearance. Do you have a box of tissues we can stuff inside it?"

"Of course," Mavis nodded.

They cleaned up their dishes from supper and walked outside to the trailer. Thankfully it had remained somewhat organized over the years, but there was still no telling what all had been shoved in the cabinets. Mavis was almost sure that Maude and Opal had deposited some of their things over the years.

Wilbur opened the screen door and unlocked the main door of the old trailer. He flipped on the light and looked around to make sure that it was safe to go inside. He had found some critters in there before that had entered through a hole in the floor, but he had made sure to fix that as soon as he discovered it. One time a bird had gotten trapped inside and wouldn't come out no matter how many windows and doors they opened. Maude eventually got it out by turning on the leaf blower. She blew the bird, a stack of papers, and a few picture frames out of the window before Mavis managed to snatch the piece of yard equipment from her.

"Alright, if you were a ceramic cat, where would you be hiding?" Mavis asked aloud.

"I'll check the kitchen," Wilbur offered. He searched through the cabinets while Mavis poked around the living room and front bedroom. She ran her hands over the framed velvet Elvis that Ruby had acquired from one of her trips to Memphis back in the 1980s before Mavis was born.

"I don't see anything in here," Wilbur frowned. "Any luck?"

"Not in here. But there's that storage closet off the back bathroom," Mavis remembered. "I wonder if it got put in there?"

They walked towards the back of the trailer and looked in the bathroom. "This joker needs a good cleaning," Wilbur said.

"I'll call somewhere out here next week," Mavis agreed. She had not been in the trailer in months. She promised herself that she would make time to organize the contents of the storage trailer and keep it cleaned in the new year.

"Here it is!" Wilbur cheered. "It looks just like I remember it!"

The green-eyed ceramic cat was orange with white paws and weighed about six or seven pounds. The cat had a creepy sort of smile on its face which always gave the onlooker a weird feeling. No wonder it had ended up on the top shelf of the closet. "I can't wait for everyone to notice it tomorrow," Mavis grinned. "I think a nice little Santa hat will liven it up."

"Let me wipe it with a cleaning rag first," Wilbur cautioned. "There's no telling what's been on it in the past thirty plus years."

Chapter Twenty-Three

Wilbur woke up the next morning to a sound in his kitchen. He hadn't set an alarm since he was up fairly late the night before. He rubbed his eyes and thought that he was surely dreaming. Then he heard a kitchen cabinet close again. Someone was in his house! None of his alarms had gone off and he didn't have time to check the camera app on his phone. There was definitely someone or something in his kitchen.

He edged to the bedroom door and opened it slightly. The smell of bacon and eggs wafted into his room. "Merry Christmas!" Emily called out from behind the counter. She opened the oven and pulled out a glass casserole dish that sizzled when she set it on the stove top. "Good morning! I didn't mean to wake you," she smiled.

Wilbur opened the bedroom door and walked over to her. "Merry Christmas," he said as he hugged her. "How in the world did you get inside?"

"A little bird let me in," Emily smiled. "I hope it's ok!"

"A little bird named Mavis, I suspect," he chuckled. "Of course it is. What can I help with?" He stretched his arms over his head and yawned again.

"Not a thing! The casserole just needed to be heated up, and the coffee should only be another minute or two. I had to drop something off to Mavis early this morning and she lent me her key. You promise you aren't mad?" Emily asked.

"Never," Wilbur said. "What did you need to take to Mavis this early?"

"Don't you worry about it," she giggled. "Now go get ready for the day and I'll finish breakfast."

Wilbur laughed and walked back to his bedroom to take a quick shower and get dressed. There was no telling what kind of holiday mischief Emily and Mavis were involved with. He would find out soon enough.

When he returned to the table, Emily had scooped out portions of the casserole onto two plates. The bacon, egg, and cheese mixture smelled heavenly mixed with the biscuit base. "This looks good," Wilbur nodded. He added some cream to his coffee and sipped the warm liquid. "And I love the Christmas shirt," Wilbur nodded approvingly. Emily had chosen a green sweater with a Christmas tree adorned with blinking lights.

"I thought I might leave the reindeer pajamas at home this time," Emily laughed. "I brought you a Christmas sweater, too, unless you already have one."

"Oh, did you?" Wilbur said. "How about that!"

"Here you go," Emily said. She pulled a folded black sweater out of the bag by her feet and passed it across the table to Wilbur.

He took it slowly and held it up in front of him.

It was solid black with a red tractor on the front. The tractor had a wreath tacked to the front with the words Seasons Greetings emblazoned across the front.

"You don't have to wear it," Emily said. "I just saw it and thought of you."

"I'll put it on after breakfast," Wilbur smiled. "Thank you. That was really nice."

"That's not your gift by the way," Emily said.

They finished breakfast and cleaned up the kitchen together. Wilbur changed into his new sweater and posed for pictures. Once Emily was satisfied with the amount of photos, she tasked Wilbur with helping her prepare the sweet potato casserole and macaroni and cheese. Wilbur had already dropped off the bottles of sodas and rolls the night before, so he was free to peel and cube the sweet potatoes while Emily boiled the macaroni noodles and grated the various cheeses for the baked macaroni and cheese. The morning passed quickly as they cooked together in the kitchen. When it was time to head over to the Manor, they loaded up in Wilbur's truck and drove through the pasture.

Maude and Opal were just pulling up. Wilbur almost had to slam on brakes to keep from getting in Maude's way. She veered into the driveway from the main road and almost slammed into the magnolia tree. It was a Christmas miracle that she didn't end up driving straight through it.

"Merry Christmas!" Opal called out from the window. "Love the sweater, Wilbur!"

Wilbur and Emily hurried over and helped

Opal out of the car and carried in the charcuterie board. Maude opened the trunk of her car and carried in what wrapped gifts she could. Emily and Wilbur made several trips until all the food and gifts were safely inside.

Mavis was carving the ham with her electric knife when Wilbur brought in the last load. Emily set the table while Maude stacked the gifts she and Opal had brought. Wilbur turned around and saw Opal staring at the colorful tropical fish in the giant aquarium. Maude shuffled in behind them and issued a firm warning. "Don't you dare jump in there, Opal."

Opal rolled her eyes and followed Maude to the table where the food was waiting. "This all looks plum good!" Maude shouted. "Oh my word! What in the hell is that thing doing here?" She pointed to the counter beside the stove where the ceramic cat had been displayed. She pulled a tissue out of its end and stared at it.

"We thought it might do everyone good to see it again," Mavis giggled. She told Emily all about the history of the cat and moved it to the center of the table so it could join them for the meal.

They all dug into the feast before them and filled their bellies. Even though they were sure they hadn't saved any room for dessert, Wilbur and Emily couldn't turn down a slice of pie each. Mavis chose to sample each of the desserts while Maude cut half the cake for herself. Opal walked over to the fridge and pulled out a container she had brought from home.

"What is that?" Maude asked warily.

"Ambrosia," Opal shrugged. "Want some?"

"Hell no," Maude frowned. She had vowed decades ago to never eat anything Opal brought in funny looking containers.

"Suit yourself," Opal shrugged.

"More like shit yourself," Maude mumbled under her breath.

"Oh dear Lord," Mavis wailed. "Can we not talk like that at the table!"

"Can't take her anywhere," Opal shrugged again.

Once they were finished eating, they all quickly cleaned up the kitchen and retired to the living room to open presents. Each person had their stack of gifts in front of them ready to pass out to their intended recipients.

Maude had put most of the wrapping paper she had bought on their last shopping excursion to good use. Each recipient had their own style of wrapping paper. Emily's gifts were wrapped in rollerblading snowmen, Wilbur's gifts were wrapped in dancing reindeer, Mavis' gifts were wrapped in hula-hooping penguins, and Opal's gifts were wrapped in ethnically diverse Santa Clauses. There was a fifth set of gifts wrapped in Christmas trees wearing sunglasses. "Who are those for?" Mavis asked.

"Those are for me," Maude said.

"From whom?" Mavis asked.

"Me," Maude said pointedly.

"She buys herself gifts all the time," Opal snickered.

"Alright, who wants to go first?" Wilbur asked.

"I'll go first," Maude volunteered. She handed each person two gifts wrapped in their respective wrapping paper. Mavis and Emily each unwrapped matching anklets with their own initials engraved on a charm. Mavis also received a new stockpot while Emily opened a new casserole dish with her name on it. Opal unwrapped an automatic water system for her pet chickens and a new coffeemaker for her kitchen. Wilbur grinned when he opened his gifts. He received a new grill utensil set and a new electric drill to replace the one the thieves had stolen weeks ago.

Meanwhile, Maude opened the gifts to herself and acted fascinated by each one. "Oh, a new shirt. And a hand-held radio? How nice! A new pocket knife? I love it! I really needed a new one."

"She ain't right," Opal sighed. "I'll go next!"

Emily loved her beekeeping suit and accessories. Opal had bought her a bee suit, veil, bee gloves, a bee smoker, a hive tool, an uncapping tool, and a brush. She had most of the supplies needed to run her own hive now. Mavis jumped for joy when she opened a brand-new set of cookware. Maude clapped Opal on the back when she opened her gift of a subscription to the wine of the month club. Maude would be receiving two bottles of wine every month delivered straight to her door. "I sprang for the added dessert line, too," Opal added. "That means you get a whole dessert like a cake or pie each month, too."

"What did you get Wilbur?" Mavis asked. While Opal was explaining how the wine and dessert subscription line worked, Wilbur silently opened his gift. Opal had wrapped up two books for him to open. One was a new book that detailed all of the birds in the southeastern region of the United States. She knew he was an avid birdwatcher. The second book is what caught his attention and made his eyes start to water. "Wow," he said. "I can't believe it. You're really giving this to me?"

"No one better to have it," Opal smiled.

The book had to be more than sixty years old. It was faded and falling apart in some places, so Wilbur held it up gingerly. He had seen that book for as long as he could remember on Opal's counter in her kitchen. It was a book that detailed all of the plant life in the state and surrounding area, as well as natural gemstones and wildlife. Opal's beautiful handwriting filled in almost every inch of available space. She had made copious notes over the years on the pages.

"I will treasure this forever," he whispered. He laid the book back in its box and stood up to hug Opal. He never expected to receive something so special.

"I guess I'll go next," Mavis smiled. She handed out her gifts and watched as they all marveled at how beautiful the wrapping paper was. Mavis had always insisted on wrapping her own gifts, even as a child. Thankfully she had become quite the perfectionist as she got older. The gifts were all wrapped in identical white paper with candy canes printed on every square inch. "Ok, so this might be a doozy, but y'all all open your gift at once."

"All identical boxes?" Maude questioned.

"Go on," Mavis smiled. "It's a gift certificate for a cruise that can be used anytime over the next two years. We can all go together or separate or whatever you choose."

"That's amazing!" Emily gasped. "Thank you!"

"Thank you!" Wilbur echoed.

"We're going to have to go together," Maude said. "I can't take Opal on a boat by myself!"

"Right, I'm the problem," Opal rolled her eyes. She and Maude both hugged Mavis who smiled giddily.

"Cruises are the most fun ever!" Emily announced.

"I like the food situation on the boats," Maude nodded.

"It's a ship," Opal corrected.

"Same difference," Maude shrugged. "Who's next?"

"Why don't you go, Wilbur," Emily suggested.

"We'll save the best for last," he winked at her. "Alright, Mavis, why don't you open up this one first?"

Mavis took the oddly shaped package and tore into it. It was a vinyl album signed by her favorite Broadway actress. Her eyes widened and she was speechless. After a few seconds of staring at the record, she mouthed, "thank you!"

Maude and Opal opened their gifts next. Opal loved the water fountain and bird bath combination that Wilbur had ordered for her garden. Maude loved the solar lights for her driveway that Wilbur promised would light up her yard like a runway.

"And Emily," Wilbur smiled. "You have all the beekeeping supplies except for a hive." Wilbur pushed two large boxes towards her from behind the couch. "It's not my first time building a set of hive boxes." He winked at Opal who beamed. "Once it's time, we'll help you start a colony."

The hive boxes were hand carved from cedar wood. Wilbur had engraved magnolia flowers along the side of the stand. It was the most beautiful set of beehives that Emily had ever seen.

"That's amazing!" Emily smiled. "Thank you!" She kissed Wilbur and hugged Opal tightly. "Ok, my turn." She handed Maude a box and waited for her to open it.

"A slow smoker? I can smoke my own brisket! Nice!" Maude gasped.

"I bet it'll smoke eggplant and mushrooms real nicely," Opal added.

"Not in my new smoker!" Maude countered.

"And for you," Emily turned to Opal. "A fruit and vegetable dehydrator."

"Perfect! All the rabbit food you want to preserve," Maude nodded.

"I love it," Opal smiled.

"Alright, Mavis! I saw this and thought of you," Emily said. She handed Mavis a gift bag. Inside was a book for Mavis to write down all of her travel adventures. "And this one, too." She handed Mavis an envelope. "It's a gift certificate to an immersive art experience in Atlanta. They have a Van Gogh exhibit next month that I think you'll love."

"That is seriously cool!" Mavis said. "We'll

have to plan a day to head over and check it out. Thank you!"

"And Wilbur," Emily smiled. "I went out on a limb here." She handed Wilbur a large gift bag and told him to wait before opening it. She and Mavis walked out of the room quickly leaving Wilbur confused. He looked at Maude and Opal who grinned like children. Clearly they knew what was coming. He wanted to peek in the bag but had a feeling that Maude and Opal might snatch the bag out of his hands if he broke the rules. A few minutes later, Mavis came back into the room. "Are you ready?" she asked Wilbur.

"Um, I think so," Wilbur said.

"Close your eyes," Emily called out from the hallway. Wilbur did as he was told. "Ok, open your eyes!"

As Wilbur opened his eyes, something jumped into his lap and licked his face. It was a beautiful chocolate Labrador puppy. "He's all yours, Wilbur!" Mavis grinned.

"Do you love him?" Emily asked.

"What's his name?" Maude asked.

"Calm down, let him breathe," Opal laughed. "He's a good boy though!"

"Wilbur's always been a good boy," Maude agreed.

"I was talking about the puppy," Opal chuckled.

"Say something, Wilbur!" Mavis begged.

"He's mine?" Wilbur asked. The puppy snuggled against Wilbur's chest and wiggled his whole body.

"Yes!" Emily said.

"He needs a name," Maude reminded him.

"He looks like a Charlie to me," Wilbur nodded. "And yes, I love him. Thank you." He held the puppy close while Emily sat down next to him and opened the bag. "Here's his food bowl and water bowl. I got him some treats and a bed. Oh Wilbur, do you really love him?"

"I do," he nodded. "He's perfect."

"And we kept the secret!" Maude high-fived Opal.

Mavis opened a container of gingerbread cookies she had stashed under the Christmas tree that was now devoid of Christmas gifts. She passed the container around and looked around at the faces in front of her. She was so blessed. What a wild year this had been. She looked forward to all the adventures next year was certain to bring.

Chapter Twenty-Four

Charlie made himself right at home as soon as Wilbur brought him to his cabin. His bright red collar and rabies tag jingled as he pranced around the hardwood floors. While Wilbur and Emily set up his food and water bowls, Charlie jumped up on the couch and promptly fell asleep. He settled in quite nicely during the next week. He grew leaps and bounds every day. Wilbur took him out with him whenever he drove into town. He made sure his shiny new name tag had all of the information necessary in case he got out.

When Wilbur hosted the New Year's Eve get-together on the final day of the year, Maude, Opal, Emily, Mavis, Harry, and Mona all sat around and played with the lively puppy after their dinner of pizza until he was thoroughly exhausted.

"What a year!" Mona held up her glass of champagne. "This was the year that Harry and I sold the cafe and really started living."

"And I found a whole other side of family I never knew existed," Mavis added. "I can't wait for you all to meet them

"And I found the love of my life," Emily offered. Wilbur put his arm around her waist and held up his glass. "So did I," he grinned.

"I bought a new car," Maude cheered.

"And no one got run over yet," Mavis mumbled.

They all turned towards Opal to see what she would contribute to the toast. "I'm just thankful to be here with all of you," she smiled.

"I'll drink to that!" Harry nodded. They all clinked their glasses and drank the chilled bubbly liquid. "Now for the real celebration!" Harry walked over to Wilbur's refrigerator and pulled out two chocolate pies he had made earlier that day. "Mavis, I'm finally going to sit down and write that cookbook you've been nagging me about. It's a brilliant idea."

"That's wonderful!" Mavis said. "But don't think sharing the recipe will stop you from having to make these delicious things. No one makes a pie like you can!"

They all sat around the table and ate the pies that Harry had made. Mavis wasn't kidding. Harry was an artist when it came to any type of pie. He had a true talent for baking.

"Harry shared one of his new year resolutions," Wilbur said. "What about the rest of you?"

"Work out more and eat better," Mona said. "Ever since I quit smoking, thanks to Mavis, I've wanted to get better in all aspects of life. I need to get back in the gym and work on myself some more."

"You're doing so well!" Mavis gave her a high-five. "I'm so proud of all the hard work you've been putting into yourself. You deserve all the good this world has to offer."

"Well I ain't changing a thing," Maude

shrugged. "Life's good. I'm good. No need to change perfection."

"That works, too," Harry chuckled. "What about you, Wilbur?"

"I've been thinking about creating some sort of foundation. Mavis, I'd really like your help with this, too. I was thinking of finding a way to honor Big Mama and Big Daddy and continue their legacy. They changed so many lives when they were alive, and I think it's really important to keep that going. You all know they changed mine. Mavis, we've talked about how they've changed yours. Everyone who knew them was better for it. I'd really like to continue their legacy," Wilbur detailed.

Mavis wiped a tear from her eye and stood up to hug Wilbur. "I would love that so much," she whispered.

"Count me in," Maude agreed. "I'll finance whatever you need."

"Me too," Opal nodded. "No better people in the world than those two."

"We're all in," Emily said. "I see the wonderful people in front of me who always speak so highly of Jameson and Ruby. I want to be a part of that for sure."

"Look at this! So many good things," Mona smiled.

"I've got another thing to add while we're at it," Harry said. "Mona knows already, but I'm getting married. I know it's sudden and y'all haven't even met her yet, but she defies all logic. I'm headed out in the morning to pick her up from the airport. She's been in Philadelphia for the past week. Y'all are all invited to the wedding. We're looking at doing a small ceremony in Birmingham in the summer."

Everyone congratulated Harry on his exciting news. Harry had certainly evolved from his days of running the Starlight Cafe. Most customers couldn't remember him saying more than five or six words a day when he ran the kitchen. Many had no idea that he was a brilliantly educated man who could run circles mentally around most people. He was quiet and often stoic, but ever since he and Mona sold the restaurant, he had relaxed and seemed to find real joy in life.

"I've met Tamara and she's wonderful," Mona said. "She's so smart, too. She's a professor at UAB and travels all around giving lectures about, what is it again?"

"Socioeconomic privilege," Harry grinned. "I can't wait for you all to meet her."

"We can't wait!" Mavis smiled. "This coming year I plan on meeting more of my dad's side of the family and getting to know them. I want to expand my love of travel and adventure. There's no time like the present!"

"I agree," Opal nodded. "Y'all are all getting older fast. Especially Maude. Live each day like it's your last."

"She's right," Maude nodded. "Even though she said it rudely." She turned to Emily and explained, "And I'm only four months older than she is."

"A lot can happen in four months," Emily

smiled.

"Which is why we're going to finally do it," Opal announced. "Right Emily?"

"Right!" Emily agreed. "We are going skydiving next week!"

"Who is we?" Maude asked again.

"I booked the entire afternoon for whoever wants to go," Emily explained.

"Again, hell no," Maude said. "I'll watch from the ground."

"I better stay on the ground and catch you all if you need it," Mavis agreed.

"It doesn't work that way," Wilbur started to say.

"If we fell on you, we'd crush you down through the earth," Opal explained. "We'll be like a speeding bullet!"

"It's so exciting!" Emily agreed. "You're going to love it!"

"I can't wait to hear all about it," Harry laughed.

"What about you, Wilbur?" Mona asked.

"I think I better keep an eye on those two," he looked at Maude and Mavis.

"Come on, Wilbur, you only live once," Opal smiled.

"I say go for it, Wilbur," Mavis encouraged.

"I'll think about it," Wilbur said.

As the clock ticked closer to midnight, they all huddled around the television and watched as the various celebrities sang their latest hits. Once the countdown began, they all raised their glasses and cheered for the new year. 2022 had brought so many wonderful changes to their lives than 2023 would have to be even greater to top it. Wilbur thought it just might!

After everyone went home, Emily stayed on the couch rubbing Charlie's belly. He had gotten a second wind by the time that everyone cheered when the clock struck midnight.

"You know how you were looking at that land the other day?" Wilbur asked out of the blue.

"Yea?" Emily answered.

"I was thinking a place with some land might suit you," he nodded.

"Oh yea? Any particular land in mind?" Emily smiled.

"I was thinking twenty acres with a beautiful cabin not too far from an adjoining twenty acres with a built-in best friend already lives," Wilbur said.

"It's funny that you mention that," Emily said. "I was just thinking about that exact thing. Know where I can find something like that?"

"I think I might," Wilbur smiled. "You know, depending on how this goes."

"I like the sound of that," Emily drawled.

Over the next few days, Emily and Opal grew more serious about skydiving. When the fateful day arrived for Emily and Opal to metaphorically spread their wings and jump, Mavis picked up everyone and drove to Atlanta where the blessed event would occur. They dropped Charlie off at Mona's house on the way so he wouldn't be kenneled all day. Mona told Wilbur not to worry because she had a full day of adventures planned.

Emily and Opal chatted the entire way to Atlanta. "Y'all can always change your minds," Mavis kept repeating.

"And I ain't feeding your death chickens if you die," Maude said. She was afraid of birds, but especially Opal's chickens whom she swore went out of their way to peck her. "I'll fry them up though," she whispered to Wilbur.

"It's going to be fine," Emily promised.

"Fine and fun," Opal agreed.

"We have very different definitions of those words," Mavis squeaked. She pulled into the parking lot of the facility. There were signs all around that boasted that this facility was the best place to jump out of an airplane.

"Thirty minutes?" Mavis gasped. "Did you see that?"

Wilbur walked over to the nearest sign and read it. "With less than thirty minutes training you can jump attached to an expert instructor! Wow, that sure is interesting."

"Thirty minutes? That seems like a long lesson," Opal frowned.

"A long lesson?" Maude snapped. "I spent more time in the bathroom this morning."

"Oh God," Mavis gagged. "Are you sure you're serious about this?"

Opal nodded. "Of course I am."

"This is a world class facility," Emily said. "It's safe, I promise. If they fly around and determine it's not safe, they will ground us. And if we get up there and she changes her mind, that's perfectly fine."

"She ain't gonna change her mind," Maude said. "Once Opal sets out to do something, she's gonna do it."

"Let's go!" Opal said. She had put in to jump alone, but after Emily explained to her that that wouldn't be possible today, she relented and met with her instructor. Tomas was in his mid to late twenties and was perfectly tanned and toned. Wilbur held back a laugh when Maude insisted on being in a few of the photos of him and Opal that Mavis snapped with her phone.

After Emily and Opal filled out the paperwork, they all filed into a room to watch a video of safety and the proper technique of jumping. When it was time to attend the short class conducted by a licensed instructor, Maude, Wilbur, and Mavis sat on the bench outside to wait for them. When they came out a few minutes later, it was time for them to be fitted in their gear.

"We learned about everything," Emily explained as they walked to the room where they'd be outfitted. "We got an overview of the process, learned the correct freefall body position, what to do in case of emergencies, the proper way to exit the aircraft, how to operate the parachute after freefall, and the proper landing approach."

"Alright," Tomas said. "Let's get your jumpsuit, harness, goggles, altimeter, and helmet. The harness attaches to the parachute directly at four separate points so there is no chance of coming loose." He made sure everything was tight and that no matter what Opal did, she wouldn't be able to snake her way out of anything. "It's about an eight-minute ride to the most beautiful part of the skies you'll ever see," Tomas continued.

"How long does the actual free fall or whatever you call it last?" Mavis asked.

"Maybe for one minute or so," Tomas grinned. "Fourteen thousand feet from the sky to the ground. A little over one hundred miles per hour free fall and then we'll pull the cord to slow her down. Then we coast back to the earth."

"And I get to pull the ripcord," Opal boasted.

Wilbur looked at Emily for clarification. "They did give her the option," she whispered. "But don't worry, Tomas will really be in charge of everything. After one of them pulls the cord, they'll be back in under ten minutes. He will steer her to the ground. He'll make sure she's ok."

"And what about you?" Wilbur asked.

"I'm jumping tandem, too," she smiled. "Angela is perfectly qualified to guide me back down to earth. She's not quite as animated as Tomas, but Opal was quite sure she needed to be partnered with him. Sure you don't want to come up with us?"

"I'm quite sure," he nodded. He looked over and saw Opal eating some trail mix she had brought with her. "Should she be eating right before y'all jump?"

Emily shrugged. "Guess we'll find out!"

When it was time for them to walk towards the waiting plane, Opal and Emily hugged everyone goodbye and listened as the instructors gave them some final instructions. Maude, Wilbur, and Mavis waved as they watched the airplane take off.

"I can't believe she's finally doing this," Maude said. "She's been talking about it for years."

"Why didn't you go up there with her?" Mavis asked. She had bit her nails down to nubs.

Maude looked at her like she had two heads. "Because I ain't crazy," she snapped.

They watched on the television screen in front of them as Opal and Emily turned on the cameras attached to the front of their jumpsuits. When they were at the appropriate altitude, one of the attendants opened up the sliding door and Angela and Emily volunteered to go first. Before Wilbur could catch his breath, they jumped.

"I knew she was crazy!" Maude howled. "And good Lord, there goes Opal and the sexy man."

They watched as Opal and Tomas sailed out of the airplane after Angela and Emily. They all had big smiles plastered on their faces. Suddenly both sets of parachutes flung open into the sky and Maude, Mavis, and Wilbur were ushered outside to watch them land. Wilbur paced while Mavis kept her eyes glued to the sky.

"There they are!" Mavis pointed into the sky.

A few minutes later, they landed. Once they were untethered from the parachutes and their instructors, Emily grabbed Opal by the hand and they walked over to where Wilbur, Maude, and Mavis were waiting.

"That was amazing!" Emily grinned.

"Let's go again!" Opal shouted.

"Your brains are all probably scrambled. Dear God!" Maude shouted back. "You ain't going again. I'm starving! Can we finally get some lunch!"

"I don't know if Emily and Opal will be ready to eat," Wilbur whispered to Mavis. He knew he wouldn't be able to eat anything for hours if he had just jumped out of an airplane.

Once Emily and Opal were back in their regular clothes, they went to the gift shop and received their free souvenir shirts and a USB with the video and pictures of their jumps. They couldn't wait to get home later that evening and watch it on the television screen. After they both assured Wilbur that they would be able to hold down food, they piled back into Mavis' car and headed towards the restaurant district. Emily found an alehouse that boasted an extensive menu. They were seated after a few minutes of waiting and ordered drinks and appetizers. Wilbur wondered if skydiving had affected Emily and Opal's hearing because they both tended to shout a little louder than they normally did.

Chapter Twenty-Five

Opal's birthday was less than a week away. Mavis had the wild idea to throw Opal a surprise party and roped Emily and Wilbur into helping plan it. Even though they all hoped and prayed that Opal would live forever, they knew that there might not be many more birthdays to celebrate with her. She was doing well at the moment, but things had changed on a dime before. Opal was big on birthdays. She always made a big deal out of everyone's birthday. She constantly reminded them that age was a privilege denied to many. She lived each day to the fullest, and they wanted nothing more than to celebrate her.

"We could have a salad bar," Emily suggested late that Sunday evening as they talked about what kind of food to have.

"Maude would call it a rabbit food bar," Mavis giggled. "But that is a great idea. Opal loves fresh vegetables and fruits."

"Ok, speaking of Maude, do we tell her about the party or keep her in the dark?" Wilbur asked.

"Will she be upset if we don't tell her?" Emily asked.

Mavis and Wilbur looked at each other and shrugged. They knew it would probably be easier to keep Maude out of the planning stages because she did have a hard time keeping a secret, especially from her best friend.

"I'm taking Opal to her next physical therapy appointment in the morning. Wilbur, you could always talk to Maude about it while we're gone in the morning. I don't know. I guess we could use her help with finalizing the guest list," Mavis surmised.

"She would definitely know who to invite. What all do we have figured out so far?" Wilbur asked.

"Her birthday is Friday, so I think we should have the party then," Mavis said. "We can have it at the Manor, but we need to figure out how to get her there. That might be another good reason to include Maude."

"Friday is the thirteenth," Emily gasped. "Friday the thirteenth! How cool!"

"I'm pretty sure she was born on Friday the thirteenth," Wilbur said. He pulled out his phone and went back on the calendar to 1939 when Opal was born. "Yep, it was a Friday then, too."

"That is seriously cool," Emily said.

"How in the world are we going to get her to the Manor Friday night?" Wilbur asked. There was a lot more to this surprise party than any of them had originally thought.

"We can always tell her we're having a party to celebrate Friday the thirteenth," Mavis giggled. "She'd be all for that!"

"Or we can Maude figure that one out," Wilbur said. He continued to make notes on the pad of paper in front of him. "All right, Mavis, you're in charge of the cake and punch. Emily and I will get the rest of the food. I say light hors d'oeuvres and definitely a salad bar. We need flowers. Opal loves flowers."

"I can take care of that, too," Mavis said. "We just need a guest list."

"Once word gets out about this, half the town is going to want to come. We may need to do it somewhere besides the Manor," Wilbur pointed out.

"Where is big enough to host a legend's birthday party?" Emily asked.

"The church might be too small," Mavis said. "What's the weatherman saying for Friday?"

"It's bound to change from now to then," Wilbur frowned. "So far it says no rain, but who knows. Until we know an estimated headcount, we can't plan for food."

"We could do a potluck," Emily suggested.

"But where?" Wilbur wondered.

"We could call the civic center," Emily mused.

"Great idea! I'll call Tariq," Mavis said. She pulled out her cell phone and searched through her contact list.

"It's Sunday night," Wilbur pointed out. "They're closed. We'll have to call tomorrow morning."

"Oh Wilbur, I have his cell phone," Mavis laughed. "He's an old friend of mine. I should have thought about the civic center in the first place."

"Of course," Wilbur chuckled. Tariq was

indeed an old friend of Mavis'. They had been very close friends in high school and kept in touch after Tariq joined the United States Navy after graduation. When he returned to Rhinestone and ran for local office a few years ago, he and Mavis ☐ were still good friends. True to her assumption, Tariq assured her that it wouldn't be a problem at all. He would lend her the entire auditorium in the civic center Friday and make sure it was beautifully decorated.

"You're a wildcard, Mavis," Emily marveled.

Once they had the venue set, everything else was certain to fall into place. Wilbur agreed to talk to Maude while Mavis chauffeured Opal to her appointment.

The next morning Mavis picked up Opal and headed to her doctor's office in Junction. As soon ☐ as the coast was clear, Wilbur headed over to Maude's house. He stopped at the bakery along the way and picked up a few pastries to sweeten the deal.

"She ain't gonna fall for it," Maude warned. "She ain't as sharp as she used to be, but I'm telling y'all, you can't pull anything over on that woman."

"That's why we need your help," Wilbur said.

Maude swallowed the last bite of her apple fritter and poured herself more coffee from the coffee pot on her counter. "You want me to get her to the birthday party without telling her about the birthday party?" Maude asked. "What am I supposed to tell her?"

"Anything you want. Whatever you need to,"

Wilbur said. "And we need a guest list."

"A guest list? A list of everyone she knows or knows her? I don't reckon any place around her will work for that," Maude shrugged.

"We thought the same thing," Wilbur nodded. "The civic center should be big enough. I don't think we should invite the whole town, but she's pretty popular."

"Pretty popular? As much as I hate to admit it, she's a near celebrity, Wilbur. Lord, we can't go anywhere without people coming up to her. And she acts like she knows them, too. Never met a stranger, that one!" Maude said.

"We've got a pretty good list so far, but we don't want to leave anyone out," Wilbur continued. "And everyone won't be able to come, of course. It's kind of last minute."

"You might be surprised," Maude replied. "This could be the happening thing! Make sure you put it out on your socially apps."

"Social media apps?" Wilbur asked.

"Whatever you want to call it," Maude shrugged. She gave Wilbur a list of names to add to his list. This party was going to be bigger than Mavis had originally intended, but it was for Opal, and that was what mattered. "Make sure you tell folks to bring a gift," Maude added.

"But I don't think Opal wants a gift from a hundred people," Wilbur frowned. Opal loved to give gifts. She was very thoughtful and put time into her gift giving, but she wasn't one who liked to receive gifts.

"It's rude to come to a party without a gift,"

Maude interjected.

"Maybe we can say something about in lieu of a gift for Opal, people can make a donation to a charity she supports or do a random act of kindness," Wilbur suggested.

"Yea, that could work," Maude nodded. "She would like that. But then again, she would like dinner at the Manor with all of us just as much if not more."

"You're right," Wilbur said. "Are we doing too much? She doesn't even like a big fuss."

"She would like anything that you kids do for her, but I think she would be just as happy, if not happier, having dinner and just spending time together," Maude said directly.

"I think you're right," Wilbur said.

"Of course I am," Maude huffed. "It don't have to be some big spectacle to let someone know you care about them."

Wilbur distinctly remembered that she was the one months ago who told him that he needed to do a grand gesture to ask Emily to be his girlfriend, but he decided to keep that to himself. She was right about Opal in this moment.

"You know what, let's make an executive decision here," Wilbur said. "Let's go back to the original idea and have dinner at the Manor. It can still be a surprise. We can still have a salad, bar and all of that. Mavis can be in charge of decorating and making the cake, Emily and I will take care of the food. We'll get all of her favorite foods."

"Maybe not all of her favorites," Maude

cautioned.

"Do you think you could get her there?" Wilbur asked.

"She can't drive, Wilbur," Maude reminded him. "I can throw her in the car and get her anywhere."

"Right," Wilbur said. He was sure that Opal could drive if she wanted to. She had agreed not to drive any longer after her strokes. Even though she was very fairylike, she could still put a hurting on someone if she wanted to. Not that she and Maude had ever tied up physically, but he wasn't sure which one would win in an all-out rumble. "Which brings us back to the guest list," he frowned after making a new set of notes.

"Me, Opal, you, Mavis, Emily," Maude shrugged.

"We're always together," Wilbur said. "We want this to be a special time."

"That's all that matters. It's always special," Maude assured him. "When you get our age you'll understand."

Wilbur called Mavis after lunch after she had dropped Opal back at her house. She took the news surprisingly well. She called Tariq and explained the situation and promised to meet him for lunch one day soon. Mavis agreed that keeping it simple would make Opal happier than a big celebration. She planned to make Opal's vanilla birthday cake and researched the best way to make homemade buttercream icing with a honey drizzle. Wilbur and Emily made a new list of Opal's favorite foods that weren't too outlandish.

They settled on a salad bar, potato soup in the crockpot, and eggplant parmesan.

Wilbur had one more surprise up his sleeve. He knew a guy in town who could take old VHS tapes and convert them to DVDs. With Maude's help, he had taken a few of the tapes from Opal's collection at her house that contained a lot of memories of Maude, Ruby, and Opal throughout the years. Once the tapes had been successfully transferred over, he stayed up every evening to put different clips together in a video for the party.

On Friday morning, Mavis woke up in a jolt. She called Wilbur in a panic. "Wilbur! What do we tell Opal today? We can't act like we forgot her birthday, but if we see her or call her, she might figure out that we're planning something."

"Just act normal," Wilbur said.

"Wilbur, none of us have ever acted normal a day in our lives," Mavis countered.

"True," Wilbur laughed. "I get what you're saying. We can't lie and pretend we forgot her birthday, so we'll need a distraction."

"Like we've got something going on tonight that we can't get out of but we'll celebrate her birthday another day," Mavis suggested.

"But that's a lie," Wilbur frowned.

"Or maybe it doesn't have to be," Mavis said. "Wilbur, I saw the ring on your dresser the other day."

"What?" Wilbur asked.

"You asked me to put the hat I borrowed back in your closet and I did. I didn't open the box or anything, but it sure looked like a ring now,"

Mavis' voice trailed off.

"Oh sheesh," Wilbur laughed. "Well, if you must know, it kind of is a ring box. Do you remember when we were kids and I found those three opals by the creek?"

"Yes!" Mavis gasped.

"And I gave one to each of them," Wilbur continued. "Well, Big Mama gave me her stone back before she passed away. I've kept it in that box ever since. I wanted to talk to Maude and Opal about it first, but I'd like to have it made into a ring for Emily."

"To propose?" Mavis asked.

"Yes," Wilbur chuckled. "Nothing gets by you."

"When?" Mavis pestered him.

"I don't know," Wilbur said. "I haven't talked to Maude and Opal yet. I don't think they'd have a problem with it, but I want to make sure."

"This is perfect, Wilbur! This could be the distraction!" Mavis cheered. "Call Opal today and talk to her about it. She can go with you to the jewelers and everything."

"I can't propose tonight," Wilbur said. "I have a lot to do before we get to that point."

"But you can distract Opal by talking to her and taking her to the jewelers with you," Mavis explained. "She already knew the time was coming. Wilbur, she's already bought her outfit and updated her certification at the courthouse." Mavis filled him in on all of the details from the past few weeks.

"How did she know I wanted her to perform

the ceremony?" Wilbur asked.

"It's Opal," Mavis shrugged.

"Of course," Wilbur nodded. His day had suddenly been planned for him and he had to admit that he was excited. "Ok, let me call over there and see what she's up to. I'll offer to take her and Maude to breakfast for Opal's birthday. I'll keep you posted."

Mavis looked at the clock on her nightstand. "You better hurry. You know Maude's schedule is built around mealtimes."

Wilbur hung up the phone with Mavis and called Maude first. She was still at home, but he had called in the nick of time. She and Opal had planned to have breakfast at the Starlight Cafe in a few minutes. Wilbur asked if he could meet them there, and Maude said that Opal would be thrilled. He grabbed the box that held the stone and hurried to his truck to meet them.

When he pulled up in the parking lot, he saw Maude's car already there. He walked inside and found them at one of the front booths. He wished Opal a happy birthday and gave her a big hug. He slid in the booth next to her and looked over the new menu. When the waitress came over to take their order, Opal went first. She ordered the vegetarian omelet with extra tomatoes. Maude ordered a stack of blueberry pancakes with a double side of bacon. Wilbur decided to try the chicken biscuit sampler that came with two chicken biscuits, one spicier than the other. While they waited for their food, Wilbur pulled out the box and showed them the stone and told them about the day Ruby had given it to him.

"I still have mine," Opal smiled. "It's in my armoire."

"Me too," Maude nodded. "I still love it."

After the waitress refilled their coffee cups, Wilbur outlined his plan for the stone and asked for their blessing.

Chapter Twenty-Six

Opal looked at Maude with knowing eyes and winked. Wilbur knew that neither of them were surprised. "She's definitely the one for you," Opal smiled.

"Ruby would love this idea," Maude nodded. "So when are you going to do it? You need our help? He needs our help," she nodded to Opal.

"I haven't decided on a time just yet," Wilbur said. "I just wanted to talk to y'all about the stone first. I was thinking about taking it over to Corey at Hamlin's Jewelry at some point to see if he could set the stone in a ring for me."

"Of course he can," Maude said. "We've all been using him for years. He knows how to do it."

"I just meant I needed to get with him to see when he could do it," Wilbur explained. "He's a very busy guy."

"Opal and I will go with you as soon as we're done here," Maude said. "He'll get you taken care of. Now where do we want to do the proposal at?"

Wilbur wasn't sure how the word we got tossed around in that sentence, but he let it go. "I've been thinking about that," Wilbur said. "I want it to be somewhere special for the both of us."

"Good one," Maude said. "Where is that?"

"I was thinking about down on the river where we went fishing that first time," Wilbur said. He and Emily had been fishing many more times since that first trip a few months back, but that was where they had talked about the direction of their relationship. It was a pivotal day in their lives.

"But what if you drop the ring and it gets swallowed up by the river, or worse, a gator or a turtle or some fish?" Maude gasped.

"I'll be extra careful," Wilbur assured her.

The waitress brought over their food and he was saved from answering any more of Maude's questions. The Starlight Café had always been a town favorite, but Wilbur had to admit that this breakfast was some of the best he'd ever had there. The two sisters that had bought the café from Mona and Harry had changed things decor-wise and menu-wise. They had elevated the food in a way that Harry nor Mona had ever thought to do. It was still down to earth home cooking, but it seemed more elegant. Maude and Opal both seemed to enjoy their meals. Opal said the new menu reminded her of the Starlight Cafe when it first opened back in the 1980s under Harry and Mona's parents.

Once Wilbur paid the bill, he left his truck behind in the parking lot and climbed into Maude 's car. It was against his better judgment, but he had not ridden in her Maserati yet, and she was itching to give him a spin around town. He made sure to buckle up in the backseat for safety. He always wore his seatbelt, but he made sure that it was extra secure any time he rode with Maude Cooper, even if it was only a few miles down the road.

Maude pulled into the plaza that housed the jewelry store, a gym, and a smoothie restaurant. Hamlin's wasn't very busy for a Friday morning, so he was able to talk to Corey in person instead of leaving a message with one of his assistants. Wilbur explained what he wanted while Corey took notes. When Wilbur asked when Corey thought he would be able to get around to it, Maude jumped into the conversation. "We'd like it by this afternoon. It's just a simple thing to do," she said matter-of-factly.

"I don't know," Corey began, but he was cut off quickly.

"It's very important," Maude stated. "How often do you find the love of your life? Do you know the story about this gemstone? Wilbur, go ahead and tell him." Before Wilbur could launch into the true story of how he had found the set of stones by the creek one morning, Maude jumped back in and explained her version of the tale. "So you see we're on a real tight deadline," she continued.

Wilbur was unsure what deadline Maude was referencing, but it would be nice to have the stone set ring in his possession as soon as possible. Emily had planned on taking off early at four o'clock that afternoon so that she and Wilbur could wrap up the rest of the things needed for the party. The plan was for Maude to bring

Opal over to the Manor around six o'clock that evening. She hadn't told them how she planned to get Opal there, but they didn't need to know that information.

"I'll do my best, Wilbur," Corey said. "Call me around one o'clock and we'll see how far I've got."

"Thank you," Wilbur said. He shook Corey's hand and ushered Maude and Opal outside.

"Alright Wilbur, we've got things to do. We're going to drop you back off to your truck and then will see you later," Maude said. She winked at him when Opal wasn't looking. Wilbur wasn't sure what all they had planned to do that afternoon, but he had a list of things that he needed to focus on without worrying about them.

Maude peeled out of the parking lot as soon as Wilbur climbed out of her car at the café. She turned down one of the main streets and booked it down the road. He could hear her exhaust long after she was out of view. He started his truck and drove to the Piggly Wiggly to pick up the rest of the food items needed for that night. He got different kinds of lettuce, cherry, tomatoes, red onions, and various salad dressings for the salad bar. He even found some packets of dried seaweed that Opal liked. Mavis had already texted him to remind him to buy extra croutons because Maude preferred to make her salad an entire bowl of the dried bread. She had also sent him a picture of the cake which looked beautiful. Mavis had made a round vanilla cake three layers high with white buttercream icing. She had piped little bees on the top and drizzled the top with honey.

Wilbur picked up a couple of cartons of ice cream and various toppings for it. He knew that Mavis and Emily both loved caramel sauce and hot fudge when they made their sundaes. He circled back to the produce aisle and grabbed fresh bananas and found a jar of rainbow sprinkles that would be perfect for the ice cream sundae bar. He stopped at the bakery for fresh bread and went over his list one last time. Mavis was making the sweet tea and Emily was bringing the bottles of wine, so he was ready to checkout.

They had all agreed to forgo the crockpot potato soup and pick up a catering sized dish of homemade Italian soup from the best Italian restaurant in town. It wouldn't be ready until later that afternoon, so he checked out and drove the groceries over to the Manor where Mavis was busy decorating. She had ordered various plants and cuts of fresh flowers to decorate the dining room. Opal had always love fresh flowers. They remembered when they were children when she had dated Eddie Walker, the premiere florist in town. He showered her daily with fresh bouquets and exotic plants from all over the world. Eddie was a wonderful man who had proposed to Opal often, but she always gently turned him down. After a while he finally started seeing a woman from Junction and got married not long after. Opal sang at their wedding.

"Hey Wilbur! How did this morning go?" Mavis asked when he brought the bags of groceries inside.

Wilbur laughed and told her all about his

conversation with Maude and Opal over breakfast and how Maude had steamrolled Corey at the jewelry store.

"I bet Opal thinks you're going to propose tonight," Mavis said.

"Why would she think that?" Wilbur wondered. "I'm planning on proposing down by the river. I told them both that I had too much to get ready for it though. I didn't tell them I was going to propose today."

"You know how they are though," Mavis said. "I bet Opal gets here this evening and thinks the party is for you and Emily."

"Good grief," Wilbur said. "And I can't warn Emily about it because I want to keep the proposal a secret. I haven't even talked to her parents yet. It's on my list."

"Do you need Maude or Opal to call them for you?" Mavis teased.

"That would scare the daylights out of anyone," Wilbur laughed as he unloaded the groceries. "What can I help with here?"

"Nothing I don't reckon," Mavis said. "When Emily gets off and y'all get back here, we can set out whatever food needs to be set out. I'm just about done decorating. I need to wrap her gift, but I think we're nearly ready."

"I'm going to pick up the soup around four and then pick up Emily from her place. Then we will head over here," Wilbur outlined.

"I'm so glad you made the decision to keep things simple," Mavis said. "I don't know what in the world I was thinking."

"Your heart was in the right place," Wilbur said. "Alrighty, I'll see you in a few hours if you're sure you don't need any help."

"See you soon!" Mavis said. "Don't forget to call Corey later!"

Wilbur drove home and finished up some chores around his house. He waited until a few minutes after one o'clock before he picked up his phone and called Corey over at the jewelry store.

"I got it ready," Corey said. "Couldn't have Ms. Cooper get mad at me again."

"Thank you!" Wilbur said. "I didn't intend on having her jump in like that."

"Trust me, I know how Ms. Cooper is," Corey laughed. "I've been fixing her jewelry for years. There's only been one time that I couldn't fix what she broke. She was madder than a nest of hornets that had been stirred up. Her dog had eaten one of her aunt's necklaces and well, she had gotten it back, but the emerald was missing and she needed me to find one to fit it. I had to special order one and she was, well, we'll just say she was pretty impatient. I ended up having to order a new chain and everything because that dog's system had torn it up."

Wilbur couldn't help but laugh with Corey as he told the story. He had never heard that story before. It was always something!

"But yea, it's ready for you whenever you want to come get it," Corey continued.

"I'll see you in a bit. I've got an errand to run not far from you around four o'clock, so if it's alright, I'll come by then," Wilbur said.

"I'll be here," Corey nodded.

When it was time to pick up the soup, Wilbur changed into a nice pair of jeans and a button up shirt. He made sure his hair looked all right and drove to the Italian restaurant and loaded up the soup. He stopped by Hamlin's and picked up the ring. Corey had done an amazing job on it. The smooth white stone looked radiant against the white gold band that Wilbur had picked out earlier. He took it out of the box and held it up to the light to further marvel at it.

"This is amazing," Wilbur said. "Thank you, seriously."

"Anytime!" Corey smiled. He walked back to his office while one of his associates rang Wilbur ⬜ out at the cash register. The woman put the ring box in a nice gift bag and handed it over to Wilbur with the receipt.

Wilbur hid the bag underneath his seat in the truck and called Emily to make sure that she was ready and she was. He spoke to Mrs. Beulah and Bart who were in the kitchen cooking their supper. Bart had sprained his wrist while working in his garden earlier that week. Beulah kept nagging him to go get it seen about at a doctor's office, ⬜ but Bart was being stubborn. Wilbur tried to stay out of their way while Emily finished wrapping her gift for Opal.

"I'm ready," she said a few minutes later. Wilbur was thankful she was finally ready to go because Beulah had successfully dragged him into the argument after making Bart take off the wrap around his wrist and showing Wilbur. Bart's wrist was swollen and had already turned purple. Wilbur agreed with Beulah that Bart definitely needed to go get it checked out. As they walked outside towards Wilbur's truck, Wilbur heard Bart reluctantly agree to let Beulah drive him over to the emergency room after supper.

"Keep me posted!" Emily ordered. Beulah promised to call her the moment she knew anything. "It's like herding cats," Emily said to Wilbur once they were inside his truck.

"I know the feeling," he chuckled.

Once they were back at the Manor, Wilbur brought the soup in while Mavis and Emily set out the rest of the food on the counter and organized it so that it all looked perfect.

"The cake looks amazing!" Emily gushed. "It looks like it came right out of a magazine."

"Oh, thank you!" Mavis blushed. "I just hope it tastes good. I found the recipe in one of Big Mama's old cookbooks. It didn't call for honey, but Opal loves honey, so hopefully it will all work out."

"If it tastes half as good as it looks, it's going to be amazing," Emily said.

Wilbur stacked the presents on the coffee table in the living room and walked back to the kitchen to see the women looking at the different flowers Mavis had chosen. "Opal loves lilies," Mavis explained. "And I made sure that none of the plants I ordered were poisonous or anything. You know she has a whole bunch at her house that can kill people!"

"I know!" Emily said. "I love them."

Mavis' eyes grew wide behind Emily's back and she looked at Wilbur. "You better be careful, Wilbur," she breathed.

Emily giggled and said that one day she hoped to have a garden just like Opal complete with honeybees and butterflies.

"Speaking of butterflies," Mavis said. "I found this butterfly bush!" She pointed to one of the potted plants in the corner of the room. "I'm hoping it'll last through the winter and I can plant it and a few others out front. I would love to attract butterflies in my garden."

"They're so good for the environment," Emily agreed.

Wilbur checked the time on his watch and noticed that it was almost six o'clock. "They should be here any minute. That is if Maude's on time," he added. He looked out the window and winced. "Um, Mavis, how attached are you to that frog statue out front?"

"I love it!" Mavis replied. "Why?"

"Well, I hope it's not worth anything because it's in two pieces now," he gulped.

Maude's tires screeched to a stop in front of the rose bushes and they heard the car doors open.

"This is why we can't have nice things," Mavis mumbled.

Chapter Twenty-Seven

Wilbur rushed over to the front door and held it open for Maude and Opal to walk inside. Mavis and Emily scrambled behind him and they all shouted "Happy Birthday" to Opal who looked perplexed.

"Oh! Thank you!" she smiled. "What's going on here?"

"It's a surprise party for your birthday!" Mavis smiled. "Happy birthday!"

"Oh! Maude said we were here for Wilbur," she began, but Maude stepped hard on her foot to shush her.

"For Wilbur?" Emily asked. "But your birthday isn't for another month." Wilbur shrugged his shoulders and pretended like he had no idea what Opal was talking about.

Maude took Emily by the arm and asked her to help her get the present for Opal out of the trunk. Once Emily was outside, Wilbur turned towards Opal and explained that he had not proposed to Emily yet. Apparently Maude had told Opal that they were going to the Manor for a surprise party for Emily and Wilbur as a ruse to get her to the Manor.

"It's really a party for you!" Mavis exclaimed.

"Oh," Opal shrugged. "I'm just glad she didn't tell you no, Wilbur. Not that she will! And thank you! But y'all didn't have to go to any trouble for a little old me."

"It was no trouble at all!" Mavis said. "As soon as they get back, we'll show you what we have planned."

Emily came back inside a few seconds later carrying a large rectangular shaped present. Wilbur helped her set it on the coffee table in the living room with the other gifts.

"Right this way," Mavis directed Opal to the kitchen where the food was set up. Opal was amazed by the cake and different foods they had lined up. Even Maude was impressed by the spread.

"I see you got a lot of rabbit food," she whispered to Wilbur. "And extra croutons for you," he smiled back.

They all piled their plates high and filled their bowls with potato soup. They ate in the dining room that Mavis had decorated. Opal loved the fresh flowers and potted plants.

"Reminds me of the Comb Over when you were dating Eddie," Maude said in between bites of bread.

"That's what we said," Wilbur mentioned. "We were just talking about him earlier."

"Eddie was a great man," Opal smiled. "He owned the flower shop next to me for decades," she explained to Emily.

"I don't know why his grandkids moved the shop to Junction after he died," Maude said. "It was fine right where it was."

"That was their right," Opal shrugged.

"Didn't you date Eddie at the same time you were dating someone else?" Mavis asked. She was a young child when Opal dated Eddie, but she remembered things here and there.

"Ha!" Maude bellowed. "Try two someone elses."

"Two?" Mavis asked. "So, three men? Wow!"

"You sound just like Ruby," Opal grinned. "Yes, they were all perfectly content with the time I spent with them."

"I remember," Wilbur smiled. "Mr. Walker, Mr. McNeal, and Mr. Raven."

"That's right!" Mavis exclaimed.

"What a trio they were," Maude nodded. "An obsessive florist, a flamboyant dressmaker, and the undertaker."

"This is amazing!" Emily said. "Tell me everything."

"Ricky McNeal was, well, he was Ricky," Maude shrugged.

"He was fabulous," Opal nodded. "He was, still is, the most talented man I've ever met. He could write a play, sew the costumes, and sing and dance for days. He moved to New York and became famous."

"He became semi-famous on their harbor cruise ship line," Maude corrected.

"All the same," Opal smiled. "He still sends me a postcard every Christmas."

"Eddie Walker got married and ran the flower shop for ages. Passed it down to his nephew and eventually great-nephews," Maude said. "Still bugs me that they moved the shop to Junction."

"And Mortie was the county coroner," Opal said.

"And an undertaker," Maude continued.

"What happened to him?" Emily asked.

"Life happened," Opal smiled. She suddenly stood up and walked back to the kitchen to get more salad.

"Mortimer died back in '92," Maude explained. "I'll admit that he was a nice man. This old town has always been full of saints and sinners. Sure, he was creepy as hell. Wilbur, I know you remember him. But he was a nice man. Opal was crazy about him. I think he might've been the only man that she would have ever said yes to if he proposed, but to my knowledge, he never did."

Mavis took an extra sip of iced tea from her glass. She was certain that Mortimer Raven was the man that Opal had been referring to a few weeks ago. She vaguely remembered Mortimer Raven, but not well enough to remember anything specific about him other than he was very tall and had a certain affinity for the color black.

"What happened to him?" Emily asked quietly.

"He got hit by a car," Maude winced. "It was late one night at a crime scene. He was there to pick up a body and one of the deputies accidentally backed into him. Didn't see him. Mortimer always wore all black. Crushed him right then and there. It was awful."

"That is terrible," Emily whimpered. "Poor Opal."

"Oh God!" Mavis gasped.

"She never talks about it," Maude said.

Wilbur understood why Opal didn't talk about him. He remembered when Mortimer passed away. Jameson and Ruby had gone to the funeral. Opal wasn't herself for weeks after the accident. None of them had ever seen her so quiet and withdrawn. Wilbur understood all too well. When his father had died, he too withdrew and professed things on his own. He and Opal were alike in that fact. They were both generally pretty easygoing and happy, but certain things rocked them to the core.

"Shh, she's coming back," Mavis said. Opal walked back into the dining room right as Mavis changed the subject to her llamas. "And they just loved their holiday themed treats. Emily and I have had the greatest time teaching them little tricks. I swear that Morgan is part dog. She is so clever!"

"How's your dog, Wilbur?" Maude asked.

"Charlie's good. He's growing like a weed," Wilbur said. The Labrador puppy had grown so much in the last three weeks.

"You should have brought him with you. I know he misses his auntie Mavis!" Mavis crooned.

"Next time for sure," Wilbur nodded. "I'm sure he's spread out on the couch snoozing right about now."

Once they were all finished eating, Mavis went to the kitchen to get the cake. She brought it back to the dining room table while Wilbur and Emily cleaned off the retired plates and bowls and took them to the kitchen sink. Emily passed out new plates and forks to everyone around the table while Mavis stuck a few candles in the cake and lit them with a match.

"You didn't want to put the right amount on there?" Maude asked. "Good thinking. It would probably burn the house down."

Opal stuck out her tongue at Maude while they all sang to her. When the song was finished, Opal took her napkin and waved it vigorously over the candles to snuff them out. "I never liked the idea of blowing out candles," she said. "My my, I can't get over how beautiful this cake is."

"Not too beautiful to not eat though!" Maude added. She watched hungrily as Mavis cut the cake into slices. The cake was indeed delicious. Mavis had added just the right amount of honey drizzle to balance the already sweetness of the homemade buttercream. The cake was light and moist. Mavis had really outdone herself with this one.

After the cake dishes had been put away, they retired to the living room to give Opal her presents. Maude opted to give her gift first.

"Whatever it is, it was heavy!" Emily leaned over and whispered to Wilbur.

Opal gingerly peeled the electric blue wrapping paper off bit by bit. Maude must have used an entire roll of tape and wrapping paper for this gift. "What a beautiful frame," Mavis said.

"It's my octopus," Opal gasped.

"It's a photograph I had blown up and framed accordingly," Maude said. "I can't remember if you took that one or not. It was in a big old box of photographs I found in your house when we cleaned out the guest room."

"I did take this one," Opal nodded. "When I went diving off the coast of California with that travel group. They had underwater cameras we could use."

Opal had joined a senior travel group in the early 2000s where they traveled across the United States visiting various national parks.

"There were some amazing photographs in that box," Maude said. "Wilbur, can you come hang it up for her one day?"

"Of course! Just let me know where you want it," Wilbur said. "I'm going to go last for gifts if that's ok?"

"I'll go next," Emily offered. She handed Opal a small gift bag that contained a jewelry box. Opal opened it and saw a beautiful silver anklet that had charms of bees and butterflies on it.

"I love it!" Opal smiled. "Thank you!"

"Me next!" Mavis said. She pulled an envelope out of her back pocket and handed it to Opal. "Ok, so I was inspired by Emily's Christmas gift to Wilbur."

"Oh God, she doesn't need a puppy," Maude howled. "Kiss those chickens goodbye! A dog will tear through them!"

"I didn't get her a puppy," Mavis interrupted.

"Emily got Wilbur a puppy," Maude said. "I was there. Did you forget already, Mavis?"

"I remember," Mavis said patiently. "I was merely saying her gift inspired me. Anyway," she turned towards Opal. "You've always said how much you loved tortoises. I know you went to the zoo and got to pet one last year."

"It was so spiritual," Opal nodded.

"It was like touching leather," Maude countered.

"Well, I have been in touch with the zoo and after talking with them back and forth, I have donated a bench in your honor in front of the tortoise habitat," Mavis explained. "You also have a lifetime pass to visit the zoo and the tortoise exhibit anytime you want to."

"That's amazing. Thank you," Opal breathed. She opened the envelope and pulled out the information packet and lifetime pass. "What a great gift."

"My turn," Wilbur said. He picked up the remote and turned on the television. He had previously set up the DVD in the player. He explained that he had taken some of Opal's VHS tapes and had them converted to DVDs. "Then I made a video of some clips of you three." They all knew that he was referring to Maude, Opal, and Ruby. He pressed play and they watched the three best friends on the screen throughout the years.

"Wilbur!" Mavis said. "This is amazing."

"Thank you," Opal said. She reached over Emily and patted Wilbur's hand.

They watched the video for the next hour of Maude, Ruby, and Opal. Occasionally Jameson would pop up on the screen with Mavis and Wilbur. Nadine, Teddy, and Patsy made appearances as well. When the video was over, they all sat around and reminisced some more late into the night while they ate ice cream sundaes.

"Thank you all for my party, the food, and gifts," Opal said. "What a special day."

"And tomorrow we're continuing the celebration! We're going to Birmingham for the day, so don't wait up for us," Maude said.

"Oh Lordy," Mavis laughed.

"Y'all have big plans this weekend?" Maude asked.

"I'm going yardsaling with my grandmother in the morning. Mavis, want to join us?" Emily asked.

"Absolutely!" Mavis said.

"I was thinking of going fishing Sunday afternoon," Wilbur shrugged. "What about it, Emily? Do you have plans?"

"Sounds like I've got plans to go fishing," Emily smiled. "But I thought you liked to go early in the mornings?"

"He's going to be installing my new garbage disposal Sunday morning," Mavis covered for him. "Right Wilbur?"

"Right," Wilbur nodded. Mavis' disposal really did need replacing. It hadn't worked right in weeks after she had accidentally got a spoon caught in it.

When Wilbur took Emily home later that evening, they pulled into the driveway at the same time as Beulah and Bart. Bart's wrist was indeed broken. The doctor in the emergency room had reset the bone and cast it so that he would still be able to get around. Once the swelling went down, they would reassess to see if he needed surgery on it.

Maude and Opal set out for Birmingham early the next morning. While Mavis and Emily were scouring the county for a good deal, Wilbur spent the morning talking to Emily's parents on the phone. They both gave him their blessing and sounded very excited.

After his phone call, Wilbur picked out flowers for Emily and checked the weather for the tenth time. Sunday afternoon was supposed to be perfect. The weatherman said the forecast called for sunny skies and no chance of rain.

Wilbur wanted to keep things simple. He made sure his tackle box was ready to go and went ahead and put it and the fishing poles in the truck. He ran to the grocery store and picked up a loaf of bread and different meats and cheeses from the deli. He wanted to have a picnic on the riverbank and propose there on the water's edge. He was almost certain that Emily would say yes, but on the off chance that she declined his proposal, they could easily pack up the picnic basket and blanket and he could take her home.

He wasn't nervous at all. When Mavis called him later that afternoon, he sounded almost giddy. He outlined his plan for her and asked if she thought that Emily had any suspicion that he might propose to her tomorrow. Maybe shook her head and said that she didn't think so. She and Emily had a wonderful time with Mrs. Beulah driving around town in search of different yard sales and then at lunch afterwards. She said that Emily sounded excited to go fishing tomorrow. She loved being outdoors and she loved Wilbur.

"Can I host your engagement party whenever you're ready?" Mavis asked.

"That would be great," Wilbur smiled. "Thank you."

"Just let me know when," she replied. "Good luck tomorrow. Not that you need it!"

"Thanks Mavis," Wilbur said.

Wilbur hung up the phone and checked underneath his bed and made sure that the gift bag with the ring box was still secure. He put a few dog treats in his pocket and put on his shoes. He grabbed Charlie's leash and attached it to his collar and walked out to his front porch. Emily was headed over to his house for them to take Charlie on a walk through the woods down by the creek. Emily loved the grounds of Magnolia Manor just as much as he did.

Life was good.

.

Acknowledgments

This book would never have been possible without the love and support of my family and dear friends. To my children, I love you more than you will ever know. Thank you for being the greatest blessings I could ever hope to have.

To the many family members and friends who are represented here, thank you for providing me with years of laughter and entertainment.

Finally, thank you Victoria, from Between Friends Publishing. You have always encouraged me and you've always believed in the Magnolia Manor series.

About the Author

Wanda Jennings lives in middle Georgia with her family. When not writing the Magnolia Manor series, Wanda enjoys traveling, spending time with her family, and rehabbing wild animals.

Dear Reader,

I hope you enjoyed Over Yonder. I am truly blessed that you took the time to meet some of my favorite characters in the great town of Rhinestone. Some of you may have even traveled to Rhinestone, or a town just like it, before. If you're like me, you may even be related to a few of these characters yourself!

I am currently working on the next book in the Magnolia Manor series. This next project will be all about Maude, Opal, and Ruby during the 70s. You'll find out how the Ladies Auxiliary began and see more pranks between Maude and Nadine. Join the "Stone Sisters" as they deal with repercussions from the Vietnam War, trials of raising a teenager, and their typical hijinks around town. Bless Your Heart will be available this fall!

Thank you again for reading Over Yonder. I would really appreciate it if you could take a few minutes and leave this book (and the other books in the series) a positive review on Amazon.com and Goodreads.com. Your feedback is very important and it helps spread the word about the series.

Thank you again for humoring this dream of writing a successful southern comedy series. I have always wanted to share the Rhinestone gang with the world. found a way to do it. I look forward to the last few books in the series.

Love,

Wanda

Books in the Magnolia Manor Series:

Dirty Laundry

Saints & Sinners

Color Me Crazy

Double Trouble

Now and Forever

Round Trip

Hold Your Horses

Over Yonder

The Rhinestone adventures will continue in

Bless Your Heart

Available Fall 2023!

Made in the USA
Columbia, SC
05 September 2023